WAR-TORN HEART

WAR-TORN HEART

ALLISON WELLS

Ambassador International
GREENVILLE, SOUTH CAROLINA & BELFAST, NORTHERN IRELAND

www.ambassador-international.com

War-Torn Heart

ISBN: 978-1-62020-845-8
eISBN: 978-1-62020-859-5
Library of Congress Control Number: 2019931078

Cover Design & Typesetting by Hannah Nichols
Ebook Conversion by Anna Riebe Raats
Edited by Katie Cruice Smith

AMBASSADOR INTERNATIONAL
Emerald House
411 University Ridge, Suite B14
Greenville, SC 29601, USA
www.ambassador-international.com

AMBASSADOR BOOKS
The Mount
2 Woodstock Link
Belfast, BT6 8DD, Northern Ireland, UK
www.ambassadormedia.co.uk

The colophon is a trademark of Ambassador, a Christian publishing company.

For Laura, Sarah Bradley, and Michelle.
The three most wonderful women in my world. I love you dearly.

ACKNOWLEDGMENTS

A big thank you to Ambassador International and all their staff for taking a chance and believing in my work. Releasing your "baby" into the hands of others is never easy for a writer, and I am so glad I did.

A special thank you to Michelle and Kim, who have been listening to me talk about this book since 2005 when I first started it. They read chapters, gave input, and were a source of great encouragement.

And the biggest thanks to my two biggest cheerleaders—my mom, Laura, and my husband, Marshall. They have always welcomed my ideas and pushed me to succeed in all of my hairbrained ideas. Look! This one worked!

A final thanks to the Good Lord, who has blessed my life so. I know You will always catch me when I falter, may I lead a life pleasing to You!

CHAPTER 1

IT WAS SUMMER. THE KIND of summer where your clothes stick to you and even the slightest breeze leaves you drawing your arms up behind your head to catch the air under your shirt. Not that raising your arms did much to catch the cool, but if you believed hard enough, you could feel a false cool come over you. It's times like this that the ladies say they get the vapors and have to go inside to sip their iced tea.

Abby was glad she was still considered a girl, for the most part. She could still get away with wearing thin cotton dresses, as little dress as she could get away with in her modest South Carolina town. Young boys ran around with just their underwear on, and little girls could get away with the same. Abby longed to be little again, so she could do that, but at sixteen she knew that was inappropriate. Her parents said it was indecent for a good Christian girl to go around like that at any age, even though her younger siblings could still do that in the backyard, where no one could see them.

Abby spent most of her summer days helping her mother with the younger children; she was the oldest girl after all. And she spent a lot of time in the kitchen, which she always enjoyed because baking was her favorite thing to do. When she had free time, she enjoyed sitting under the oak tree in their yard, daydreaming about opening her own bakery or about getting married.

Abby looked forward to getting married, but not to the chores that came with it. Her momma would say that all good Christian girls should have joy while anticipating getting married and having lots of children and tending house. It made Abby a little nervous because she feared no boy would ever have interest in her.

She wasn't thin and pretty like her sister Reba, nor was she curvy and full like Momma. Abby saw herself as round and maybe even a little lumpy—the type of girl that made people think her family had plenty of food on the table, because not all families in their area had that luxury. Her bosom was ample, causing some boys to tease her, which she hated. She walked with her arms around in front of her chest most of the time. She had dark-as-night hair that encompassed her face in curls if left down, which was too hot to do during the summer. Usually, she wore it in a braid to keep it off her neck. She knew the current fashion was for shorter hair, but she couldn't bear to part with her long locks. Abby had brown eyes as well, not the clear blue her sisters had, and they were as big as doe eyes. Her nose was small, and her lips were plump. She felt out of proportion. But, as her momma said, that's what God gave her, and she ought to be happy with it.

Her mother, Grace, told Abby not to worry about how she looked or getting a boyfriend. She said not to worry about looks because Jesus and God never paid no mind to how anyone looked and that vanity was a sin. But Abby guessed she sinned every day because she did care. She had even secretly bought some lipstick from the pharmacy in town and would wear it when no one was around to tattle on her.

**

This summer, their church was holding Bible classes for children and adults alike. Abby had been put in charge of caring for the young children, so others could attend the pastor's classes. After dropping her younger siblings—Reba, Eliza, and Jacob—off in the Sunday school room, Abby made her way to the back of Mount Olive Baptist Church, where the little ones were being kept. It was the coolest room in the building because it had a set of fans to move the air about. A few small toys were scattered around, along with a high chair and a few gates to corner children off from the others. Abby at least remembered to thank God above for fans and allowing her to be in the one area of the church that had them.

Eight children were left in her care, and she had no help whatsoever. It felt hot as Hades in the room, and Abby thought she would never want to have children after this summer was over. With only two arms and three bottles, Abby found that bottle-feeding four infants was not exactly easy.

Long after the other parents had dropped off their children, a man arrived with a ninth child to put under Abby's charge. She didn't know him, and that made her curious. New people didn't walk into church often—especially not on a Sunday night. Abby was immediately taken with the stranger. He was at least a head taller than Abby and had pitch black hair that was tousled and hung in his eyes. And oh, his eyes. They were an intense green, like nothing Abby had ever seen before. His jawline was strong, and his forehead was high. His skin was tanned, but obviously tanned out of luxury and not necessity. It was apparent he didn't do much hard labor because his hands were smooth and unsoiled. He wore blue slacks and a white button-down shirt that looked more suited to a big city than their lazy, little town. He was crisp and clean and the most handsome thing Abby had ever seen in her life.

"I'm sorry; I wasn't expecting any more children tonight. I don't think I have enough arms," she explained with a nervous twitter, trying not to stare at him. As Abby blew loose hair from her face, she realized that, aside from the children, she was alone with him, and she wasn't supposed to be unchaperoned with any man.

"Sorry about that," he said quietly, staring back at Abby. "My aunt just said to take Freddy back here, so she could get the other kids in their classes." He looked across the room, counting the children already there. "You have your hands full. Do you need help?"

"What do you know about tending children?" Abby asked him with a laugh, still pushing loose curls from her face. "Surely you have never changed a diaper or given a child a bottle. Isn't that considered women's work?"

"Maybe," he said, smiling. He held little Freddy casually, comfortably, as he leaned on a table. Abby had never seen someone smile like that before. It gave her chills instantly. "Well, this here is my little cousin, Freddy Newman. My Aunt Doris is his mother."

Abby nodded and said that she knew the family. Freddy's cousin set him down and picked up another baby. Amelia Henson was the youngest in the room.

"Now, you be careful with her," Abby warned, stepping toward him. "She's very young. Are you supporting her head?"

The man just turned away from her and started humming to little Amelia, and he had her asleep in no time at all. He did that with two other babies before it was time for parents and older siblings to retrieve their youngsters.

"Look. I don't think many parents would be too happy that a newcomer was in here with their children and alone with me. Maybe you'd better leave and find your aunt," she warned him.

"Whatever you say," he responded. "I'll be back." With that, he slipped out the door before anybody else arrived. Abby was relieved nobody would find him in there, but was instantly disappointed to discover she hadn't learned his name.

When most of the children were gone, Reba, Jacob, and Eliza came in to sit in front of the fan and wait for the stragglers.

"Can we go now?" Jacob asked.

But little Freddy Newman was still there, waiting to be claimed.

"No, we have to wait for Mrs. Newman to come for him, Jake," Abby said.

They waited and waited. A good thirty minutes passed before a whole troop came in to pick up Freddy. Four boys filed into the room. Excited to see the fan, they ran over to bask in its not-quite-cool glory. They were followed by the fellow who had been in before, as well as Doris Newman.

"Oh! I am so sorry we're late to get Freddy, but it took us a little while to round up this brood!"

"It was no problem," Abby lied. *Sorry God*, she thought. "Freddy was very sweet." Not a lie.

Doris Newman scooped Freddy up and scanned the room to see that all of her children were still present. Freddy was the youngest of five boys; Edward, Richard, Gregory, and Oliver were all older. Freddy was what some people called a surprise baby. The next youngest, Oliver, was nearly ten years old. Richard and Gregory were twins, about thirteen, and Edward topped out the Newman children at fifteen years old.

"Abby, did you meet my nephew?" Mrs. Newman said, turning around, looking for the young man hiding behind the door. "Harvey?

Harvey Nicholas, where did you go? Come introduce yourself." She grabbed his hand and pulled him forward into the light.

Harvey. Abby's heart stopped for a brief second. Why did it do that? She took a deep breath to regulate it again.

Harvey Nicholas came forward and said hello. He raked his hand through his dark hair and smiled shyly. Abby immediately looked to the floor; she couldn't help herself, since she was blushing madly. *Stop,* she told herself. *Don't act crazy.*

"Hello, I'm Abigail Walker, and these are my sisters, Rebecca and Elizabeth, and my brother, Jacob," she prattled on, looking up at Mrs. Newman, but talking to Harvey. "And I have an older brother, Peter."

Harvey simply repeated her name, "Abigail." She could actually hear his smile when he said her name. She felt her heart skip again. *Stop that, heart,* she commanded it.

Mrs. Newman spoke up to fill the silence. "Harvey is my nephew, here from Charleston to stay with us this summer and help out while Frank is gone. Harvey's going to be a senior cadet at Clemson College come fall."

She smiled, but sadness shown through her eyes. Frank Newman had just signed up for the army and left only a month before. The Newmans were among the poorest of the poor in their town, and they often hurt for some necessities. In order to provide for his family, Mr. Newman had sold most of his farming tools and joined the army for a steady paycheck that would keep the family afloat. Abby guessed Harvey was up to help out on their small farm.

After a moment, Mrs. Newman and her large brood of boys made their way out of the church and down the road that led to their house. Abby turned out the light and locked up the church, and they also made their way down the road, turning to take the path that led to their house.

As they walked, Abby holding Eliza's hand, she prayed that she would see Harvey Nicholas again soon. Maybe not the next day, but the day after that would be nice. He was nice to look at, and he talked to her like a person—not like she was Nathan Walker's daughter. Her daddy was a deacon at the church and the banker in town. Everyone in town knew she was Nathan Walker's daughter, and Abby felt they were all treated differently for it. She couldn't pinpoint how, though—just different.

Nathan and Grace Walker had gotten home before their children and were in the living room, dancing to the music on the radio. The children could see their outlines through the curtains, and it warmed Abby's heart to see her parents so in love after so many years together. Even though they were a traditional southern couple, Nathan treated Grace extraordinarily, and they loved to dance in the evenings.

Their eldest child, Peter, was nowhere to be found, but that wasn't unusual. He had a girlfriend named Emmeline Madison, who lived a few houses away, and he liked to visit her. The lovebirds mostly sat on the front porch in white rocking chairs where her daddy could check on them, and then Peter would come home.

Dinners during the summer were always served after dark. Grace lit candles and placed them along their long, narrow table. They ate by candlelight, so the room didn't heat up. When Peter finally got home, they ate cold fried chicken and potato salad with iced tea. The table was crowded, but it was full of love and conversation.

"How was it tonight, Abby? Did you have many children to tend to?" Nathan asked his daughter. He always stopped and looked to whomever he was addressing and waited for a reply.

"Yes, I ended up with nine children, but I had no help," Abby said after finishing her tea. "I may ask Barbara Bennett to help me next week."

Nathan only nodded and then asked Eliza what she did.

Abby's mind began to wander, and it kept going back to Harvey Nicholas. Abby kept trying to tell herself to stop thinking of him, but it was no good. She kept seeing his green eyes flash through her mind. She tried to engross herself in her potato salad. Too bad potato salad didn't have dashing green eyes.

As soon as dinner was over, all the children changed into their nightclothes and got ready for bed. Abby, Reba, and Eliza shared a long, narrow room. Along one wall, there were three beds in a row—Abby's nearest the window, Eliza's in the middle, and Reba's nearest the door. Across from the beds was a chest of drawers, where the girls each had a drawer for their clothes. They also shared a closet. The room was sparsely decorated, but they didn't know any different. Abby liked sharing a room, but the older she got, the more she wished she could have her own room.

Their house was considered big compared to others in the area, and it needed to be to accommodate their whole family. It was all on one level and was described as a bungalow style. The largest bedroom was for Nathan and Grace, and there was one for the girls and one for the boys. Grace would be having a baby at the end of summer, and all the girls were really hoping it would be a boy, so they wouldn't have to put another girl into their room. It was cramped enough.

Abby lay down in bed, exhausted—partly from the night of caring for children and partly from the heat—but sleep didn't come. Again, her mind turned to Harvey Nicholas. *Why is he in my head tonight?* She wondered if she would ever think of anything else ever again. Abby tried not to think of his dark hair hanging in his eyes. She refused to think about those green eyes, the color of magnolia leaves when they first bud. And she really wouldn't think about how his tall, muscular body towered over her and how she could see his muscles through his shirt. She was getting warmer by the second trying not to think of him.

When one of the younger girls stirred, Abby came out of her trance and scolded herself. "Momma would say that good Christian girls don't think about such things," she whispered to herself. "Do they?" She turned on her side, squeezed her eyes shut, and begged sleep to come. She didn't want to think about Harvey Nicholas if it meant sleepless nights. Abby prayed for God to take the thoughts away.

Abby awoke the next morning to little Eliza shouting. She moaned and rolled over. "Eliza, stop it."

"But, Abby, we're going over to the Newmans' house today, and Momma said I could hold baby Freddy," Eliza gushed.

Abby bolted up in bed. The Newmans? *Drat,* Abby thought, God didn't answer that prayer. I've not even been awake a full minute before Harvey Nicholas invades my mind again. She dressed and ate a quick breakfast before heading out with her mother and youngest sister.

At the Newmans' house, the young boys were in nothing but their underthings, running around in the dusty clay soil. Abby felt ashamed for Mrs. Newman, but she didn't seem to care at all. Without trying to look obvious, Abby scanned the property for Harvey. He wasn't anywhere she could see, and she felt both relieved and disappointed.

Abby sat on the porch with her mother and Mrs. Newman. Eliza and Freddy were on the dirty floorboards, Eliza trying to teach the baby *Pat-A-Cake.* Grace and Doris Newman exchanged pleasantries and talked a little of the war in Europe. With Frank Newman in the Army now, both women said they hoped the United States would stay out of it.

When Doris' eyes began to get red-rimmed, Grace changed the subject. "Now, Doris, where's that nephew of yours? I was so hoping to meet him today. My husband, Nathan, said he looks to be quite the helper this summer while Frank is away."

Abby secretly groaned. She had just gotten Harvey off her mind, and her mother brought him right back.

"Well, he should be along shortly," Mrs. Newman replied, offering her guests some iced tea. "He had to go to the college. I still can't believe my sister Jane's boy is going into his final year of college. I just hope he doesn't have a mind to actually join the army like Frank did. Especially with all this war talk going on."

"Surely it will be over before he graduates next spring," Grace assured her friend. "But it is sad that those Germans are trying to get rid of all the Jewish people. Don't they know Jesus Christ was a Jew Himself?"

There were no Jewish people in town—or anywhere that Abby could think of, for that matter. But they had all heard on the radio about Adolf Hitler and his army trying to kill all the Jewish people. Maybe her mother was right, Abby thought—maybe someone needed to tell him that Jesus was Jewish.

As she was thinking, Harvey walked up in a Clemson Cadet's uniform. "Well, Aunt Doris, what do you think?"

He showed off his crisp uniform and tipped his hat at the ladies. He was dressed in a snug suit of dark blue with bars and medals across the front. A spotless white shirt lay underneath the jacket with a matching tie. Harvey wore a military cap on his head, covering his hair and hiding his eyes. He looked magnificent and aloof. Abby felt so small and helpless. She liked the feeling, and then she disliked herself for liking it.

"Lovely, Harvey!" Doris gushed. "Harvey, this is Mrs. Grace Walker, and I think you met her daughters, Abby and Eliza."

He nodded to Grace, then turned his attention to Abby. "Oh, yes, Abigail Walker, we met at the church," he said, smiling. "Happy to see you again."

Words escaped Abby, and she could only nod back to him. Remembering her goal to forget about Harvey, she thought it was probably better not to speak. But she couldn't tear her eyes away from him. Before she could think further on the matter, Harvey had excused himself into the house and the weathered screen door shut behind him.

The mothers carried on their conversation, but Abby turned to stare out into the yard. She didn't know how long she sat like that before the front door of the Newmans' home creaked opened again, and Harvey walked back out. This time, he was wearing a thin, white cotton shirt and denim pants. Abby could only gape, even though she tried to avert her eyes. He looked so natural, yet at the same time, too good for the farming clothes. He smelled crisp and clean against a dingy-smelling background.

Mrs. Newman poured him an iced tea, and he drank it down in two gulps. Harvey raised an eyebrow to Abby and winked, which neither older woman noticed. Abby certainly noticed and felt a wave of heat roll over her body, unsure of its origins. He ran his hand through his newly sheared hair before setting out for the yard to work on a busted fence.

"He's a godsend," Mrs. Newman said. Abby could only shudder in agreement.

Back home and after dinner, Abby took her turn in the shower and reveled in the quietness of the cascading waters. Relaxation didn't last long. With only one bathroom for the entire family, time alone was very precious. Within minutes, Reba was knocking on the door, waiting her turn. Abby imagined having three or four bathrooms one day so that there was never a line, never a rush.

Abby fell asleep that night dreaming of taking a long, hot shower and getting her fingers all pruned. But those dreams were taken over by dreams of Harvey in the white shirt and blue jeans.

CHAPTER 2

A WEEK LATER, THE ENTIRE Walker family was sitting in their living room. Nathan was reading his paper, and Grace was teaching Abby and Reba knitting stitches. Peter and his friend Jack were listening to the radio and quietly discussing the Nazis while the little ones played on the floor.

Jack moved closer to Abby through the evening, and it didn't go without notice. Her parents thought he was a good boy from a good family. Grace only smiled with each scoot, but it bothered Abby. She wished he would go away. He seemed nice enough, but Abby thought there was something amiss about Jack Williams. He wasn't particularly tall, only a few inches taller than Abby herself. His hair was mousy and fell limp over his forehead. He was constantly jerking his head back to wave the hair out of his face. His eyes were small and a muddy brown color. He wasn't necessarily bad to look at, just not, on the whole, pleasant, either.

On the last scoot, Abby felt like she was going to scream if Jack got any closer. She needed to get away from him and fast. She jumped up from her seat, spilling her knitting on the floor.

"I'll get you a fresh drink, Momma," she said, grabbing her mother's glass and rushing for the door.

But when Grace bent down to pick up Abby's spilled yarn, alarm came over her.

"Nathan," she said calmly. "The baby's coming tonight."

"Grace, it's not time yet. Surely you . . . "

"No, sweetheart, my water's broke. The baby's coming now."

Nathan bellowed to Abby, who was frozen in the doorway. "Abigail! Get your mother's hospital bag! We're having a baby!"

Abby ran into her parent's room with Reba on her heels to help.

"It's too early, Abby," Reba whispered.

"Yes, by weeks," she whispered back as she stuffed whatever clothes she could find into Grace's suitcase. As the girls worked, memories from the past flooded their minds.

Years ago, Grace Walker had a baby too early—after Reba was born and before Jacob. She had a baby—a boy—too early, and he died after only a few days. When it came time to bury him, Pastor Phillips asked if he had a name. Grace thought a minute and said the baby was an angel now, so to call him Michael, like the archangel. The family never talked about Michael, but it was years before Jacob was born. If Michael were alive, he would have been eleven years old now.

"Abby, is this it?" Reba asked.

"Oh, oh, yes. Take that to the car. Tell Daddy I'll stay here with the kids," Abby said, handing her sister the suitcase. Reba rushed out the door.

Later in the evening, after the little ones were sleeping and Abby had made Jack leave, she and Reba sat in the kitchen, sipping iced tea and chatting.

"Abby, do you remember Michael?" Reba asked.

"Yes, he was so small," Abby replied, resting her head on her fist. "You were just a baby yourself, and I was Eliza's age, but I do remember him a little. I remember he was tiny and fit in Daddy's hands. Peter and I wanted to hold him, but we couldn't. He had to stay at the hospital.

He never lived outside that hospital. Momma told me and you after he died, that he had been an angel sent to earth to give us all a message."

"What was that message, Abby?"

"Momma said Michael was named Michael because he was an angel sent to tell us that God loved us very, very much and that we should never doubt what God does, even if it makes us hurt."

Reba laid her head on the table and sobbed, crying for the lost brother she couldn't remember, crying for her mother's heartbreak, and crying for the new baby she could not help.

"Shh, Reba," Abby wrapped her arms around Reba, tears flowing from her own eyes as well. "Michael was born way too early. This baby is early, too, but not as early as Michael. Momma was only in her seventh month when Michael was born, but she's further along this time. I'm sure they'll both be okay."

"Do you promise?"

"Let's just pray that God will take care of them," was all she could say. She lifted up prayers to heaven for God to protect her mother and the baby she carried.

They stayed up as long as they could, but eventually drifted off to sleep on the couches in the living room.

The girls woke the next morning to Peter bounding through the door.

"Well, it looks like we have a brother!" he exclaimed.

Abby and Reba held their breath, waiting for any addendum to that statement.

"He's fine. Momma's fine," Peter said and smiled.

They all embraced and gave shouts of joy that woke Jake and Eliza. They promptly joined in the fun as well. They all loaded into the Walkers' car and headed to the hospital to visit their parents and new brother.

The baby was tiny, but strong. He fought and kicked at his blankets. His hair was dark and his eyes darker. His skin was wrinkly, pink, and soft. Tiny squeals escaped from his mouth, and Abby wondered what he was saying. As if on cue, the baby began to wail, needing to be fed. The men left the room as Grace latched the baby onto her breast. Young Eliza did not hide her amazement at how their mother's body worked. Abby did her best not to stare.

"God gives all mommas milk to feed their babies," Grace explained to her youngest daughter. "It comes from their breasts."

Abby cautioned a glance toward her mother and watched as the baby wriggled closer to Grace. Abby was in awe that God designed women to do such things, that He made them able to nourish their children. It made her wonder if she would ever suckle a babe on her bosom, and the thought made her blush.

To avoid her own personal embarrassment, Abby asked, "Does he have a name?"

"Well, since God decided to send this angel a little early, we hadn't thought about it much," Grace started. "But I think I want to name him Gabriel, like the angel."

From behind a curtain, Nathan answered, "That's a fine name. Gabriel it is."

A day later, the newly expanded family was all at home. And they started to settle into a routine again.

Over the next several days, many visitors came to the Walker home, including the Newman family. Mrs. Newman sat with Grace and the baby in the living room. Abby was busy working in the kitchen when Harvey walked in the door.

"Abby," he said, catching her off guard as he entered the kitchen. "Looks like you're having a busy day."

Abby didn't even look up. She pretended to be engrossed in slicing bread. "Oh, Mr. Nicholas, I'm so glad you could stop by to see the new baby," she said, still not looking up. Abby glanced around quickly for Reba, but her sister was nowhere to be seen. She was alone with him, much to her chagrin.

"I told you to just call me Harvey," he said. "My Aunt Doris said she was very relieved to hear your mother and brother are healthy. I understand he wasn't expected this soon."

Abby distracted herself more by pouring Harvey a glass of iced tea before answering. "Yes, he came a bit earlier than we expected. But Gabriel is healthy—praise God."

"Gabriel, huh? That's a great name."

"Yes, isn't it? He was named for the angel," she said, stopping and looking at Harvey. She smiled at him before she realized it and promptly looked back down at the kitchen counter.

"Of course," was all Harvey said in reply. Abby wished she had something interesting to talk about; she was afraid Harvey would think she was boring. After a moment, he asked, "Where's Peter?"

Ah, that was why he's hanging around. He wants to talk to Peter. "Oh, he's around here somewhere. He's got a girlfriend, Emmeline Madison. She lives down the road. He visits with her a lot these days."

"Ah, okay." Harvey began to drum his fingers on the table. *I knew it; he is bored. What can I do?*

"Um, I think he'll be back soon," Abby stammered. "Or I can run and find him for you, if you like."

"No, that's okay," he said, sighing. "I'd like to just sit and chat with you a while." Abby's head shot up to look at him, sending her dark curls flying over her shoulder. Harvey was grinning and staring back intently. She looked back down.

This is not helping, Lord, Abby thought to herself.

"What do you do, Abby?" Harvey asked, peeking under her loose curls to see her eyes. She didn't dare look up until the red in her cheeks subsided.

"I take care of the house, especially now with a new baby home. And I'll take care of Eliza, Jacob, Reba, Peter, and Daddy until school starts back up," she said, laughing. "When Momma has a baby, I become the momma for a while."

"How about aside from tending to your family? What do you like to do?" Harvey emphasized the word *do*, causing Abby to look up at him again.

She smoothed her loose curls back into her braid as she thought. Abby figured Harvey was just being polite. But he raised an eyebrow at her, waiting for a response.

"I like school. And I like to read. But what I really love is baking," she said, concentrating on her bread again.

"That's terrific, Abby. I like a girl who likes to cook. Maybe you can cook for me one day," Harvey said, sitting up straight. He raised an eyebrow and smiled at her. Abby watched as he took a long drink of the iced tea, and as he put it down, he stood up. "Well, I better get going. I have work to do."

He started for the door to the living room when out of nowhere Abby heard herself pipe up, "What about you?"

Harvey turned on the balls of his feet. "Excuse me?"

"What about you?" she stammered. "What are you going to do? After Clemson College, that is."

"Well," he said as he turned completely and took a few steps toward her. "I want to go into the army, perhaps. Or maybe I'll farm. I'd think I would also like to become a preacher. But this summer . . . this summer, I think I want to get to know you better."

With that, he winked and walked through the door.

When the door closed, Abby fell back into a chair, her heart racing. There was something about Harvey that drove her wild. She put her hand to her heart as if that would slow the pounding. She closed her eyes and took a deep breath, unsure what to think of this mysterious and friendly new visitor.

***

The next day, many family members came to visit. Grace's sisters, Judy and Dottie, came to visit. Everyone wanted to *ooh* and *ahh* over the new baby.

Grace's sister Judy lived about thirty minutes away by foot, and she usually walked. She brought her only child, Harold, Jr., with her. He was about Jacob's age, and they played together often.

Dottie, who was still unmarried at the age of twenty-five, also came to visit. She cooed over the new baby, saying how she couldn't wait to get married and have children. Dottie had received several marriage proposals, but turned them all down. She had eyes for only one man—Pastor Phillips. He was also young and single, and everyone thought he was enamored with Dottie as well. If only he would tell her so, Abby often thought.

After everybody had held the baby, the ladies were sitting in the kitchen chatting. The smell of fresh biscuits and roasting ham filled the room and made Abby's stomach grumble.

"Abby, you have one more year of school left. What will you do then?" Dottie asked. "Are you planning on getting married right away? Or do you think you'll wait awhile?"

"I don't even have a boyfriend," Abby said, knowing she could be honest. Her Aunt Dottie understood all about being an independent woman. "I would love to go to school to become a chef and maybe open up a bakery."

"You can't be serious!" Judy chimed in. "No man wants to marry a woman who won't be waiting on him at home with dinner—especially if she were off somewhere else making food for other people!"

"Why not?" Abby didn't understand what the difference was between working at home all day or working at a job. At least the job paid extra money.

"It's just not proper for a good, Christian wife," she replied. *Surely God isn't against women working,* Abby thought. It helps with finances, which means more money for the church, which should please God. "I hear you have some beaus. Who are they?"

Grace answered, "There are a few who are sweet on our Abby, but she's still looking for the right gentleman. Aren't you, Abby?"

"Yes, ma'am. Nobody has caught my eye yet. Of course, I don't think I've really caught any eyes myself."

Abby nodded, then excused herself. She was tired of her aunt's constant nagging about getting married. She decided to sit outside with her father for the rest of the evening.

At church the next morning, Peter headed straight over to the pew the Madisons sat in, so he could talk to Emmeline. The Madisons had one married son and one married daughter, who were much older than Emmeline; she was the only child left in the house. That made Mr. Madison very protective and Mrs. Madison very emotional.

When the sound of the organ announced that the service would start soon, Peter made his way three aisles back to his own pew, staring at Emmeline the entire time. As Peter sat down next to Abby, Jack Williams headed over to their pew and sat down next to Peter.

"Hey, Peter, I see you have Emmeline eating out of your hand."

"Yeah," Peter said, stretching his arms in front of him. "She's a great girl. She's not only great to look at, but she loves to look at me."

Abby rolled her eyes. Secretly, Peter would do anything Emmeline Madison asked him to; it was more like Peter was eating out of her hand. Abby knew boys had to make themselves look better in front of their friends.

Jack turned his attention from Peter. "Abby, how are you doing?"

"Fine, Jack." She kept her answer short. There was just something about Jack she didn't like.

"You know, I would love it if you would look at me like that," he said in a quiet voice. He leaned in closer, and Abby was overwhelmed with the scent of Jack's smelly aftershave. "I would do anything for you, if you were my girl."

Before Abby had a chance to push him away, her father came to her rescue. "Jack Williams, how are you doing?" He smiled down to Abby.

Jack stood straight as an arrow. "Fine, sir, just fine. How are you and Mrs. Walker doing, sir?"

"We're just fine. But you're in my seat," Nathan said. "Besides, I think your father is looking for you."

"Yes, sir. Excuse me, sir." Jack looked at Abby and made his way back to his own family's pew.

After the service, Dottie went up to Pastor Phillips to congratulate him on his sermon, which she did every week. "John, that sermon was riveting. I love the way you make God so accessible."

"Well, Dottie," he gulped as she put her hand on his arm, "God is always accessible." He looked nervous, but added, "Is there anything I can pray about for you, Dottie?"

Dottie leaned in to the pastor and talked low to him. She rested her hand on his arm again, clearly making him uncomfortable. Abby and Reba just laughed. Their aunt had a way with the pastor. Maybe before long, he would be their uncle.

CHAPTER 3

AS THE SUMMER DAYS PASSED, Abby adapted to her new routine. In the mornings, she would help Momma clean, make lunch for the family, and then start dinner. But the evenings were solely for her. Even though she sometimes opted to sit outside snuggling little Gabriel, letting her mother have a small break from the demands of a new baby.

One particular night, she sat holding the baby, dreaming of her future—living a successful life and wearing sophisticated clothing. It took her a few moments to notice someone approaching her from the yard. It was Jack Williams.

Lord, let him be here to see Peter. Abby winced as he bound up the steps. She angled herself away from him and turned her complete attention to the baby. She cooed and giggled at him, hoping for Jack to pass her by.

"Hi, Abby," he said with a smile. He sat next to her, too close for comfort. He always smelled too strongly of aftershave. She prayed for the smell to bother the baby and make him cry.

"Jack," she nodded. "What brings you out here in this heat? I don't know where Peter is."

"Well, actually, Abby," Jack looked down at his shoes and licked his lips. He was clearly nervous. "Actually, Abby, I wanted to see you."

No! Not that!

"Like I told you a while back, Abby, I would love it if you looked at me as your boyfriend. If you would look at me the way Emmeline looks at your brother. I thought if I came around a little more, maybe you would look at me. Like that. One day." Abby didn't say anything, and Jack took that as an invitation to continue. "I would love to talk to your folks about it, Abby, and see if I could call on your regular-like. And maybe one day, we could have our own baby like this one."

Abby cringed inwardly and outwardly, hoping it wasn't too obvious. She pulled the infant closer to her, keeping him away from Jack. She tried to smile. "Jack, I'm flattered, but why me? I'm nothing special."

"Why not you? You're my best friend's sister. We've practically grown up together," he said, getting closer to Abby as she lifted Gabe to her shoulder. Gabe made an excellent blockade from Jack. "And you're great with kids, so you'll be a great mother some day. And, Abby, I think I love you."

Lord, help me! Abby stammered, "No, Jack, you don't love me. Look at me; I'm a mess, certainly not suitable for you to want to marry. Ever. And besides, I'm not near old enough to marry. I'm only sixteen."

"I'll wait."

"Jack—" she was cut off by the baby's crying. Thankful to God for the chance to escape, she stood and stepped away from him. "Jack. I've got to get the baby inside. Please go."

Abby took the baby into her parent's room and laid him in his crib. Her mother was folding laundry. Abby sat next to the pile of clothes and groaned, "Oh, Momma. Jack's here."

"Is he? Peter's not here; are you entertaining him?"

"Apparently. Momma, he said he loves me. Can you believe that?" she demanded an answer.

"Well, of course I can. But it seems you don't return the affection?"

"Not at all," Abby replied with a scowl. She took a deep breath and pressed her hand to her forehead. "Momma, I don't even know Jack well. And I don't think I could ever love him; he's kind of peculiar." Abby's thoughts drifted to a man she met who was not peculiar or smelly. Though she hadn't seen Harvey Nicholas recently, he still drifted into her thoughts regularly.

"But there's someone else who has caught your eye?" Grace sensed, watching her daughter keenly.

"I don't know, Momma. Even if I did, I'm too young to think about marriage."

"Well said, Abigail," her father said from the doorway. He came into the room and laid a hand on her shoulder. "I just saw Jack outside, and he confessed his undying love for you. Very dramatically." Nathan tried to hide a snicker unsuccessfully. "But I take it you don't return the, uh, fondness?"

She shook her head. "No, Daddy."

"Very well, then. I told Jack you were too young, anyway, since you're still in school. I tried to send him home, but he said he wanted to see you first. Please go say goodbye."

Abby went to the porch, where Jack was still sitting on the step, just as she left him. She stayed in the doorway and cleared her throat before speaking. "Jack, you need to go. It's late."

He stood and smoothed his shirt out. "Abby. I spoke with your father," he said excitedly.

"Yes, Jack, I know." She didn't budge from the doorway. She wanted space between them.

"And I want you to know that I won't give up on us." He took a step toward her, but Abby stepped back over the threshold. "He said you're too young yet, and I guess maybe you are, but you'll be seventeen soon. I'll come back then to talk to your father." He made his way down the steps, but turned back. "Will that be enough time, Abby?"

"I'm sorry, Jack," was all she said. She turned back into the house, hoping to escape the heat that seemed to want to engulf her. Tonight she wished it would.

***

One evening after church, Harvey was waiting for Abby under an old oak tree. He joined her as she walked home, her siblings laughing and running ahead. From that point on, he was always waiting after church. When they reached the fork in the road, they would go their separate ways, and Abby always turned to see Harvey disappear around the bend.

Over the course of several weeks they learned a lot about each other. She felt comfortable around him now. They talked about school and his home in Charleston. Abby told him about growing up in her sleepy little town and marveled at his talk of the big city. He told her about the ocean, and she longed to see it. Usually, they walked home with the kids in tow and chatted.

But tonight, Harvey had other ideas. "Can we go somewhere? Alone?" He asked her quietly as the last child was collected by his mother.

Abby looked down and turned red. "I have to get my brother and sisters home." She couldn't believe he was asking her to be alone with him.

"Already taken care of. I asked your friend Barbara to escort them and tell your father you'd be along shortly after you did some finishing up around here," Harvey said with a smile, his eyes bright.

Within seconds, Barbara promptly appeared, giving Abby a small wave and smile. She hurried the Walker children out the door and winked at Abby as she followed them. Harvey waited until the door closed and turned to Abby with a grin. "Let's go."

"Where?" Abby was uneasy, but not enough to turn down the offer. *Was this a date? Where did he want to go? And more importantly, what did he want to do once they had gotten there?*

"That's the only problem. I don't know where. I'm still not entirely familiar with the places here."

Abby thought a minute, and the perfect spot sprang into her mind. "I have an idea. Follow me."

She took the lead and grabbed Harvey's hand, pulling him behind her. She felt the heat from his hand and wondered if he felt the same. She tried to put it from her head; she and Harvey were just friends. He probably thought of her as something like a sister, even if she did feel her heart flutter whenever she saw him.

"Where are we going?" Harvey asked. Abby just smiled and didn't speak. She led him along a back road and down a dusty driveway that hadn't seen visitors in decades. The sun was dipping below the treeline, and the light to see by was growing dim. When Harvey saw that they were becoming more and more secluded, he asked, "Aren't you worried of being with me alone? Out alone at night?"

It hadn't occurred to Abby lately to worry about being alone with Harvey. Surely, her father would disapprove; but they were nearly at their destination, so she pushed the notion from her mind and told Harvey she wasn't worried at all.

"Here we are," she announced, splaying her arms to present her secret hiding place to Harvey.

"I was thinking a diner, but this will do. Where exactly is *here*?" he asked, stepping through a stone doorway with no door.

"This is the old Lachlan plantation house. It's been around since well before the War Between the States. It's been deserted forever; the roof is long gone; and it's just walls now. I've been coming here for years as a kind of secret hideaway."

The house had been monstrous. As a former plantation, the Lachlan house was once full of grandeur. Stone walls traveled up two stories before ending abruptly without a top. Some walls were crumbling, and stones had been stolen by thieves in the night. At the opposite end of the grand room they were in was a free-standing brick fireplace that had once warmed the entire house. Dusty, iron benches were scattered throughout.

Harvey looked around and found a not-too-dirty bench to sit on. He cleared a spot for Abby and patted the seat beside him.

"I wanted to ask you a question," Harvey said, his voice quiet, his eyes searching hers.

"Please do." Abby tried to keep the conversation light to counter the weight of her heart thumping in her chest.

"Lots of the cadets at school talk about their girlfriends," Harvey started. "And how they write to them while they're in school. I've never had that in the past three years." Abby's heart fluttered. "There's one girl from Charleston who writes me. She wants to be my girl." Abby's heart sank. "But, you see, I don't feel that way about her," he continued. "At least, not when I compare it to how I feel about you."

"I don't understand." Abby searched Harvey's eyes, trying to figure out what he meant.

"You, Abby. I was thinking of you." He swallowed hard. "I was thinking maybe you could write me a few letters. I have really enjoyed getting to know you this summer, and I don't want to lose that when I leave for school in a few weeks."

"Me? You want me to write to you?" Abby asked, flushed. What did this mean? Did he want her to be his girlfriend?

"Yeah, we can be like pen pals."

Back to the sinking feeling. "Pen pals? Okay. Sure," Abby whispered. She had hoped he would ask her to be his girlfriend, but realized that was foolish. Harvey was several years older than her and would never be interested in her romantically. *Lord, I shouldn't feel this way. He's made no mention of being sweet for me, so I should not feel this way. God, as I've begged You before, take away these odd feelings I have for Harvey Nicholas.*

With the matter settled, Harvey smiled and continued talking. He didn't notice the disappointment on her face. "Great. I'm so glad, Abby. You're about to start your last year of school, too. What do you plan to do then?"

"What?" Abby was still trying to grasp the pen pal idea, and he was asking more questions of her.

"Your life," he said again. "What do you want to do with it?"

"Oh, well, Momma and Daddy want me to get married and have a big family like them. I guess when I get out of school next year, I'll settle down like I'm supposed to," Abby explained. "In a small town like this, that's what is expected of me."

"That's not what I asked." Harvey shook his head and licked his lips. "What do *you* want to do? Not what your parents want you to do. You said before you like to cook, right?"

Abby was honest. "Well, I do want to get married one day. But I do love to bake. Cookies and cakes and breads. That's where I feel most at home. I've thought about having a bakery one day."

Harvey nodded. "That's great. I like that modern girls want to be useful outside the home."

Abby couldn't believe he actually agreed with her. No one ever did. She lifted an eyebrow to Harvey, questioning his response.

"Really," he assured her. "I think it's great."

Abby's eyes lit up. "I would love to go to Charleston one day," she gushed, grabbing his hand. "Especially if they have people who think like you do."

"Well, not everyone thinks that way," Harvey admitted. "But they're coming around. One day, I'll take you to Charleston."

Overcome with excitement at the prospect of going to such a far-away place, Abby bounced into Harvey's arms and gave him a tremendous hug. "Oh, Harvey, that would be wonderful!"

Harvey embraced her back, not letting go. Neither moved, and Abby was suddenly aware of how alone they really were. She could feel Harvey's breath on her neck and his chest pressed to her own. Finally pulling away from one another, Harvey lingered for a moment, inches from her face.

Suddenly yet slowly, he leaned back in and kissed Abby. It was short and sweet, Harvey's mouth squarely on Abby's. She could feel his breath, hot and musty. His lips were soft, but she could tell they could easily be rough and demanding. She felt his freshly shaved skin on her, and she could have sworn that she felt his soul.

It was Abby's first kiss.

Harvey backed away, more surprised than Abby was. "I'm sorry, Abby," he whispered, standing. "I shouldn't have done that." He turned away from her.

Abby stood after him. "It's okay."

She stepped closer to him and put her hand on his shoulder. She wanted to get closer but wasn't bold enough to do so.

"No, it won't happen again; forgive me." His voice was sullen, his eyes shadowy. He led Abby out of the old house, and they walked in silence in the dark.

She was afraid she had done something wrong. Was he not attracted to her? Did Harvey regret kissing her? She wanted to ask, but wasn't sure what to say and wasn't sure she even wanted the answer. When they got close to Abby's house, he bid her goodnight and turned away. Abby was too confused to say anything, and she went home to bed.

Abby walked around bewildered for days, until her friend Barbara visited.

"Oh, Barbie, I need to talk to you!" Abby exclaimed. They settled outside, sitting in the dirt under the oak tree with their backs against the trunk. "Promise to keep a secret?"

Barbara gasped and turned to her friend. "A secret? Of course! Did something happen with the Newmans' nephew? Harry?"

"Harvey." Abby gulped as she bit her lip. She felt the breeze flutter through her hair and refresh her in the midday heat.

"That's right, Harvey," Barbara repeated with a smile and took the correction as a sign of guilt. "Where did you two go the other night? He asked me to walk the kids home, so he could talk to you, but I saw you two take off from the church. You can't hide it from me."

Abby told Barbara everything that had happened. Barbara's mouth dropped when she mentioned going to the Lachlan house. "Alone? Abby weren't you scared? What if he were a pervert or something?"

"Hardly." Abby sighed, knowing that Harvey would never look at her passionately. "He definitely doesn't think of me that way. In fact, after he kissed me, he said he was sorry."

"He kissed you?"

"Yeah, but then said it would never happen again, and he was sorry he did it." Abby looked down, mortified. How could things have gone so wrong?

Barbara hugged her close. "I'm sorry, Abby. But it was your first kiss. How exciting! You have to tell me all about it." Her friend always had a way of putting a positive spin on things in the end.

As Barbara prattled on, Abby wasn't sure if it was exciting or not anymore. Now, she wished it had never happened.

CHAPTER 4

ABBY'S BIRTHDAY FINALLY CAME, WHICH meant school was right around the corner as well. Abby was looking forward to her final year of school and the prospects it would bring. But for this one day, everything was about her, and Abby reveled in the attention.

On the morning of her seventeenth birthday, Abby's father surprised her with a package wrapped with bright blue paper. "Happy birthday, honey."

"Aw, thank you, Daddy," she said with a big smile, loving the attention from her father. When he gave her a nod, she tore into the paper and opened the box. Inside was a gorgeous dress of green with little yellow and blue flowers. The fabric was luxurious and soft. Abby felt like it was a very grown-up dress, the kind a well-to-do woman would wear.

Abby hugged her father's neck in excitement and peppered him with thanks. "We don't need all this." He shied from the affection, but held his daughter tight. "It's just a dress."

Grace told Abby to put her new dress away for later, and she did as she was told. When she came back, there was a gift from her brothers and sisters at her seat. Inside were two dress patterns and some calico fabric. She was quite a handy seamstress and was happy for the opportunity to make new dresses. Abby thanked and hugged her siblings one by one.

That evening, friends and family gathered in Abby's honor for a meal. Her favorite dish of pork chops with mashed potatoes and fresh snap beans was on the menu. The kids had all taken turns churning away on the ice cream maker to make fresh butter pecan ice cream for dessert. Pastor Phillips, who was there with Dottie, said a lengthy prayer over Abby and the meal. Abby sat between Reba and her cousin Alice, and despite being hotter than Hades, she was very happy to be surrounded with the people she loved.

Well, almost all the people. She still had Harvey Nicholas on her mind. And even though she was sure he hadn't thought of her again, she certainly felt head over heels for the handsome man.

After dinner, the guests started to leave one by one. Once she had given her guests plenty of hugs and thanks, Abby helped her mother clear the table. On a return trip outside, she found a Shasta daisy—her favorite—sitting where her plate was. She smiled and looked around for whoever had left the flower. She wondered who had secretly given her such a lovely flower. Was it one of her sisters? Or maybe Barbara or Emmeline? Seeing no one, she picked up a note that simply said, "Steps."

Abby picked up the daisy and the note and went to the steps she had just come down. There was nothing on them. She creased her brow and peeked on the side. To her delight was another daisy laying in the grass and a note that read, "Laundry." Laughing now, Abby ran out to the laundry line and weaved her way through the clothes and sheets. Inside an empty clothespin, four more daisies waited for her—pure white with a yellow center—along with a note.

August 16, 1941

Dear Abby,

You didn't tell me it was your birthday. If you can, meet me at the Lachlan house at nine. I have a gift for you.

Hope to see you then.

Happy Birthday,

D. Harvey Nicholas, Jr.

Abby was relieved. She had been afraid the flowers were from Jack. But knowing they were from Harvey made her stomach flip and her heart swell. She wondered what else Harvey could have for her aside from a half-dozen of her favorite blooms. And how had he known what her favorite flowers were? Had she told him in one of their summer night talks? She knew it was already after eight, and she was unsure if her parents would knowingly let her go to meet him.

She went back into the house and put her bouquet into a small vase of water and carried it to her room, placing them beside her bed on a nightstand. She sat down for a minute, realizing her feelings for Harvey were stronger than she recognized. She figured that this was God's plan because it certainly hadn't been hers. She fished her Bible out from under her bed and opened it, praying for God to lead her to a verse that would help her.

"Trust in the Lord with all thine heart; and lean not unto thine own understanding," Abby read quietly to herself. "In all thy ways acknowledge him, and he shall direct thy paths." Abby wished she knew more about what the Bible meant. She reread the verse from Proverbs,[1] taking it to mean that she needed to trust in God and not question Him. She closed the heavy book and slid it back under her bed.

---

1 Proverbs 3:5-6

Abby peeked out of her room, keeping the rest of her body behind the door. All was quiet. She quickly closed the door, changed into her new dress, and stood before the mirror. She felt like a grown woman—and a beautiful one, at that. The dress gathered at just the right places, making her waist look tiny. The folds of fabric fell down her legs and swirled around her knee. She undid her braid, running her hands through the strands, and let her hair flow down to the middle of her back. She pulled only the top away from her face and pinned it up, letting the rest cascade down.

Abby hurried past the living room where her parents were and made a beeline for the door. She found Reba and told her she would be back later but to tell her parents she was very tired and had gone to bed. She pleaded with her sister not to tattle on her. Before Reba could ask questions, she fled the house and ran down the driveway. She ran all the way down the street to the Lachlan driveway. She stopped and caught her breath. Smoothing her skirt and hair, she tried to stroll casually down to the house, but her heart beat furiously against her ribs in anticipation.

She arrived right at nine o'clock; and as she stepped through the doorway, she straightened her back and pressed her lips together.

"Harvey?" she called out. "Are you here?"

She walked around from room to room, peeking through hidden doorways. She finally found him at the back of the house, hidden behind the monstrous fireplace. He had cleared a spot for them to sit. Abby prayed for her heart to calm as she saw him sitting before her.

"Wow," Harvey said with a sigh as he got to his feet. He was wearing well-worn blue jeans with a light blue buttoned shirt. His sleeves were rolled up around his elbows, exposing strong, tan forearms. The cadet haircut was already growing out, and his dark locks started to fall over onto his brow. His green eyes shone in the dark, seemingly calling for Abby to come to him, and she could do nothing but obey. A smile came across Harvey's face, and Abby vowed to remember it forever.

"Sorry I didn't dress for the occasion. You look wonderful."

Abby blushed and pushed her hair over her shoulder. She bit her lip out of nervous habit.

"You didn't tell me it was your birthday. I found out from a little birdie," he said, stepping closer and taking her hand. Abby's pulse quickened, and she wondered if he would notice.

"You didn't ask," she said playfully, then turned more somber. "And I haven't really seen you since . . . "

"Yeah, I know," Harvey replied, and his chest fell. "I'm sorry, again, about that. I was out of line."

"Don't be sorry," Abby said, still not understanding him. Her eyes searched his, and she got closer to him.

"No? I wanted to kiss you, but I didn't want to scare you or move too fast."

"You wanted to kiss me?" Abby was suddenly aware of just how close they were. Their hands nearly touched, their bodies mere inches apart.

"Yes, but I wanted it to be special. It was your first kiss, wasn't it?" he asked tenderly as he put a hand to her hair and swept it out of her face.

"Yes, it was," Abby admitted, her face turning red. "It was special." Harvey smiled wide. Then Abby noticed that Harvey was keeping one hand behind him. "Harvey, what's behind your back?" Abby grinned and tried to peek, but he wouldn't let her.

He took a step back, slowly revealing a wide, flat package and handed it to Abby. Without looking down, she unwrapped the package little by little. Abby pulled out a stack of mint green paper with little blue flowers across the top and the initial *A* on the upper left corner. Along with the paper was a stack of envelopes in a matching pattern. Each envelope was affixed with a stamp, ready to be posted. Finally, a ballpoint pen rolled out of the wrapping.

"Harvey, this is lovely," Abby said running her fingers over the paper. "Thank you. I love to write, you know. And now you can get stylish letters from your . . . pen pal." She had chosen her words carefully. Abby loved the gift, but wanted to make sure Harvey knew she understood exactly what she was to be to him.

Harvey's eyes flashed in the dark. He looked bothered, but then softened. "I wanted to talk to you about that," Harvey said, stretching his torso closer to her. "I thought maybe instead of 'pen pal,' it could be 'girlfriend.'"

Shocked, Abby could only squeak out, "Pardon?"

"I would like it if you would call me your boyfriend," Harvey said, moving closer still, putting his large hands around her waist. Abby had never been touched like that before, and her heart raced. "Abby, I've liked you since the first time I saw you. And I thought being here this summer would be dull. You've livened it up. You've livened me up like I've never been before. I don't want to lose that when I leave in a few weeks."

"No?" Abby's doe eyes shone in bewilderment.

"No." Harvey laughed. When she didn't respond, he prompted, "Well?"

Abby laughed. "Of course!"

They embraced, and Harvey kissed her neck, sending chills down her spine on the warm August night. She felt wonderful and alive in his arms.

"I have to go," Abby said after a while. "No one knows I'm gone; I've never snuck out of the house like this before. My sister is covering for me."

She started to pull away, but instead, Harvey brought his arms in tighter, enveloping Abby. Harvey held her close. She could feel the heat radiating off his body, and she breathed him in. His scent was intoxicating, a mix of sweat and faded cologne. She wrapped her hands around his middle, and Harvey's hands went into her hair. Abby could feel his breath on her face, hot and sweet.

Before she knew what was happening, Harvey's mouth was upon hers. It was hot, passionate, his teeth scraping her lips. She melted when he lightly nipped her lower lip, and she did her best to respond. It was a kiss Abby would remember her entire life. Time seemed to stop, existence outside the rundown house ceased to be. Abby could feel a ball of warmth start at her belly and spread throughout her arms and legs, carrying that warmth to parts of her body she didn't know existed.

Abby heard a moan escape from between them. Was it her? It must have been, because Harvey moved away and looked into her eyes. "Are you all right?"

"More than all right." Abby breathed heavily. She had never been intoxicated, but she imagined this was what it felt like.

Harvey stepped back, and Abby felt a rush of cool air between them. It made her feel empty.

"While I would love to continue, you should probably get back home. Happy birthday, Abby."

Abby pouted at the idea. She wanted to stay, but she knew he was right. She gathered up her gift and went to the doorway. As she looked back at Harvey, she blew her hair up out of her face. He stuck his hands in his pockets, and his biceps flexed. It made Abby want to giggle. She wished she could bring him home right then, but it was too late.

"I'll see you at church tomorrow?" he asked, his breaths still deep.

Abby nodded and slipped out the doorway and headed home. *Lord Jesus, help me. I'm falling in love.*

Days later, Harvey found time to have dinner with Abby and her family. Abby wasn't sure if her parents would approve of her dating. They encouraged her to find someone and get married, but she didn't think they were ready for her to date just yet. She guessed her father wanted her married before she ever dated. Besides, Harvey was nearly four years older than she and surely more experienced. Abby frowned as she figured her father would probably disapprove of that.

But the dinner happened anyway. Abby held her breath the entire time. Harvey had been to the house before, but this was in a new capacity. He wasn't there to pal around with Peter or talk shop with Nathan. He was there as Abby's boyfriend. Her mother seemed aware of that fact and placed the additional place setting to Abby's left side.

The evening was hot and muggy, one of the worst of the summer. Everyone's hair was matted down and stuck to the backs of necks. Abby was trying her best to look cool and collected, but to no avail.

Dinner was cold roast beef sandwiches with coleslaw and fresh melon. Certainly nothing special, and Abby prayed Harvey wouldn't care. Iced tea flowed freely as Grace fanned herself. Words were few, but Nathan was gracious and asked Harvey questions about Clemson College, which Harvey answered obligingly.

After the meal, Nathan invited Peter and Harvey into the living room, as was his custom with male guests. Harvey grabbed Abby's hand and squeezed it before he stood. He winked at her as he followed her father and brother out of the room. Abby didn't usually care what the men discussed in private, but now she was aching to know.

She didn't have much chance to dwell on it, as there was plenty of cleaning up to do. While she cleared the plates off the table, her mother smiled at her. "So you two are a couple?" Abby blushed in response. "He's a very nice young man, Abigail. But he's quite a bit older than you."

Abby took a deep breath, knowing her parents would bring it up. "I know, Momma. But think about it. Now, I'm seventeen, and he's almost twenty-one; but in twenty years, I'll be thirty-seven and he'll be fortyish. That's not such a big difference."

Grace laughed at her eldest daughter. "That's true; your father is four years older than me." She put her hands on Abby's shoulders and locked her blue eyes on her daughter's brown ones. "He's a very nice boy, Abby. Your father and I like him very much. We just hope he doesn't break your heart."

With a sigh, Abby admitted, "Me too."

After an hour or so, the men emerged, laughing and shaking hands. Abby was thrilled to see her father clasp Harvey's hand in his. With a fresh glass of tea swallowed, Harvey said it was time for him to go.

"Mrs. Walker, this was very nice. Your family is wonderful." He looked directly at Abby as he said that. "Thank you so much for your hospitality."

"You're quite welcome, Harvey. And please, call me Grace," she said with a nod. "We hope you can join us again one day."

"So do I." He then turned to Nathan. "Sir, I appreciate everything. Thank you very much."

Nathan only nodded and shook Harvey's hand again. As Harvey walked to the door, he looked at Abby. She, in turn, looked to her father for permission to walk Harvey out. Her father waved his hand at her and laughed. Without a word, Abby smiled and followed Harvey outside.

They gazed at the stars for a few minutes in silence before Harvey spoke. "Your family is wonderful—so boisterous, nothing like mine."

"Oh, we're a wild bunch, aren't we? Your family isn't like this?"

"Well, we didn't have six children in the house. There was only my sister and me . . . " he trailed off. "Your father seemed quite approving of our dating."

Abby blushed again. "Really? I was afraid he'd say you were too old for me."

"Nah, he said you've never seemed happier than you have this summer." Then he added with a grin, "It would seem that he's noticed our attention to each other this summer all along."

The pair sat atop the picnic table and held hands. The night air was still warm, but it had cooled considerably from when they were eating. A slight breeze moved through the air, and Abby's hair and skirt waved. The air felt wonderful on her skin, and then she noticed that it wasn't the air on her arm, but Harvey's fingers tracing them up and down.

His touch was light. He ran his fingers along her bare arms and into the crook of her elbow, tickling Abby slightly. She inhaled deeply as his fingers then traced the outline of her face. She didn't move, instead watching him intently as he studied her with both eye and hand. He cupped her chin in one hand, pulling her in for a very light kiss. It felt like the breeze and was over as quickly. But despite the briefness, it still lit a flame in the pit of Abby's stomach, and she longed for more.

Knowing she was most likely being watched by her parents, Abby whispered goodnight and slowly stood and walked toward the house. As she opened the screened door, she looked back at Harvey. He was still sitting, his arms resting on his knees, his black hair shining in the moonlight, his eyes sparkling, and his skin glistening. Abby realized she wasn't just falling in love; she had already fallen. She smiled at him and disappeared as the door closed with a clang.

***

Within two weeks, it was time for Harvey to leave for Clemson. Those weeks seemed like mere hours to Abby. She was heartbroken at the idea of his leaving, even though he would be a short car drive down the road. It might as well have been hours away, Abby thought. He was still leaving. She had spent the entire remainder of her summer by his side, and she loved it. She loved him.

The entire Walker family went to the Newmans' home to bid him farewell. They had all gotten to know him better, since he had been around the house so much. The young children hollered goodbye as they ran off to play. Peter helped Harvey load his trunks into his car.

Harvey shook hands with Nathan and Peter, promising to help them pick out a new car for Peter the next summer. Grace patted Harvey on the back and hugged him, wishing him blessings in college.

Mrs. Newman cried over her nephew. "Call me, and write."

"I will, Aunt Doris."

"Visit anytime you can for a good meal." She sniffed as she held onto him.

"Yes, ma'am," he promised. They hugged, and Mrs. Newman ran into the house. Abby's family also retreated from the scene to give the lovebirds some privacy.

Harvey looked at Abby and held his hand out to her. "It's time. I have to go."

He raised an eyebrow when Abby hesitated to come toward him. Fighting tears, Abby fell into his arms. He held onto her tightly. She could feel his heartbeat beneath her, and she felt hers slow to match his.

"You'll be back soon?" She curled her fingers around the collar of his shirt and breathed him in. He smelled like aftershave and summer heat.

"As soon as I can," he promised. Abby met his gaze through tear-filled eyes.

Wiping her eyes, Abby took an envelope from her pocket. "I already wrote you a letter. But you have to wait till you get settled before you read it."

Harvey smiled. "Okay." He held Abby close again, kissed her fore-head, then her lips. "I wish I could take you with me."

Abby giggled. "That's probably against the rules. I'll be right here. I'll see you soon, right?"

"Yes, soon. I love you." He kissed her again, and her heart soared to hear him say he loved her. "You're my angel. God brought you to me at just the right time."

Abby smiled and blushed. "I love you, too."

As Harvey climbed into the car, Abby did her best to brush tears away. She looked down, so she wouldn't watch him drive off. But when she didn't hear the car roar to life, she raised her eyes. He was leaning out of the window, waiting for her. Abby ran to him, and he kissed her with a long, deep kiss. His hands were tangled in her hair, pulling her closer to him. His teeth bit her bottom lip, and Abby felt her pulse quicken. Despite the heat around them, Abby felt chills run down her back, following his arms. She felt as though she could stay in that kiss forever.

When Harvey broke away from her, Abby let out a small cry of pain. Letting him go hurt, and she hated the feeling as her cheeks cooled. But she released him, and he released her. Harvey was breathing heavy, and Abby could feel her own chest heaving like she had been running a long distance.

The vehicle started, and Harvey waved to her.

God help me, Abby prayed. *Give me strength. Keep our love strong, Lord. I can't believe only a few short months ago, a few short weeks ago, I was so naïve and thought I would never feel like this. I couldn't imagine anybody wanting to kiss me the way Harvey just did. And now, I can't imagine my life without him. Keep him safe; bring us together again soon, please!*

And the car disappeared around the corner. Abby fought to control her *crying*, but she felt her chin quiver and hot tears roll down her cheek. She ran home and buried her head in her bed for the rest of the day.

***

Letters went back and forth between Abby and Harvey during the fall semester. They wrote each other nearly every day. Most letters were only about their daily routines, but Abby kept every single one. She pulled out an old shoebox and put each letter inside carefully, as if they would disintegrate if she treated them harshly.

Dearest Abigail,

I hope my letter finds you well and in good spirits. I am settled in here at Clemson and wanted to write you right away.

I room with a fellow named Walter McBie. He's a senior as well, and he's a good friend up here. We've been roommates since we were 2nd year cadets. He has a fiancée back home named Mary. He's from Charleston as well, but not really near my family.

We do have chapel twice a week on Tuesday and Thursday. It's got me thinking maybe to go into seminary, but I don't know. I don't think my father would like that too much, as he expects me to pick up his shipping business when he retires.

How are things going back where you are? I miss you already, and I read your letter the minute I got to Clemson. I, too, can't wait for the day we can see each other again. I often recall our kisses and am warmed by the thoughts.

How is your family? How is Peter? I wish he could be here with me; he would love it. There's lots of talk about the war in Europe. I hope it doesn't cross the ocean.

I'm getting ready for classes to start and am looking forward to all my professors and courses.

Football will start soon; I hope you can make it for a game. My parents will be coming to Homecoming, and I hope you and your family can come, too. I want you to meet my parents soon.

Until we can meet again, my heart remains with you.

Love,

David Harvey Nicholas, Jr.

Song of Solomon 6:8-9

Abby loved looking up the verses Harvey noted at the end of each letter. Song of Solomon reads, "There are threescore queens, and fourscore concubines, and virgins without number. My dove, my undefiled is but one; she is the only one of her mother; she is the choice one of her that bare her. The daughters saw her, and blessed her; yea, the queens and the concubines, and they praised her."

Abby fell back into her pillow after reading that verse and squealed. She had never considered herself beautiful, but Harvey did. Her feelings for him made her feel like her chest would burst open at any minute. She couldn't imagine loving him any more, but she expected that she would. She decided to include verses back in her letters to Harvey as well.

Dear Harvey,

It's hard to believe it's been a week since I last saw you. I was so happy to get your letter. The Scripture you included embarrassed me. I was so glad nobody was around, but I was all too happy to look the passage up and read what it says. I've included a passage for you as well.

I'm getting ready for school myself. I can hardly believe I have one year left, and I will be done with school. I wonder what I will do when I am through. I still aspire to become a baker. There's an empty shop in town, and I keep thinking it would make a great little bakery, where I could serve dough-nuts, muffins, and warm breads. We don't have a bakery in town anymore, since the Millers' place closed a few years ago. Wouldn't it be nice?

I would love to see a football game. We usually go down every so often to see the cadets march or play sports. I'm sure Peter will love it, but will be jealous not to be a cadet himself.

Meeting your parents would be great, though I admit the notion scares me. Have you told them about me? Call or write to Daddy and invite the family for a football game. I'm sure he'd be happy to take us.

Remember that first night we went out and ended up at the Lachlan house? Then we met again for my birthday, and you have given me the best birthday gift ever. Not just the paper, but your kiss. Does that sound silly? Maybe, I don't know. But it was the best gift of my seventeen years.

Momma would have my hide if she knew I wrote that. It's improper, she would say, not for a Christian girl to say. Oh well!

Let me know how your classes are going. School starts here soon. I look forward to your next letter with the anticipation of a child who longs to see snow.

With Great Love,

Abigail R. Walker

Song of Solomon 3:4

***

School started back for Abby, and the distraction from Harvey was welcome. She spent time studying and fantasizing about her future. The possibility of marriage, of a career—she felt nothing could get her down. Abby did her best to get good grades, but now that all seemed trivial compared to spending her life with Harvey. She didn't ignore her studies, but spent more time in the kitchen baking than doing homework, daydreaming of becoming Mrs. Nicholas, rather than doing her algebra.

Abby knew she shouldn't put all her future plans on Harvey. She knew it was a risky thing. She knew other local girls who were swept up with Clemson cadets, only to have their hearts broken when they left. But Abby thought Harvey was different. Surely anyone who first got to know each other at church—and not a dance hall—would have a more promising future than anyone else.

After a particularly harried day at school, Peter sat Abby down for a surprise.

"What is it?" Abby begged, her eyes dancing. She loved surprises. "Peter, what's the surprise?"

Peter skipped around Abby for a minute, annoying her and enjoying it. He felt it was his right as her brother to annoy her. "We're going to Clemson, for a football game," he finally said.

Abby jumped up, knocking her chair over. She threw her arms around her brother. "What? We are? When?" She was grinning ear to ear at the news.

"Calm down now," Peter taunted, enjoying the chance to tease his sister. "One of the guys I work with has football tickets he can't use. So, he offered them to me. So, next week, we'll be going to a Clemson College football game, and you can see Harvey there."

Abby shrieked and jumped as her parents walked in the room.

"Abby must know about the football tickets," her father said with a chuckle. His dark eyes twinkled as he recalled how his wife used to get just as excited in her youth. Abby hugged everyone in the room and bounded off to find something to wear to see Harvey.

The day before the game, Harvey called the Walker house. Abby couldn't hide her excitement at the call. It was the first one she'd ever had just for her. She did her best to press her form to the kitchen wall and talk low to avoid eavesdropping. She knew little ears were everywhere.

"Harvey?"

"Abby, hello!" He sounded as excited as she was. "Abby, I'm so excited that you're coming this weekend. I just wanted to tell you that my parents will be here. I can't wait for you to meet them."

Abby gulped, and her palms began to sweat right away. "Your parents?" She tried not to sound terrified, but she was. The idea of meeting Harvey's parents made her insides turn over. "You said you told them about me?"

"Yes, Mother and Father will just love you," he gushed. "I've told them all about you. They'll be so happy to meet you finally."

"That's great, Harvey. I can't wait. When will I get to see you?"

"I'll be sitting with the other cadets at the game, but I can sneak away and see you during halftime and then after the game, of course." Harvey continued talking about the game and the cadets, but Abby was too worried about meeting his parents to listen.

"Abby?"

"Yes, sorry, Harvey."

"So I'll meet you behind the cadet bleachers during halftime? I'll find you, because I'll look just like the rest of the cadets."

"No one looks like you, Harvey," Abby said with a laugh and a blush, even though she was on the phone. "But I'll see you there, at halftime."

After hanging up, Abby sought her mother for advice on meeting Harvey's parents. Grace was all too calm for the situation as far as Abby was concerned.

"Isn't that nice? I'd love to meet Mr. and Mrs. Nicholas," Grace said as she fanned herself while the baby nursed.

Abby stood, mouth agape at her mother's sense of calm. She burst out, "Momma. Did you hear me? His parents will be there. They're rich society people from Charleston, Momma!"

Grace tapped the chair next to her bed, indicating Abby to sit. Abby obeyed, but felt too nervous to sit still. "Abby, dear, don't worry. The Nicholas family is just like our family. They work for a living; they raised a family; and I would hope they're church-going people. If they raised Harvey, I'm sure he's just like them. You have nothing to worry about."

Abby took a deep breath to calm herself but just wasn't certain. "Are you sure? What if they're different, and they think I'm not good enough?"

"Why on earth would they think that?" Grace asked, putting her hand on her daughter's arm. "You're perfect just how God made you. I know that, and Harvey knows that. They will know that tomorrow."

Feeling reassured, Abby thanked her mother and hugged her lightly. Excusing herself, she went to ransack her closet for a suitable outfit to wear. She wanted to look every bit as sophisticated as she thought they would be.

The next morning came all too soon for Abby, as she hadn't slept well. She was still scared about meeting Harvey's parents. What would they think of her? Would they treat her like a little girl? Worse yet, a poor little girl?

Her mother woke her gently by rocking her shoulder. "Abby," she whispered into her daughter's ear. "Abby, get up. I'm getting you up earlier than the others, so you can get ready first."

"Thanks, Momma," Abby mumbled as she rolled out of bed. She went to the bathroom and peered in to the mirror. She scrubbed her face until it turned pink and brushed her teeth till her gums bled. She wanted to look her absolute best for Harvey.

Lord, she prayed, *please help the Nicholas family to see me for who I truly am—a young woman who cares deeply for their son. And, Lord, please allow Harvey to find me in the crowd of people. And, Lord, one more thing. Thank You for everything You've given me. I have a blessed life, and it's full of Your grace. Thank You, even, for the opportunity to see Harvey again. Amen.*

Abby started to work on her hair. She had washed it the night before, so it was clean, but a little frizzy. She used a wide-tooth comb to get the tangles out, along with some water to tame it. She parted her hair to the side and used pins to hold the curls out of her face. She then knotted her hair into a tidy bun at the nape of her neck as she had seen done in a magazine. Abby topped the look off with a borrowed hat, hoping she looked elegant and mature.

Once every one else was awake, Abby rushed to get some food on the table, so they could leave all the sooner. Her father told her to slow down, that they had time, but Abby didn't care. The quicker they left, the quicker she got to see Harvey. It had been well over a month, and Abby was feeling desperate to feel his touch again. After what seemed like hours to Abby, the family was ready and piled into the car.

"Daddy," Eliza bellowed from the backseat after a few minutes. "Daddy, when will we be there?"

Abby was glad her younger siblings were there to ask those questions, because she had them on her mind as well.

"About five more minutes, Eliza. It's a short drive. We should see the campus in just a minute," he said.

Abby craned her neck, trying to be the first to see Clemson College. She had seen it several times before, but this time was different. This time, it housed the man she loved. She hoped to see Harvey before anything else, but knew that wouldn't happen. But just being at Clemson put her all that much closer to Harvey, so it would do for now.

"There it is!" Abby shouted, pointing at the tall clock tower that announced Clemson to the troupe. The Main Building of Clemson was a landmark of the campus. It stood out in front, like a beacon for all who came near. Housed in the top was a gigantic bell that chimed and sang each hour. Abby had always loved the sound when she heard it, but the chimes were all the sweeter to her now.

The clock got bigger, and Nathan parked the car nearby under a tree. Harvey had written that the field used for parking was known as Bowman Field and used for military exercises, as well as recreation. Abby was amazed at all the cars there just for a football game. She didn't realize it was that popular a sport. The family made their way to Riggs Field and found their seats.

"Abby, do you see Harvey?" Jacob asked, taking a seat next to her. Abby thought Jacob missed Harvey almost as much as she did. Harvey was always great with Jacob, taking time to talk to him over the summer.

"Not yet," she said as she scanned the students for a familiar face. Abby's eyes followed each row of cadets, searching for Harvey. It took a few minutes, but she finally spotted him. "There, Jake!" She pointed in the crowd. "There he is! Second row, do you see him?" Abby could feel tears burn her eyes with excitement.

Jacob stood on the bleachers to get a better look. "Harvey! Harrr-veeey!" He waved his arms wildly, but the distance was too great and the crowd too loud for Harvey to hear Jacob's call. "Oh well. I guess we'll have to wait," he said, sitting in defeat.

The game began, but Abby didn't pay attention. She was too busy watching Harvey across the field. When Clemson made a good move, Harvey would stand and cheer with his friends. He chatted with the cadet to his right when he wasn't cheering. If only he would look up, Abby was sure he would see her. During time-outs in the game, Abby could see Harvey scan the crowd. He was looking for her. She tried to stand out, but that was hard to do with all the people, and she never caught his eye in the first half of the game.

When the referees called halftime, Abby made her way down behind the cadet bleachers. She fought through the crowd of uniforms and girls in tight sweaters. She scanned the masses of people, unable to find Harvey. Frustrated, she stopped under the bleachers and stayed still, praying he would find her as he promised.

Luckily, Harvey found her without much problem. While she waited, craning her neck to catch a glimpse of him, he snuck up behind Abby and put his hands over her eyes. She gasped and twirled around, knowing it was him. Harvey picked her up and spun her around.

"Abby, oh Abby," he said, putting her back on solid ground. "Abby, I missed you so much." He kissed her cheek and kept his hands linked behind her back.

Abby felt flushed. "I'm so happy to see you." She looked into his eyes and smiled. Harvey leaned down and kissed her right in front of everyone—not that anyone was watching—but it made Abby blush just the same. The kiss was light and quick—but physical evidence of Harvey's presence there with her.

Their rendezvous was brief, as Harvey had to be back in his seat at the end of halftime, but it was enough for Abby. At least, it was enough until the game would be over, and Abby prayed for it to end quickly.

It seemed to take an eternity, but finally, the game was over, and Clemson had won. Abby had no idea what the final score was, but she knew Clemson had won by the cheering.

"Abby," Reba called. "Abby," she called louder, and finally caught her sister's attention. "Let's go."

"Oh, wait," Abby protested, grabbing her father's sleeve. "We're meeting Harvey's parents behind the stands. I promised you would meet them."

He smiled at his daughter and said, "I know. That's where we're going."

Nathan picked up Eliza and kept moving with the crowd. Abby's mom winked at her, while she tried to console a hungry Gabriel.

Once out of the bleachers, Abby tried to nudge everyone to where Harvey said to meet him. She kept repeating Harvey's instructions: "He said behind the stadium there are two large magnolia trees, and we're to go there."

No one was hurrying, which was leaving Abby exasperated. *Why did we have to come from a place where people don't know how to rush? This is the time to rush,* she thought. *God, tell them to hurry.* And in response to that prayer, God told the family to stop.

"I need to feed the baby," Grace said. "Let's stop and do that while the crowd thins." Before Abby could say a word of objection, Nathan announced that it was a good idea and parked himself under a nearby tree. Abby sighed and leaned against the tree herself, not wanting to sit and spoil her dress. She was fidgeting with anticipation.

"Don't worry, Abby," Peter said from the other side of the tree. "They have old friends here; they'll be a while, anyway."

"You think?"

"Yeah," he said, and then whispered, "Emmeline and I will wander that way, and if we see them, we'll tell Harvey you're on your way."

"Thanks, Peter." Abby knew she had lucked out with a brother so willing to help her out. Not all brothers were as nice as Peter. He smiled and took Emmeline's arm, and they sauntered off together, waving to the rest of the family as they went.

Abby stood in the shade and watched Reba, Jacob, and Eliza play with leaves that were starting to fall. She then looked at her parents. *I don't fit in this picture,* she thought. *I would have loved to play with my sisters and brother, but I'm too old. And I am certainly not old enough to be married with children of my own either.* Abby wished she could fit into one of the two groups, but wasn't sure which one she wanted more—to play or to be responsible. She decided to be happy with where she was because God had made her this age at this time for a reason. And that reason was Harvey.

"Abby," Grace called to her daughter. "Abby, what are Harvey's parent's names?"

"Mr. and Mrs. David H. Nicholas," she replied matter-of-factly. "His father is in shipping." Abby prattled on about what she knew of the Nicholas family, while Grace finished feeding Gabe.

Once the baby was satisfied and had drifted off to sleep, they walked through the thinning crowd toward the place Harvey had told her to find him. She spotted him in an instant. He was joined by Peter, Emmeline, and some well-dressed people. He was laughing, which made Abby feel jealous that she wasn't in on the joke. She immediately felt inadequate, but had no time to run and hide as she wished because Harvey had seen them. Abby and her family went to the group, and the introductions began. Harvey, being a polite young man, started with the Walkers.

"Mother, Father, I would like to introduce to you Mr. and Mrs. Nathan Walker," he said, holding his hand out to Nathan and Grace. "These are my parents, David and Jane Nicholas."

Pleasant hellos and how-dos were exchanged, and hands were being shaken all over. "Father, Mother, these are their other children—Reba, Jacob, Eliza, Gabriel, and Abigail," he said, pausing before Abby's name and smiling.

"Yes, we've met Peter and his friend," Mr. Nicholas said. "These are our good friends, Jean and Nina Renard. And this is their daughter, Clarice. I believe she's the same age as your Abigail."

"Yes, pleased to meet you," Nathan said, extending his hand to Mr. Renard. While they shook hands, Mrs. Renard kissed Grace on the cheek, which took her by surprise.

"Ouí, Monsieur Walker. It is so nice to meet you all," Mr. Renard said with a heavy accent. Harvey whispered to Abby that the Renards were French, but had lived most of their lives in Charleston.

Clarice came up to Abby and Reba and kissed them on the cheek as her mother had done to their mother. "Abigail, Reba, so nice to meet you," she said in a southern drawl completely unlike her parent's accents.

Clarice Renard was considerably shorter than Abby, which she didn't know was possible, given her age. But she held her back impeccably straight and her chin taut, giving herself a regal appearance. Her yellow hair bounced in formed curls with the front swept up like a Hollywood starlet, most likely done with a hot iron, Abby thought. Her eyes were small and deepset, but were the color of the sky. Clarice's mouth was tiny and puckered, and she wore too much rouge on her cheeks. Abby immediately disliked her.

Reba answered when Abby didn't. "Clarice? Yes, nice to meet you, too."

"How do you know our Harvey?" she asked as she smiled toward the cadet.

Reba, ever perceptive, said, "We met him when he was helping out on his aunt's farm. He's friends with our brother, Peter." She seemed to know not to mention that he and Abby were a couple.

"Oh, okay," Clarice replied, putting a hand to her bouncy hair. "I've known the Nicholas family since I was practically a babe. Harvey and I grew up together. Our families go way back."

"How nice," Abby said, lying. She didn't think it was nice, and she hated the heat of jealousy that rose up in her body. *Lord, forgive me.*

Harvey came over to join the girls, as did Peter and Emmeline. Abby was glad to have the crowd on her side, if there were sides. Harvey stood between Clarice and Abby in the circle they had created, and he allowed his hand to brush against Abby's, his rough hand across her delicate skin. She knew it meant that he was there with her. Abby wanted him to grasp her hand and profess his love for her, but knew that it would be inappropriate.

Emmeline spoke out in an effort to be polite. "Clarice, are you still in school?"

"Ouí, yes," she said bluntly, turning her attention to Emmeline. "I get tutored during the week in writing, mathematics, politics, and French." She continued to talk about her studies and how gifted she just happened to be.

While she spoke, Harvey positioned himself behind Abby and whispered, "Her family and my family are friends. She's full of herself;

I only tolerate her for Father and Mother." As Clarice began to talk in French, he added, "I admit, I can't stand her."

Abby giggled, causing Clarice to stop short, turn and glare. "Is there a funny joke?"

Thinking quickly, Abby looked immediately to her smaller siblings and said, "I'm just watching the children play." She motioned to Jacob and Eliza. "They make me laugh at times."

Narrowing her eyes to slits, Clarice turned to where Abby pointed to see Jacob pull Eliza's braid, making her turn and chase him. "Hmm, well. Aren't we glad we're no longer children?"

"I quite miss pulling on girls' braids," Harvey said as he gently tickled Abby's neck without anyone else seeing.

"Humph," Clarice said in return, and she remained silent.

The topic turned to the football game, and Harvey and Peter become engrossed in retelling the game they had just seen. Abby, Reba, and Emmeline talked about what was happening in school, and Clarice was left out of the conversation. She positioned herself next to Harvey and laughed whenever he did.

After a while, Harvey broke away from the teenagers and brought Abby over to where their parents were talking with the Renards. Abby wished she could turn and see Clarice's face as they walked away together.

"I want my parents to get to know you better," Harvey said to her, and then he spoke to his parents. "Father, Mother, Abby is considering becoming a master baker and opening her own bakery shop. What do you think about that?" Abby blushed madly as Harvey shared her secret desires with the adults.

"Splendid, Abigail," Mr. Nicholas said. "You enjoy cooking?"

Thrown into the spotlight, Abby tried her best to sound confident. "Yes, Mr. Nicholas. I love to bake cakes and breads." She glanced to her parents, who knew of her affection for baking, but disapproved of the idea of their daughter owning and operating her own business.

"Lovely. And even if you don't work, you can always use those talents at home and for your church," Mr. Nicholas said with a nod.

Before Abby could reply, Nathan interrupted, placing a hand on Abby's shoulder. "We think our Abby is very smart and talented. She'll put those talents to work one day as a wife and mother."

Abby was never so embarrassed. Didn't her father think she was good enough to make pastries or smart enough to run a shop? Or was it the money that would have to be invested that made her father so disapproving? She knew he was from an old train of thought, but she still turned red at his comment.

"Well, it's so nice to meet a girl with a goal," Mrs. Nicholas said cheerfully. Abby found it painfully clear that the Nicholases had no issues with money.

"Yes, isn't it?" Mrs. Renard said dryly. Her steely gray eyes looked Abby up and down like a piece of meat. "Do you have many suitors, darling?"

"Oh, she has several young men hanging on her every word and every muffin, don't you?" Harvey retorted as he placed his hand on the small of her back. Abby blushed and said nothing.

And for once, she was happy to see Clarice, as she gave Abby a chance to avoid the question. "Mother, I was just about to ask Harvey why he doesn't write me," she said. "Why haven't you written?"

She gave Harvey a pouty look with her small lips, and Abby thought she looked like she had just sucked on a lemon. Clarice laid her hand across Harvey's forearm, and she eyed Abby as she did it. Harvey shifted to lean on a tree, removing himself from under Clarice's grasp.

"I don't have much to write, Clarice," he said. "It's pretty boring up here."

"Well, I write to you; you should write back," she said, edging closer to him. "I'm sure you get lonely with no contact from the outside world."

"No, actually, I'm not lonely at all," Harvey said, eying Abby. She smiled and felt confident.

Clarice turned red as she followed Harvey's stare to Abby. "Oh, well . . . " She faltered in her confidence, but regained it quickly enough. "Too bad you don't have someone as educated as me to write to you."

At that, Abby turned red, which Clarice noticed right away. She looked smug, like she had just won a small victory over Abby. Without missing a beat, Harvey ignored Clarice and spoke to his father. "How are things back home, Father?"

As they began to talk about things in the shipping business, Clarice meandered behind Abby. "Don't think that just because Harvey lets you tag along and write him letters of your boring life out here in the middle of nowhere that it means anything," she hissed. "Our parents have had us matched up since we were children. We're practically engaged, so don't think you can land the rich life. Harvey would never fall for a poor hillbilly like you."

Appalled, Abby turned slowly to face Clarice and responded as calmly as she could. "We have a relationship. The only one looking to get rich is you."

"You don't mean anything to him."

"I would beg to differ," Abby said, then added, "and so would he." With that, she turned and walked away. *Father, I need Your guidance. Let*

*me be the better person here. Let Your patience and grace shine through me.
And, Lord, let that Clarice Renard fall flat on her face. Sorry, I didn't mean
it. Entirely. Give me assurance; give me wisdom.*

After another few moments, the Walkers said it was time for them
to go. Abby was relieved to be away from Clarice Renard, but sad
to leave Harvey behind, especially since Clarice would still be there.
Everyone exchanged polite farewells, and Mrs. Nicholas asked Grace
to keep an eye on her sister, Doris. The Walker family began the walk
back to their car.

"Father, I'm going to be gentlemanly and escort the Walkers to their
automobile. The parking area is still quite crowded, and they may have
a hard time locating it," Harvey said.

His father waved him on and went back to his conversation with
Mr. Renard. Clarice fumed with jealousy as she looked after the troupe
as they walked back toward their vehicle.

Harvey didn't do much escorting of the family, as they all sped
off and left Abby and Harvey trailing behind. Abby knew her family
may not have the education and breeding of the Nicholases or Renards,
but they knew all about respect for others. Abby and Harvey were
allowed to walk at their own pace behind the family. Abby knew her
father could turn around at any time and see them just fine. But he
was trusting and didn't glance back even once.

Harvey took Abby's hand right away, making her feel protected.
His hand was strong and firm as it enveloped her smaller one. It felt
like a warm summer night, even thought it was October. Abby was
reminded of when they went to the Lachlan house and shared their
first kiss. She desperately wanted Harvey to kiss her again. But she was

ALLISON WELLS   71

a good Christian girl and knew she shouldn't be kissing him behind her father's back. The pair didn't talk, just held hands and walked along.

Abby stole glances to her side of Harvey in his blue cadet uniform. He looked so sophisticated and mature. He peeked at her, and she blushed as she looked away. Once out of the crowd of football fans, Harvey put his arm around Abby's shoulder. With his other hand, he lifted Abby's chin so they were gazing into each other's eyes while they walked. They didn't look forward or back the rest of the stroll. Once they approached the rest of the family, Harvey let go of her, and Abby felt her shoulder grow cold. She became very sad that she was separating from Harvey yet again.

Emmeline met them several yards in front of the car. "Your mother has to, um, feed the baby, so it will be a while before we go. You have a few minutes before it's time to leave."

"Thanks, Emmeline," Abby said, smiling. Seeing that she wouldn't be missed anytime soon, she and Harvey quickly darted behind the nearby tree for a more private goodbye. The tree was large and shady— at least enough that her family couldn't peek in and see her easily.

"Thank goodness," he said, running his hand up her arm. "It would have killed me to let you go so soon."

"Harvey, don't say that."

"Sorry, Abby, but I have missed you. Missed looking into your beautiful eyes, touching your angelic hair, and hearing everything you think about."

Abby smiled and said, "You lie to me."

"Never."

"What is Clarice to you?" she asked, not really wanting to know the answer. She bit her lip and twisted her skirt in her hands.

"Nothing more than a nuisance," he said. "I purposely didn't give her my address, but she got it from Mother. I don't want her letters, and I would never have written back." He left it at that, and Abby was satisfied. "I don't want to talk about her. I want to talk about you. How's school going?"

"Slowly," she said, laughing. "It never went this slowly before I met you. I'm ready for this year to be over."

"As am I," Harvey said as he leaned in and kissed her forehead. Abby loved the feel of his lips on her skin; it gave her butterflies in her stomach. She leaned up against the tree for support, and he pressed his body to hers.

"After this year," he started, "I'm going to marry you, and then you're going to take some classes, so you can become a baker or chef or whatever you want to be. And then we'll have a family; I promise."

"Harvey, don't make promises you can't keep," Abby said. But her stomach fluttered with hope and promise, regardless of what she said.

"Abigail Walker, I will keep this promise. With God on our side, we can't fail. We will get married one day. And we'll have a big family like yours. You want a big family, right?"

Abby hadn't thought about it too much. Before meeting Harvey, she had not thought about marriage or a family at all. Now, she could practically see the two of them on their own front porch, watching their children play in the yard.

"Abby?"

"Well, I hadn't really thought about it," she confessed. "I want a family; how big doesn't matter."

"I want a big family," he said, holding his arms outstretched. "You and me and many children. Children with wild, curly hair," he added, fingering the curls that had come loose from Abby's bun.

"Harvey, that's improper!" she exclaimed, looking to be sure no one heard him.

"But you're my girl. I want to love you and have children with you," he said with a spark in his eye Abby could see, despite the low light. "Let you hair down. I miss seeing it down and all around your face."

"But I did it up all nice and sophisticated . . . "

"I don't care about sophisticated," he interrupted. "I care about seeing you with your curls tumbling down your shoulders. Please."

Looking past Harvey to where her family was, Abby could see she was not yet missed. She turned back to Harvey and took her hat off, resting it on a branch. Abby took several pins out of her hair and let it fall. When she started to run her hands through it, Harvey stopped her, his hand on hers.

"I love you," he whispered.

"I love you, too, Harvey," she whispered back.

He set her hands by her side and unraveled her hair himself. Abby closed her eyes and enjoyed feeling Harvey's hands in her hair. It felt like a sin, and Abby prayed it was not a sin for him to do this.

"Your hair feels like silk," he said into her ear.

Harvey kissed her neck. Abby couldn't speak, couldn't breathe. *This has to be a sin,* she thought, *because nothing feels this wonderful and isn't a sin.* She didn't move, and allowed Harvey to move around her. He stood behind her, her hair in his face, and wrapped his arms around her waist, pulling her back close to his chest. Abby could feel his breath on her bare skin and felt his hands resting on her middle, just under her chest.

"Abigail." Abby turned toward Harvey when he said her name and pressed herself against him. She held him close, unhappy with any space between them. Again, Harvey whispered her name in her ear, and Abby felt like lightning raced through her body. It was nothing she had ever experienced before.

Harvey kissed her neck, her chin, her cheeks. His lips finally landed on her mouth. Abby felt like she was being fed after fasting for weeks. Kisses that would have to sustain her for weeks to come. She thought that this is what an earthquake must be like—frightening, exciting, and full of energy.

Harvey's hands moved all over her back, sending shooting sparks down her spine. Abby locked her hands in Harvey's short hair. Abby felt electric, like the earth would crumble under her. His touch melted her skin and brought it to life as he kissed every inch of her exposed skin. Before she knew what was happening, Harvey's hand took hold of the back of her neck, and he pressed a demanding kiss onto her lips. Abby felt both shocked and excited. She gasped.

The gasp must have alarmed Harvey because he pulled away from her hastily and rested his hands on his knees as he caught his breath. "Abby, forgive me," he said, his chest heaving. "I'm so sorry."

"Sorry? Why?" Abby said, also trying to catch her breath. *Did I do something wrong?*

"Forgive me. I shouldn't have . . . you should be treated better. I shouldn't touch you like that."

But she had enjoyed every touch he had placed on her; she didn't understand. "Harvey, it's okay, it felt wonderful."

In her head, she said the Lord would have to forgive her later. Improper or not, she loved the way Harvey's touch made her feel. She felt beautiful.

"Still, it's not right. I have no right to do that," he said.

Abby still felt lightheaded and unsure. "But you want to marry me?"

"Of course. And then I will touch you the way God designed a husband to touch his wife," he said. "Until then . . . I probably need to go back."

With that, Abby's senses came back, and she felt depressed. "No, Harvey."

"Yes, sweetheart. You have to return home," he said, cupping her face in his hands. "We both have to finish school, and then we can get married."

Abby didn't want to cry, so she started to pull her hair back up, when he stopped her. "Let me look at you first. You look like an angel."

Abby stood there, under a big oak tree at Clemson College and let Harvey's eyes roam over her. Even though they did not touch, the act still felt just as intimate to Abby as their kisses. She stood in her green dress, her hair flowing over her shoulders. She took the chance to drink him in as well. He was so handsome, she thought. She missed his thick black hair that would hang in his brilliant green eyes, now given way to a cadet crew cut. But he was still the handsomest man she had ever seen.

Lost in their own world, an interruption came from Reba's voice. "Abby? Abby, come on!"

"I'll be right there," Abby called back. She quickly twisted her hair up and pinned it in place, topping it off with her discarded hat.

"I hope no one notices," she smiled at Harvey.

"It's getting dark," Harvey offered. They both straightened up before coming back around the tree.

"I hate to leave you," Abby said.

"And I hate for you to go," he said in return. "But it's just for a little while. I'll see you soon. I love you."

"I love you, too," Abby said, resting her hand on his chest. He leaned in and kissed her.

"Go on. I'll write you tomorrow," he said, pulling Abby back.

"Okay. Soon, I'll see you soon," Abby tried to hide her tears. She was unsuccessful.

As they returned to the car, Harvey whispered to her, "Don't cry, my love. We will be together again soon." He kissed her goodbye, bid farewell to Abby's family, and turned away.

5 October 1941

Abby,

How I hated leaving you last night. I can't stand to see you cry. I did my best to be jovial when I returned to my parents and guests. Father said I had been rude and been gone too long. I told him I have quite a rapport with your family and enjoyed a pleasant conversation with them before you all left.

I brought you up in the conversation with Father and Mother. Mother said you were an attractive girl, and she said she commended you for knowing what you want to do with your life beyond marriage and children. Mr. Renard said he was most impressed with your entire family, especially for not being well-educated people. He's quite the snob, isn't he? Don't mind the comment; that's actually a compliment from him.

But all I could think of, and am still thinking of, is our time alone. It was so brief, yet so sweet. The kisses we shared were almost electric. I know you sensed it too; I could feel it in your body. I'm still apologetic about the demanding way I forced that kiss on you. I should be treating you like the princess you are.

October is here, which means Thanksgiving is soon approaching. I told Mother last night that I would be spending that holiday with Aunt Doris, since Uncle Frank is still gone in the army. I'll have to return to Charleston for Christmas holiday, but at least I can see you over Thanksgiving.

Until then, I'll be living off your kisses and your touch. May God sustain me in my wait.

Happily Yours,

Harvey Nicholas

Hebrews 1:3

Abby felt better about meeting Harvey's parents after receiving his letter. His mother thought she was attractive, which made her feel good about her efforts to look sophisticated.

She still did not feel ashamed of how Harvey had touched her. She didn't tell anyone at home about it, but she wasn't ashamed. Abby did think she better ask God's forgiveness for enjoying it, so she did, and she felt completely at ease with the entire thing. She felt like a woman, a desirable woman. And if she tried hard enough, she could still feel the heat from Harvey's hands against her.

Abby looked up the passage he scrawled under his name and then took out her paper and pen and wrote him back.

Harvey,

Please don't ever worry about touching me so. Surely, you have asked forgiveness from God and me. I have granted it, and I know God has also.

I'm so pleased your mother liked me. I don't care what Mr. Renard thought, or his daughter Clarice. I know it's not Christian of me, but I don't care for her that much. That's a lie; I hate her. I don't like her around you. It makes me jealous, and I hate that feeling, as well.

Thanksgiving is just a few weeks away. Surely, we can hold out until then. We made it from August until October, didn't we?

School is going well. I had a geography exam earlier this week, and I did fairly well on it. It was about South Carolina geography. I was very interested in the topics about Charleston. I hope I can go there one day with you.

Gabriel is growing so fast. I can't believe he's nearly five months old. I promise he's bigger than when you saw him last week. He wants to sit on his own now. And Eliza knows her alphabet.

Oh, I spoke to your Aunt Doris the other day. She sends her best and wants me to tell you that Freddy is beginning to walk! She's very proud of him. She misses your uncle something terrible. When you come for Thanksgiving, you'll cheer her up so much.

You'll cheer me up, too. I'm praying for the weeks to go by quickly. Write soon.

Yours in Love and in God,

Abby Walker

Psalm 5:1-3

CHAPTER 5

ABBY ANTICIPATED THANKSGIVING LIKE A child waiting for Saint Nicholas. It was only a day away, and she was flushed with excitement. Harvey would be joining them after dinner, as he was eating with his aunt and her family. Abby was to expect him around six o'clock. Grace kept Abby busy in the kitchen to keep her from fidgeting. Peeling potatoes and tearing up bread for stuffing, Abby was happy for the distraction. Once she finished those tasks, Abby set to making sweet tea. Usually a summer drink in the Walker home, Abby was adamant on having some for Harvey. Her mother and sister only watched and shook their heads at Abby's insistence.

"Abby, it's too cold for iced tea," Peter commented as he came in the room and grabbed an apple out of a bowl.

"No, it's not. It's supposed to be warm tomorrow," she predicted. *Lord, let tomorrow be warm,* she prayed silently.

"Says who?" Peter raised an eyebrow at her forecast.

"Me," she pouted. "I think it will be warm tomorrow." She at least knew she would be warm tomorrow once Harvey's arms were around her.

Grace just smiled as she watched Abby work so hard. She remembered what it was like to want to impress a suitor and let her daughter get a little carried away in the preparations.

Abby's father came in and announced that things were looking bad in Europe. He had been listening to the radio and they're all fired up about this war and Hitler. Abby hated talk about it, so she tried to tune him out, but she kept thinking about Frank Newman and the other men in the army. Abby prayed for things to calm down over there, so no American boys would have to fight. She wasn't alive for the Great War, but she had heard enough stories to not want it to happen again.

"People are saying Japan is going to get more aggressive and attack the Indies," Nathan said.

"What's there?" Grace asked.

"Resources they need." Nathan shrugged. "They'll find some way of attacking someone. And those Nazis are going through Eastern Europe taking over every city they set their sights on . . . "

Abby did her best to close her ears off, but she couldn't drown him out completely. She excused herself; she didn't want to hear anything else that could ruin her Thanksgiving.

Abby awoke the next morning feeling giddy and euphoric. Harvey would be at her house that very evening. She could hardly wait. She knew the entire day would be agony until she saw him.

Stopping by the house early was Dottie, talking an awful lot about Pastor Phillips. They had been seeing each other a lot lately, and he even met Abby's grandparents recently. Perhaps they would be hearing wedding bells soon.

"I think he may be getting ready to propose, and I am ready for it," Dottie told Abby as they sat at the kitchen table. She extended her hand and wiggled her ring finger. Abby liked that her aunt confided in her like a friend. She was only a few years older than Abby, and they got along very well.

"I wish I could be proposed to," Abby sighed, resting her head on her propped up hand.

"Abby, you're only seventeen; you have plenty of time."

"I know, but Momma was sixteen when she married Daddy," Abby reasoned.

Dottie thought a moment. "Yes, I know. Can you imagine that?"

"No. I didn't like anyone when I was sixteen. Well, I met Harvey but wasn't thinking marriage last year. Now it's all I think about."

"Tell me about it. Now, when is Harvey coming?"

"I think six." Abby blushed and smiled.

"Well, we still have an hour or so before we eat and everything's ready," Dottie said. "How about I fix up your hair? I love to play with it."

"Sure." Abby smiled. They stood and went back to Abby's room. Abby sat on her bed, facing the window. She watched some birds fly around the yard while her aunt pulled a chair over behind her. Dottie parted her hair behind the ears and began to weave a braid around the top of Abby's head, leaving the rest free. Abby felt her hair cascade down her back and was reminded of Harvey telling her she looked like an angel. Abby's mind began to daydream, and she leaned her head back more for Dottie to continue what she was doing. With all the talk about marriage going on, Abby couldn't help but think what it would be like to get married.

Aunt Dottie is behind me, working in my hair. When she announces she's done, I'm ready to go. It's my wedding day, and I'm about to be the happiest person on earth.

I check the mirror and see myself in a white dress with lace on it, white lace in my hair and flowers in my hand. Momma is to my right, all dressed up. And my sisters are on my left, also dressed for the occasion. Everyone is crying and saying how lovely I look. My hair is down, the way Harvey likes it.

I get ready to walk down the aisle. Behind the door is my groom, waiting for me. As I take a deep breath, I can smell him . . .

Abby came out of her daze and felt nearly crazy because she thought she really could smell Harvey. She took a deep breath, and her heart skipped. Her longing for Harvey was so strong, she could actually smell him.

"Aunt Dottie," she whispered with her eyes still closed, "It's crazy, but I miss Harvey so much, I can smell him."

She felt hot breath next to her ear and then heard a voice, low and masculine. "It's not crazy, Abby."

Her eyes flew open. It was Harvey! She spun around to see him standing behind her, a huge grin on his face.

"Harvey!" Abby nearly knocked him over as she jumped up and hugged him close. "It really is you I smell."

"Yes, it is." He held her tight. She breathed him in as he did the same. Abby loved how Harvey smelled.

"It's not a dream?" She blinked her eyes as she looked at him closely.

"No, Abby," he said, laughing, "it's not a dream."

She held him close and breathed him in again. She felt Harvey's hands stroke her hair. "What are you doing here? I thought you weren't coming until after dinner."

"Well, I couldn't stand not seeing you until then, so I told Aunt Doris I had to come right over. Your mother met me at the door and said you were back here. Are you surprised?"

"So surprised. And so happy, now that you're here."

Harvey sat on her bed and looked around. "This is your room?"

Abby was suddenly very aware of where they were sitting. They were alone on her bed, and it made her hands tremble.

"Don't be embarrassed," he said. "And you don't need to blush. But I love it when you do." He ran his hand over Abby's cheek.

"Harvey, what if someone . . . " Abby panicked.

"It's okay," he said, stroking her cheek with the back of his forefinger. "Your mother is the one who sent me back here to see you. And I have been dying to see where you are when you write to me. Now I can imagine you in here. And now I know where you lay at night, where you rest your head and have wild dreams about me."

"Harvey!" Abby felt heat come over her body, and she turned away from him.

He continued, "Resting with your angelic hair falling over your shoulders and off the pillow. Oh, Abby, I wish I could watch you sleep."

Abby felt a familiar tingle in her stomach, and her faced flushed red. "Harvey, I . . . "

"Abby! Come on, we have guests!" Nathan bellowed from another room.

The heat Abby felt before was replaced with panic of her father finding Harvey in her room—her mother's permission or not. She turned to Harvey and kissed him. Hard and heavy, she kissed him, surprising the both of them. They hustled down the hall to find Pastor Phillips had arrived. Dottie was beaming. Seeing Harvey and Abby, Dottie quickly spoke up. "So, Harvey, did you get a tour of the house?"

"Um, yes," he stammered without meeting anyone's stare. "Yes, I did."

Nathan didn't know Harvey was in the house. "Harvey! So glad to see you, my boy! I didn't know you were coming for supper."

"Good to see you, too, sir," Harvey said, finally looking up and shaking Nathan's hand. "I'm afraid I can't stay for dinner. I just wanted to make sure the offer still stood for me to drop by tonight."

"Of course. Peter and I would love to talk to you some. Want to know how things are going down at that college and what you cadets are doing about this rising tension between us and those Nazis."

Harvey lit up at the idea of talking war with Abby's father. She tried not to show her disappointment.

"Yes, sir, Mister Walker! I best be off before Aunt Doris is ready to skin me. I'll be back soon." Abby and Harvey walked onto the porch. "Abby, I want to spend as much time with you as possible. But I also want to make a good impression on your father. When the time comes that we can be together, I don't want him to hesitate."

"I understand," Abby said honestly as they sat on the porch. "But I don't want you to spend all night talking about a war we're not even involved in." Also honest.

"Don't worry, Abby," he said. "I'm here to see you." And with that, he pulled Abby in close and gave her a lengthy kiss that left her head spinning. Harvey released her and ran out the door across the lawn. At the edge of the property, he turned back and waved at Abby before she returned inside the house. Abby wished she could shriek in delight, but didn't think her father would be too happy about a reaction like that.

A few minutes later, Peter and Emmeline came into the house. Abby didn't even know they had been away, as they had been around at lunchtime. Both were beaming with smiles from ear to ear. With everyone gathered around, Peter stood in front of the family, his arm around Emmeline's middle.

"Everyone, I have something to tell you." He pulled Emmeline close to him, and she shied her face from the crowd. "I spoke with Mr. Madison just this week and asked his permission to marry Emmeline."

The entire family erupted with congratulations and cheers. Grace and Dottie kissed both Emmeline and Peter. The small children talked excitedly. Pastor Phillips offered up a hearty congratulatory prayer.

Brimming with excitement for her brother and her dear friend, Abby spoke up, "So, when are you getting married?"

"Yes, when?" everyone asked at once. Peter stammered; Emmeline turned crimson.

Nathan finally spoke. "Well, they're just announcing their engagement. We'll sit down with the Madisons and talk about setting a date later. Maybe in the spring?"

"Oh, yes, a spring wedding," Grace gushed, with her hands pressed to her bosom.

Abby thought she saw Dottie give Pastor Phillips a wink and a nudge. She was a few years older than Peter, and Abby felt sure she was a little disappointed that her nephew would wed before she did. Dottie had even told Abby just an hour before that she was ready for a proposal.

The family enjoyed a Thanksgiving meal of hot turkey with stuffing, fresh corn on the cob, homemade cranberry relish, and sugar snap peas. For dessert, they enjoyed both apple and pecan pie. Afterward, everyone was again gathered in the living room, talking about the upcoming holiday season and the newly announced nuptials. When a knock was heard on the kitchen door, Abby jumped up, knowing it had to be Harvey.

Abby opened the door for him, and he smiled. "You always need to wear your hair loose and have light behind you." Harvey's eyes twinkled as he leaned in through the door frame.

"Why?" she said, laughing.

"Because it makes you glow. You're beautiful regardless, but it makes you radiant." Harvey was never at a loss when it came to praising Abby, yet she never got used to it.

"Oh, Harvey, guess what happened today? Peter proposed to Emmeline, and they're getting married in the spring!"

"How exciting," he said as he stepped through the door. He leaned close to her ear and whispered, "Maybe we will be next."

Abby looked away and blushed. "Harvey . . ." She pulled him into the living room with the rest of the family, and she prayed under her breath for their own engagement to happen one day as well.

When Peter saw Harvey, he slapped him on the back with a smile. "Harvey! Buddy! How are you?"

Shaking Peter's hand, Harvey congratulated him. "I heard the good news. I hope Emmeline can tame you." Everyone laughed, and Abby felt so happy at that moment.

Standing, Grace announced that the girls were needed in the kitchen. Abby didn't want to leave Harvey, but he whispered to her, "Just a bit, then I'll find you."

The ladies began to gather dishes and silverware and place them in the sink. The women of the Walker clan were like a well-oiled machine when it came to cleaning. Everyone knew her duty. Someone always cleared plates and put leftover food in the refrigerator for another meal; someone always swept under the table; and someone always did the dishes. Abby usually wound up with the dishes, but she didn't mind.

She donned her apron to stay dry and started scrubbing dishes. She was the first to bring up the engagement again. "How exciting about the engagement. Emme, we are going to have so much fun planning!"

Grace put her hand over her sister's. "Dottie, I'm sorry you didn't get a proposal tonight."

"Oh, I'm sorry, Dottie," Emmeline exclaimed, looking worried. "We could have announced it later."

"No, no, that's all right," Dottie said, shaking her head and smiling. "I guess it's just not my time yet. Besides, one wedding a season is all we can handle, right?"

Reba piped up, "In spring, all the flowers will be in bloom, and the latest fashions will be out."

"I don't really care about the fashion," Emmeline said. "But I do know what kind of dress I want."

"Oh, tell us," Aunt Dottie pleaded.

As Emmeline began to describe her ideal dress and how she would make it, a head popped into the kitchen. It was Harvey.

"Ladies? I just had to ask if Mrs. Walker made her famous iced tea today."

All eyes on him, Grace responded, with a smirk on her face, "No, I'm sorry; I didn't." Harvey looked a little disappointed, until she added, "But Abby did."

He entered the kitchen and looked at Abby as she washed dishes. She felt a little embarrassed that he was seeing her up to her elbows in soapy water and her frontside all wet, but she smiled as her mother poured Harvey a glass of tea.

"Thank you, Mrs. Walker," he said, taking a quick drink. "I've been looking forward to this for months. Abby, thanks for making it."

"Sure," Abby said, trying to act nonchalantly. Harvey raised his glass to the girls and disappeared back behind the door.

"She made it just for him," Reba teased when he was out of the room.

Abby turned to face her sister and stuck out her tongue. "It's a good thing I did. See? He did want some."

Grace and Dottie just giggled at her.

Well, it is a good thing, she thought. *I know how to take care of him.*

When they were done cleaning, Abby snuck back toward the living room and listened in on the men's conversation. She wanted them to hurry, so she would have more time with Harvey.

"Honestly, Pop," she heard Peter say. "I'd join the army or navy or something and go to Germany and whip those guys into shape."

Great, they're talking about that stupid war again. Will they never stop? She tried to peek in through the crack in the door, but she couldn't see any of the men.

"Peter, let's just see if those people can handle their own problems. We got enough men involved over there," Nathan replied.

"I agree," said another voice. It was Pastor Phillips. "Violence, war, and death are not the way to solve things. Christ never once lifted a hand for combat."

"This is true," Harvey finally interjected.

Good for you, Harvey; tell them to stop talking war.

"But it is a necessary evil to bring control and peace back to some people."

Abby couldn't believe her ears. Was her Harvey actually condoning war?

"With rumors that the Japs could attack our allies, there are talks in the barracks of us getting involved," he continued. "Several of the guys want to leave school and join the army."

No. No, he can't leave for the army. I won't let him. As long as nothing happens, he won't try.

"I would," Peter said. Abby really wished she could see inside the room. "I would join up in an instant."

"Atta boy," Nathan said. "If this country needs you, it's good to know solid men are willing to fight."

"That's right, sir," Harvey again. "Half of the corps of cadets is ready to sign up at a moment's notice."

Abby took a step back from the door, fresh with anger and fear. She would not let the man she loved go off to an uncertain war. She refused to entertain the idea. Feeling the sting of tears in her eyes, she went to the bathroom to wash her face. Splashing water on her cheeks, she heard the men break up their talk and dissipate. Pastor Phillips and Dottie left, and Peter took Emmeline home.

Abby knew Harvey would be looking for her, so she emerged from the bathroom to find him. She spotted him on the porch and joined him on a swing. She sat beside him, but left a large gap between them.

"See? I told you I would get to spend time with just you," he said.

"For how long?" Abby snapped, feeling the bitterness in her words.

"Well, I do have to go back to Aunt Doris' tonight." He laughed, not catching what Abby meant.

"I heard you." The chill in the air did nothing to dispel the hot anger she felt flaring.

"Heard me?"

"Yes, talking about war," she murmured. "You would go, wouldn't you? You would join the army and leave?"

Harvey knelt in front of Abby and picked up her chin with his hand. It felt cool on her flushed skin. "Yes. I would. My father fought in the Great War, my ancestors in the Civil War. I wouldn't turn down a chance to defend my country if it rose."

Abby knew she couldn't argue with him, but still needed to be heard. "But what about me? Harvey, don't you love me?"

"You know I do."

"And you would still leave me?"

"How much of our conversation did you hear?" he asked.

"Not all of it, but some."

"Well then, did you not hear your brother say the same? And he and Emmeline are going to get married soon." His eyes searched hers for understanding. She had a hard time turning those eyes down, but she did her best.

"If I were Emmeline, I would say the same thing," Abby explained. "What if something were to happen?"

"Look, Abby." He moved next to her, closer than before. "As of now, nothing is happening. It's all what-ifs. Don't worry so much. I'll never be farther away than your heart."

Abby sighed, still unsure, but trusted that God wouldn't take Harvey across the world. They stood and walked out into the yard and sat on a picnic table under the oak tree. Harvey put his arm around Abby's shoulder, and she leaned into him. *I could stay like this forever,* she thought.

"I'm sorry if I upset you," he whispered. He gathered her hair with his fingers and pulled it behind her ear. It was a very delicate touch and gave Abby a chill.

"I'm not upset," she whispered back.

"Okay. Tell me about Peter's wedding. I'm sure you girls have it all planned already."

Abby looked at him, curious as to why he was interested. He probably just wanted to change the subject, which was fine with her. "Well, Emmeline said they're going to get married in the spring. And she told us about her dress, but I was daydreaming and forgot what she said."

"What did you daydream about?"

Abby blushed and looked at Harvey. "You." She could see her reflection in his eyes and thought he was seeing into her soul.

Before Harvey could respond, a dark figure approached them from the trees and distracted them. A man's voice called to her, "Abby?"

Startled, Abby strained to see who it was. She could barely make out of the figure in the dim light. "Jack? Is that you?" She inched closer to Harvey as she said his name.

"Abby, who is this you're with?" Jack shouted, his voice angry.

As he came in to the light, Abby could see the scowl across his face. He was wearing his coveralls from the auto shop he worked at. It was smeared with grease, as was Jack's face.

As Jack stepped closer, Abby introduced Harvey. "Jack, this is a family friend, Harvey Nicholas. Um, Peter took Emmeline home if you're looking for him."

"I don't care about Peter right now." He scowled as he looked Harvey up and down with disgust. "What are you doing alone with this guy?"

Harvey spoke up. "Calm down, buddy. Like she said, I'm a friend of the family."

Jack stepped closer. "No, I'm a friend of the family. And I think you better leave my girl alone." He took another step. Abby could tell he was intoxicated. His gait was off, and his words ran together.

"Harvey, just tell him to leave. Please," she said quietly. "Jack is an old friend of Peter's who has been pursuing me. I always tell him no."

Abby saw her father appear in the doorway, but he didn't come outside just yet. He watched Jack stagger in the yard.

"You heard her, Jack. It's time for you to go," Harvey called out.

"You! You get your hands off her," Jack commanded. "Abby's my girl."

"I'm afraid you're mistaken, pal."

"No, you're mistaken. Pal." Jack lunged closer to where Abby and Harvey were sitting.

Harvey jumped off the table and in front of Abby to protect her from Jack's wild movements. "Go on, Jack. Leave. Abby doesn't want you here."

Jack stopped and looked at Abby, who shied away behind Harvey. Her action enraged him, and he leaped toward Harvey and managed to tackle him to the ground. Both went down into the dirt.

Abby screamed, "No, stop!"

Nathan ran outside and tried to break the boys up, but couldn't get between them fast enough.

"Daddy! Stop them!" Abby stood on top of the picnic table and watched, terrified. And she prayed, *Lord, please, if You're watching this, make them stop! Please make Jack leave. I'm not worth all this. Make them stop!*

Jack pulled his arm back and landed his fist in Harvey's jaw. Abby couldn't watch any longer and ran up the porch steps, yelling for her mother. Harvey got the upper hand and punched Jack in the stomach, doubling him over. Jack groaned in pain, but didn't give up. Harvey stood, chest heaving, and he and Jack threw punches. They were out for blood.

Nathan continued to attempt to pull the two apart, but wasn't strong enough or stupid enough to get in the middle. Peter appeared from across the yard and ran over to help when he saw the commotion. He grabbed Jack by the middle and pulled him off Harvey, hurling him through the air. Nathan rushed to grab Harvey to keep them apart.

Peter pushed Jack on the ground. "What's wrong with you?" he screamed as he stood over Jack.

"I love your sister, Peter. And this joe thinks he can put his hands all over her!"

Abby was shocked and called out from the porch, "He has not put his hands on me. Besides, I love him!"

With that remark, all four men stopped and looked at Abby. The silence was deafening.

"Jack, you have been drinking," Peter announced, distracting the others from Abby. "Just stay away from my family."

"I thought I was your best friend, Pete," Jack said as he picked himself up off the ground.

"So did I, Jack, but not anymore."

Grace came outside and said she had called Jack's father. She put her arms around Abby and brought her inside. Nathan told Peter and Harvey to go inside and get cleaned up; he would wait for Jack's father to arrive and have a word with him alone. Abby was in shock that Harvey and Jack had been fighting over her. *Am I even worth fighting over?*

Slightly battered, Harvey and Peter walked into the house. Harvey sat on a kitchen chair, wiping a mixture of sweat, dirt, and blood from his brow.

"Harvey! Harvey, are you all right?" Abby rushed over to his side and knelt beside him.

Still breathless, he said he was fine. Abby looked at his hands, cut and bleeding with dirt ground in. His cheek was bright red, and there was a cut above his right eye. A small trickle of blood had run down the side of his face. Abby picked up her skirt and started to wipe the dirt and blood away.

"You're getting blood all over yourself," Harvey said with a heavy voice.

"I don't care," she said, and she didn't. "Come on, let's clean you up."

Grace came into the room with first aid supplies, and Abby started to carefully clean Harvey's wounds. Abby doctored them the best she could, thankful most weren't too deep. Her mother and brother went to another room, leaving Abby and Harvey alone in the kitchen.

"Harvey, I can't believe you," Abby scolded. "Getting in a fight like that. What will my Daddy think . . . ?"

Abby looked up and cringed. Harvey's left eye was already turning purple and swelling shut. Tears sprang to her eyes, and she lost any words left in her mouth. After a few deep breaths, she went back to cleaning Harvey up, feeling guilty for his fight. When Harvey winced from pain, Abby could feel tears slip over her cheeks.

"I'm so sorry," she whispered.

"Don't be," he said. Harvey took her hands in his and kissed them gently. Harvey consoled Abby as she cried; he kissed her hands and forehead and pulled her close to him. "I'm fine, Abby. I've had worse before," he said as he attempted to smile.

"Oh, if only Jack had stayed away," she sobbed. "I have never told him I like him; I promise you. I don't know why he won't leave me alone."

"I think you're safe now," Harvey said. "If he didn't believe you before, he will now."

"Why? Because you beat him up?"

Harvey smiled. "Because, Abigail Walker, you said you loved me in front of the lot of us. I think he got the hint."

Abby had forgotten about declaring her love for Harvey. Her father had heard it. Peter had heard it. Abby was willing to bet that half the town had heard it.

"I can't believe I did that," she said quietly. "Daddy will never let you see me again after that. What a mess."

"Don't be too sure of that," Nathan said from the doorway. He crossed to where Harvey was sitting and extended his hand. "I don't condone fighting on my property. But I'm mighty glad to see you defend my daughter, son." He put his hand on Harvey's shoulder as he said the word *son.*

"We've had enough excitement for tonight," Grace said as she came back into the room. "Come on, Nathan, let's get to bed. Abby, don't you be up too late."

"Yes, Momma."

"Goodnight, dear," she said. Grace nodded at Harvey and led Nathan out of the kitchen, leaving the couple alone.

Harvey looked at Abby with concern in his eyes. "Are you okay?"

"Me? I'm fine. But look at you! Oh, I can't believe this happened," she said, tenderly feeling the bruises on Harvey. "Let me get you some ice."

Before she could get up, Harvey grabbed her hands. "I'm fine, Abby. Let's get out of here and go for a walk."

"Go? Where?"

"Away from here, where we can be alone. After tonight, I won't see you again until after the holidays."

"Oh, Harvey. I can't imagine Christmas without you." She fought back more tears. Abby thought she had cried more than ever since meeting Harvey.

"Christmas isn't about me, Abby. It's about the love of God, and we both have that," Harvey reminded her.

He was right, and Abby knew it. Christmas was about celebrating the birth of Christ. But how could she celebrate without Harvey by her side? Life had changed so much in a few short months, Abby realized.

They walked on from the house, hand in hand. Harvey's hands enveloped Abby's. They walked in silence, and before they knew it, they were standing in front of Abby's family church. Mount Olive was an old church of over one hundred years, and the Walker family had been attending from the very beginning. It was nothing special—white clapboard sides with a brown roof. The steeple was white with a white cross on the top. The windows were stained glass scenes of Jesus with lambs, apostles, and other biblical scenery. The inside was all dark wood, hand carved generations ago. Abby's parents were married in the church; Peter would soon be married there. Abby wondered if she would be married there as well.

"It's lovely, isn't it?"

Abby was pulled from her thoughts. "Hmm?"

"The church. It's quite pretty, isn't it?"

"I suppose," she answered. "I've seen only a handful of churches before; they all look pretty much like this."

"Really?" Harvey looked surprised.

"Well, yes. It's not like we travel much. And there are only two churches in town. Other than that, I've seen a few in Clemson, and a few in other towns."

"One day, I'll take you to Charleston with me and take you to my church," he promised. "It's the oldest Baptist church in the South. It survived the Civil War, earthquakes, hurricanes; it's a grand church with tall columns in the front."

"It sounds like quite a building," Abby said with a sigh. "Our little church may not be much; it may not have columns and large classrooms, but it's my world. My grandparents were married here; my parents were married here. All my brothers and sisters were born into Mount Olive. In a few months, Peter will be married here."

Harvey laughed. "I guess the size of the building doesn't really matter, does it? It's the size of the hearts inside it that matter the most. My family is much the same. Generations have been born and married there. Generations are buried there." He snuggled in to Abby for warmth and comfort.

Abby smiled. She and Harvey may be from two different worlds, but they were essentially the same. "What about you?" Harvey asked.

"What about me?"

"Will you be married in this church?"

Abby smiled and looked at the steeple. "I sure hope so."

Harvey sighed. "I wish I had a picture of you to tide me over until after the holidays. And then until Peter's wedding. I won't get to see you in between."

"I know. But you're going to come to the wedding?" When Harvey nodded, she continued, "Oh, good! I wish we had a camera."

Harvey cupped her chin in his hand and looked her straight in the eyes. "Let me look at you, so your image is ingrained in my mind."

Abby looked down and blushed. "Harvey . . . "

"No, look up," he said. "Why do you look down? You are the most beautiful person I know. Inside and out."

"No," she stammered. "I'm nothing special. Certainly not worth fighting Jack for."

"Don't lie, Abby. We are at church, you know." Harvey's smile brought one to Abby's face. "There you go. No more looking down. You're an assertive and smart woman, Abby Walker. God made you this way. I love you this way."

Abby wrapped her arms around Harvey's waist and hugged him close. He put his hand in her hair and ran his fingers through her curls. They stayed like that, not speaking, for several minutes. The night sky expanded above them into the heavens, and Abby closed her eyes.

"Abby," she heard her name very faint, like it was on the wind. "Abby?"

She shifted, not wanting to return to reality just yet. "Yes?"

"It's getting late."

"No, it's not," she lied. *Sorry, Lord, but I refuse to give him up tonight.*

"Do something with me." Curious, she picked her head up and looked at Harvey. "Come inside," he said, moving to stand.

"Why? What's in there?" she asked softly.

"God."

"God is everywhere," Abby corrected him.

"Come on," he pleaded. "Abby? Please?"

She followed Harvey to the door as he cracked it open. The sanctuary was always left open in their small town. He stepped into the empty room cautiously. It was dark, but Abby's eyes adjusted to the small amount of moonlight shining through. Harvey made it to the front and lit a candle. His face was glowing, his lips and cheeks highlighted.

"Now what?" Abby whispered.

"Pray with me."

"What?"

"Pray with me, Abigail," he repeated. "I want us to pray together."

She was intrigued. It seemed somewhat foolish to pray in the middle of the night in an empty church, but it also seemed like the right thing to do. Like it was natural.

"I don't know what to say, though," Abby told him.

"It's okay," Harvey reassured her as he touched her cheek. "I know just what to say." He took her hand and led her to kneel next to him at the front of the sanctuary. "I've been praying it for a while now."

Abby cocked her head to the side and looked at him, her eye searching his. *He's been praying about me? I know I've been praying about him, but to know that he's been praying about me!* Abby was amazed. It made her feel all the more beautiful, knowing that he talked to the Heavenly Father about her. Abby felt humbled and overwhelmed.

The pair bowed their heads, and Harvey took Abby's hand in his.

"Heavenly Father," he began, low and quiet. "Heavenly Father, I come to You now—we come to You now—wanting to thank You. I want to thank You, Lord, for bringing forth Your light into a world of darkness. For sending Your spirit to earth to watch over us and guide us. God, thank You for guiding me to this town, to this church, and to this godly woman I come to You with today.

"Lord, I am so thankful You brought Abigail into my life. She has been a source of Your light from the moment I met her. And from that moment I first saw her, I knew she would be something special to me. She's alive for You, God. She loves You; she strives to be a Christian woman in an ever-changing world. And I thank You for her.

"God, I want to ask for Your spirit to be with us, looking over us, as we cannot look over each other on a daily basis. I ask You, Father in heaven, to always guide us back to each other, even when we are miles apart. Bless our relationship, that it remains strong. Allow it to continue to grow, as a seed grows into a mighty oak tree. Lord, I want our relationship to grow as we grow with You. The seed has been planted, and a sapling has sprung forth, but it must weather heavy storms before it can turn into the grand tree You have planned.

"And we ask Your will to be done in our lives, separately and together. May we follow the path You have chosen for us. And may those paths be side by side, intertwining, down the long road of life. We don't know Your plans, but we know You have them. Whatever Your will is, Lord, we are Your servants, ready to do as You request.

"I just pray, Father, that it is Your will for Abigail and me to marry, to have children, and to grow old together. I desire to marry this fine woman, and I think she feels the same. I want to provide her with all the love and comfort I can, which are all first provided by You, Lord. I ask that You would, when the time is right, allow her father to grant us permission to wed and start a family.

"Lord, Abby and I ask You to bless our families throughout the coming Christmas season. We especially ask Your blessing on the marriage of Peter and Emmeline. Thank You, Father, for the grace You provided on the cross, most of all. In Christ's name I ask, Amen."

"Amen," Abby whispered after Harvey. When she lifted her head, she felt hot tears roll down her cheek. She didn't even know she had begun to cry. Abby was so moved by Harvey's words and the Holy Spirit; she was completely unaware of anything else. She was next to Harvey, in front of the altar at church. Very few times in her life had she ever thought about being here getting married, but now she couldn't stop thinking about it. They had met at this church months ago, stolen glances during services here, and now they had spoken to God here.

Abby sighed. "Harvey, it's late, but I don't want to go."

Standing, he helped her to her feet. "I know, my love. But we have to. Your parents will be worried."

"Not as long as I'm with you."

"Especially if you're with me," he said with a chuckle. "Your father could skin me."

She smiled. "No, he likes you. I can tell."

Harvey smiled back. He took the candle in one hand, and Abby's hand in the other, and started back down the center aisle of the church.

"You want to marry me?" Abby asked, nervous for his answer. "You said that while you were praying."

"Yes, of course."

She swallowed hard and bit her lip. "You want to have children?"

"Yes."

"With me?" Abby asked for clarification. Her heart sang, and her stomach flipped.

He laughed. "That's the way it generally works, Abby. You get married; you have children."

She bit her lip, feeling giddy and happy. "You want to marry me? And you want me to have your children?"

"Yes, I want to marry you. And yes, I want to watch your stomach grow with child and have you bring our children into the world." Harvey's eyes gleamed with promise and hope. He bent slightly and placed his hand over Abby's abdomen briefly, but it was enough. It was enough for Abby to feel a flutter of excitement and anticipation right where he touched her.

"You've thought of all this before?" Abby was dumbfounded.

"Constantly," he said. "I'm having a very hard time waiting until next year, so I can ask for your hand in marriage. And an even harder time waiting for the marriage itself. I just want to marry you and have children and a long life together."

"How many children?" She giggled thinking about what he had said.

"How many do you want?"

"I don't know," Abby thought out loud, completely unsure. "As many as God decides to grant me."

"Sounds prefect to me," Harvey said, picking her up and twirling her around.

"But, Harvey . . . " she trailed off.

"Yes?"

"In order to have children we would have to . . . " she stammered. Loving Harvey was one thing, but the idea of lying with him was another idea altogether. Abby blushed madly, embarrassed to be talking about it. She knew that the entire discussion must be a huge sin.

"Make love?" He offered to finish the sentence.

"Yes." *God forgive me!*

"Yes, we would," he said, getting closer to her. He leaned in and spoke softly. "It will be lovely, Abigail. God made it to be a wonderful experience, a man and a woman together. And one day, when we're married . . . But let's not talk about that now."

"Harvey, have you . . . ?"

"You know better than that," he admonished. "I'm a Christian man. We will get married, and our first night together will be the first for both of us."

"Okay," Abby said and giggled. She could hardly believe they were having this conversation.

"We should go," Harvey said, a little flushed himself. He changed the subject, much to Abby's relief. "So, what do you want for Christmas?"

"Oh, I hadn't even thought about it," she said. "I just want you."

"Well, I have something for you already," Harvey admitted. "I'll post it soon."

"What is it?" Abby was excited about getting a Christmas gift from Harvey. She wondered what it would be. A ring? No, too soon.

"You'll just have to wait until Christmas."

They walked to the front of the church and out the wide doors. Harvey kissed Abby, whispered his promises of love in her ear, and then they parted ways. Abby ran home and tiptoed into the house. She slipped into bed, wondering about the future.

CHAPTER 6

ABBY HAD A HARD TIME getting into the Christmas spirit that year. All around her, others were excited and bustling about with their shopping and decorating. Abby wondered if it was because she had grown out of that magical stage or if it was something else, but she wasn't feeling very festive. All around her, the Walker family were hanging garlands and wrapping packages. Abby hoped and prayed she would find her Christmas spirit when they chopped down a Christmas tree in a few weeks' time.

It was a Sunday morning, and the entire Walker clan was scrambling to get to church on time. The disorganization was highly unusual. Everyone had to make one last pit stop somewhere around the house before they could take off for Mount Olive Baptist.

Everyone piled in the car. The air was cold, and the kids enjoyed watching their breath stretch out and freeze in front of them. It was a tight squeeze with Nathan driving, Grace holding Gabriel, and Eliza sitting between them in the front, while everyone else crammed in the back. Abby had Jake in her lap, and Reba was squished between Abby and Peter. Abby felt like a sardine, but at least they kept her warm. When they finally arrived at church, everyone rushed out of the car and took a deep breath.

"Don't worry, kids," Nathan said. "With Peter leaving soon, we'll have more room. We'll have to see about getting you a car soon, Peter." His eye sparkled as he looked at his oldest son.

Peter's face lit up. "Really? I've been saving some money."

"We'll go look around right after Christmas," Nathan promised. "How about it?"

Peter smiled. "Yes, sir!"

The Walkers sat in their usual pew. Peter had taken to sitting with the Madisons since announcing his engagement to Emmeline. Abby knew it made their mother a little sad that her son was growing up, but she was happy to see him happy. And the Madisons didn't seem to mind his joining them. Abby tried very hard to pay attention to Pastor Phillips but just couldn't seem to grasp his message. She peered around the church and looked at other families huddled together for warmth.

Abby wanted to look back and find the Newman Family. Doris Newman had been having a harder time since Harvey left; the boys were acting out at school and getting into all sorts of trouble. Abby felt bad that Mrs. Newman had no one to take care of her and the boys and no one to talk to at night. She hoped Mr. Newman would come home soon.

Up in the front of the church was Dottie. Abby thought she had barely moved from her pew in months—since she and Pastor Phillips had been seeing each other. She was still waiting for her marriage proposal. Abby's mother seemed sure it would come over Christmas; Abby hoped it would. She wondered who would marry them, since Pastor Phillips was the pastor. She guessed they would have to call another pastor from a different church.

The closing prayer was said, and people began to shuffle about in the aisles. Some people stayed and chatted, but most bundled up and headed for the warmth of home. Abby felt bad for not paying attention at all and decided she had better lift up her own prayer.

Lord, forgive me for not listening to Pastor Phillips today. I guess I just needed a day to think to myself. I do read Your Word daily. And when Harvey sends me a letter, I can spend hours reading and spending time in the verse he sends for me to find. I like to see what comes before it and after it . . . And, Lord, You know I've taken to praying extra with each letter I get. So forgive me, please, for my mind wandering today. I am trying to be a good Christian girl. I hope You understand. Amen.

As people made their way out of the church, the Madisons approached the Walkers. They sat and chatted for a few minutes, trying to nail down a wedding date for Peter and Emmeline. Abby occupied the children while they waited. Soon Peter and his parents were walking out of the sanctuary. Abby and the rest of the children followed. In the car, Peter told Abby that Mr. Madison had suggested March twentieth, and it was agreed upon.

At home, the family went about its usual business. Everyone ate and settled in for a cozy Sunday afternoon. Reba was wrapped in a blanket, reading a book; Jacob and Eliza were playing with farm animal toys; and Gabriel was down for his nap. Abby and her mother were working on knitting, and the men were listening to the radio.

Abby was working on Harvey's Christmas gift. She was making him mittens and a scarf from a deep blue yarn that matched his cadet uniform. She carefully counted her steps, working diligently to make sure it would look perfect. She stuck out her tongue as she worked; she claimed it helped her concentrate, but truthfully, she didn't know why she did it.

Nathan and Peter were tuned into news of the war in Europe. It scared Abby to think of what was going on around the world; Abby realized she should be praying more often for all the troops fighting overseas. Abby tuned the radio out; she hated hearing depressing news. She focused on Harvey's gift, wondering if it got cold enough in Charleston for mittens.

Nathan's voice carried across the room, interrupting Abby's thoughts. "Grace, come over here. You've got to hear this."

Everyone stopped what they were doing and listened.

"What is it?" Grace asked, standing to her feet.

"Shh."

Nathan turned the volume up on the radio.

"This is John Daly, and you're tuned to *The World Today on CBS*," the radio broadcast. "We bring you a special news bulletin from across the nation. The Japanese have attacked Pearl Harbor, Hawaii, by air. The attack occurred at about eight o'clock this morning, Hawaii time. In two waves, Japanese pilots bombed the harbor, destroying airfields and battleships stationed at Pearl Harbor . . . "

"Oh my . . . " Grace gasped and raised a hand to her mouth as if to block it. She looked back to Jacob and Eliza, who were playing, unaware of the news.

"Daddy," Reba whispered, "what does this mean?"

"I think it means America is going to war," he said. No one else spoke for several minutes, but it might as well have been hours. They listened to the account of what happened. The radio announcer said hundreds of soldiers had been killed, many of whom were sleeping still and had no idea they were about to be under attack. After a few minutes, Nathan changed the radio dial, looking for any additional information. None said anything new, and many were already returning to their regular programs. Sounds of an orchestra filled the airwaves, and the news report was over.

America had been attacked. Americans had been attacked and killed. Abby's father was right; surely, President Roosevelt would send troops into war soon. They would just have to wait and find out. But Abby's mind raced to Harvey and Peter's conversation from Thanksgiving.

"I would join up in an instant."

"Half the corps of cadets is ready to sign up at a moment's notice."

Peter. Harvey. Would they join the army, too? Would they leave and go to the war? Before Abby could ask, her father snapped the radio off. He was angry that there were no new updates, nothing further on a course of action from Washington.

"I'll turn it back on tonight after dinner. Maybe there will be more news," he said.

Grace looked at Nathan and Peter. "Come on, Reba. Abby, let's get supper started." She made her way to the door. "Jake, honey, you and Eliza go play in your rooms, okay?"

"Okay, Momma," came the reply, and the children shuffled out.

The women went into the kitchen, and Reba stared at her mother. "Momma?"

"Shh, let's not talk about it just yet. We're not sure what's going to happen," Grace said as she pulled out pots and pans to make supper. Her hands were shaking, and the metal clanged together. "Hawaii is far away; maybe this won't affect us."

"Okay," Reba said and went quietly to work.

Abby didn't speak. She could only think of Harvey and Peter and what would happen if they did go to war. She was completely silent and automatically helped make dinner, trying to block the possibility of what may happen in the not-too-distant future.

***

The next day, everyone in town seemed to be floating around in a daze. At the Walker home, the family stayed gathered around the radio to hear an update. They listened to a speech delivered by President Franklin Roosevelt.

"Mr. Vice President, Mr. Speaker, Members of the Senate, of the House of Representatives:

"Yesterday, December 7, 1941—a date which will live in infamy—the United States of America was suddenly and deliberately attacked by naval and air forces of the Empire of Japan," he began.

"The United States was at peace with that nation, and, at the solicitation of Japan, was still in conversation with its government and its emperor, looking toward the maintenance of peace in the Pacific.

"Indeed, one hour after Japanese air squadrons had commenced bombing in the American island of Oahu, the Japanese ambassador to the United States and his colleague delivered to our Secretary of State a formal reply to a recent American message. While this reply stated that it seemed useless to continue the existing diplomatic negotiations, it contained no threat or hint of war or of armed attack.

"It will be recorded that the distance of Hawaii from Japan makes it obvious that the attack was deliberately planned many days or even weeks ago. During the intervening time, the Japanese government has deliberately sought to deceive the United States by false statements and expressions of hope for continued peace.

"The attack yesterday on the Hawaiian Islands has caused severe damage to American naval and military forces. I regret to tell you that very many American lives have been lost. In addition, American ships have been reported torpedoed on the high seas between San Francisco and Honolulu.

"Yesterday, the Japanese government also launched an attack against Malaysia. Last night, Japanese forces attacked Hong Kong. Last night, Japanese forces attacked Guam. Last night, Japanese forces attacked the Philippine Islands. Last night, the Japanese attacked Wake Island. And this morning, the Japanese attacked Midway Island.

"Japan has, therefore, undertaken a surprise offensive extending throughout the Pacific area. The facts of yesterday and today speak for themselves. The people of the United States have already formed their opinions and well understand the implications to the very life and safety of our nation.

"As Commander-in-Chief of the Army and Navy, I have directed that all measures be taken for our defense. But always will our whole nation remember the character of the onslaught against us. No matter how long it may take us to overcome this premeditated invasion, the American people in their righteous might, will win through to absolute victory.

"I believe that I interpret the will of the Congress and of the people when I assert that we will not only defend ourselves to the uttermost, but will make it very certain that this form of treachery shall never again endanger us. Hostilities exist. There is no blinking at the fact that our people, our territory, and our interests are in grave danger. With confidence in our armed forces, with the unbounding determination of our people, we will gain the inevitable triumph—so help us God.

"I ask that the Congress declare that since the unprovoked and dastardly attack by Japan on Sunday, December 7th, 1941, a state of War has existed between the United States and the Japanese empire."

The men stiffened at the word war. "War. Dad did you hear that?"

"I heard it, son."

"What does it mean?" Abby asked, searching her father's face for answers.

Peter stood and announced, "It means I'm joining the army. Those Japs can't attack my country." His nostrils flared as he punched one hand into the other for effect.

"No! Peter, no!" Grace cried as she held a handkerchief to her face.

Nathan was calm. "Peter, have a seat." Peter did as he was told. "Now, before you go joining a war, let's talk about this."

"We talked about it yesterday, Dad. I told you, I want to fight. I don't want people coming into my land, my state, and wreaking havoc. I can't stand by and watch my family and my friends get hurt. I'm nearly twenty years old; I'll be getting married soon . . . "

"And will you be getting married if you go to war?" Nathan interrupted. "What about Emmeline?"

Peter took a deep breath and closed his eyes. "I have to protect Emmeline and all of you. I can't do that working here and sitting idle."

It was Grace's turn to speak. She started slowly and quietly. "What does Emmeline think of you joining the army, Petey?"

"I don't know, but I'm going to find out," he said as he ran out of the room and headed to the front door. Nathan held a hand out to calm Grace and quickly followed.

It was a long time before Peter and Nathan returned. At least, Abby thought it seemed like a long time. No one spoke at first—the women sitting in the kitchen around the table, the men standing in front of them. It was like a stand-off. Who would speak first? Grace's eyes shifted from her husband to her son and back. Finally, Nathan shook his head, confirming all the ladies' dread. Peter would be leaving. Grace quickly stood and fled, Nathan on her heels.

Reba spoke up. "Peter, how could you hurt Momma like this? And Emmeline, too?"

"Emmeline was okay. She supports my decision," Peter said, exhausted. Abby thought his eyes looked red, as if he had been crying. "We're going to get married this weekend, and I'll be leaving after Christmas."

Abby was shocked to hear that news, and she let her brother know it. "This weekend? Christmas? This is all happening so fast." *Lord, too fast. No one should have to get married so hastily.*

"Wars don't wait, Abby," Peter said as he ran his hands through his sandy blond hair.

"Harvey. Will he leave, too?" Please, Lord. Not Harvey. Don't take him away!

Peter looked at her, then down at his feet. "Probably. I'm sure nearly all the cadets will be going."

Abby ran to her room and paced the floor. She wished she had a telephone number to reach Harvey. She needed to talk to him. Maybe he could talk some sense into Peter. Maybe she should see Emmeline and have her talk Peter out of going, and then Peter could talk to Harvey. She prayed harder than she ever had before.

Lord in heaven, I don't know what's going on. I don't know why these things are happening. Since yesterday, we've been praying for the residents and people stationed in Hawaii who were in the attack. We've even prayed for the salvation of the heathen Japanese and Nazis. But now, God, it's personal. Peter wants to join the army; he wants to fight. He wants to join in the bloodshed.

Abby felt tears trickle down her cheek and drop off her chin into her lap.

Lord, he and Emmeline are going to get married. I don't mind them marrying so soon. Maybe that's a good thing. That way he has a wife to worry about coming home to. I expect You to bring him home safely, God. Protect him; watch over him. I don't know what else I can pray, except for this, over and over.

Lord, in addition to Peter, I also pray for Harvey. My sweet Harvey. I haven't heard from him since all this transpired. I wish he would call, but I know he probably can not get to a telephone. I have to write him that Peter is getting married this weekend. Father, please don't send Harvey to war. I can barely handle Peter going, but Harvey going would kill me. Finish this war, Lord. Let the Nazis and the Japanese be defeated. Allow the Jewish people to go free. Are they not Your chosen people, Lord? How can You allow this? Let the suffering stop, Lord. Let the suffering over the entire world stop.

Abby climbed into bed without even changing clothes. She pulled the covers up over her head and sobbed herself to sleep. She wondered how many other sisters and girlfriends were also crying themselves to sleep that night.

CHAPTER 7

THE WEEK WENT BY QUICKLY for everyone, but doubly fast for the Walkers as they planned an impromptu wedding. Peter and Emmeline would be married in the morning, followed by lunch at the Walkers' home. They would be staying at the Magnolia Inn until Christmas, after which Emmeline would return home to her folks, and Peter would leave for the army.

Emmeline was at the Walkers' house getting last minute details attended to before her big day. Abby could tell she had more worry in her mind than joy. *No one should get married under such rotten conditions,* Abby thought to herself. *Poor Emmeline. She should be so happy now.*

"Will Harvey be coming up for the wedding?" Emmeline asked as Abby did some final altering on the wedding dress.

"I sent him a letter," Abby said with a sigh. "I hope so. And I really need to see him and know what's going on. Not knowing has been horrible."

"I'm sure it has."

Just then, Reba came in the room with a letter in her hand. "Abby! This just came. It's from Harvey!"

Abby tossed down the needle and thread she was holding and tore the envelope open, reading aloud, "Abby, I received your message. I, too, have to see you soon. Expect me Friday night. Harvey."

"That's tonight," Reba said.

"Yes, it is," was all Abby replied. "I can't wait to see him. Now, let's finish this dress for tomorrow."

She knew what Harvey was going to say. If he wasn't leaving, his letter would have said so. She finished the hem and excused herself from her sister and future sister-in-law and went to the kitchen. It was her job to decorate the wedding cake. Carefully, she spread the white icing over the cake in a thin layer. Once that was done, she added another thicker layer of icing over the top.

Peter walked in and admired Abby's handiwork for a moment. "Looks good so far, Abby. Just don't mess it up." He loved to tease her, and Abby was happy to have him do it today.

"I won't," Abby said with a smile. "Now get out." He made his way through to the back of the house to find Emmeline. They needed to meet with Pastor Phillips before the following morning to finalize their ceremony.

Abby went back to the cake, ready to add some pink flowers to the decoration. She added a few drops of red coloring into the white icing and mixed it. The red quickly stained the white. *Like blood on a field of snow*, Abby thought grimly. She shoved the depressing thought from her head and made the icing pink in no time. A more joyful color, she thought. She hummed as she worked, piping delicate little flowers across the side of the cake. She was hunched over, consumed in her work. Abby took her time with each flower, hoping that the longer she took, the longer Peter would stay home.

Finally done, she stepped back to admire her work. She tossed the bag of icing down. "Thank goodness, that looks pretty good," she said, wiping her hands on her apron. "I thought I would never finish."

"Neither did I."

Abby spun around to see Harvey, still in his Clemson uniform, staring at her. "Harvey!" She threw her arms around Harvey's neck and felt his arms around her waist. She could feel him breathe her in. "I can't believe you're here!"

He stepped back. "I told you I was coming. And I got your letter about Peter's wedding. You don't think I'd miss it?"

"No, of course not," she said. Suddenly aware of how she must look, Abby started to pat down her hair and fluff her apron. "Oh, I'm a mess, aren't I?"

"You look fine," he said.

"Oh, I'm sure I look a fright." Abby chuckled, reaching behind her back to take her apron off. For some reason, the knot wouldn't come undone.

"Here," Harvey offered as he turned her around. "Let me." She felt his hands on the small of her back, and he pulled the strings, letting the apron loose. "You look great. I enjoyed watching you work."

Abby stammered, "You were watching me?"

"And listening to you hum. I liked your tune."

Abby turned beet red. Humming was not something she did in front of other people.

"I think that may be the most beautiful I've ever seen you. Well, aside from Thanksgiving, with your hair flowing. You looked so natural and in your element decorating that cake. And it looks great, too. You're an amazing decorator."

"Thank you, about both. I really love to bake, as you know." Abby smiled and offered Harvey a seat. "I just hope Emmeline and Peter like the cake."

"I know they'll love it." With that, Harvey pulled her into his lap and kissed her.

"Oh, Harvey, you're here." Abby pressed her cheek to his and took a deep breath.

"I'm here," he repeated. "At least for the weekend."

"I'll take it."

That night, when everyone had gone to bed and things were calmed down, Harvey and Abby sat on the couch in the living room.

"So, it seems everything is in order for the wedding, and I'm going to be Pete's best man," he said proudly. "You all really threw it together quickly."

"Well, they had begun planning before all this, including making the dress, but it really took no time to pull it together this week," Abby said. "Peter is planning on leaving right after Christmas, so he and Emmeline can have a holiday together before he goes."

"He'll be back before next Christmas," Harvey reassured her. His arm went over her shoulder, drawing her close.

"Do you think?"

"Of course, Abby."

She looked down, knowing what was to come of this conversation. She felt a lump rise in her throat. She had to ask. "And you? When will you be back?"

"You know I have to go, Abby."

"I know; I won't argue with you."

"You won't?" He seemed genuinely surprised as he put his finger under her chin and lifted her gaze.

"I've done a lot of thinking and praying this week," Abby told him as she searched his eyes. "And I know I can't keep you from going. I wish I could, but I know I can't, and I know you and Peter need to go so you can defend our country and home. I have been praying and will continue to pray to God that you will be returned home safely."

Harvey pulled her closer. Abby buried her head in his shoulder, fighting tears, praying for them to stay away. Amazingly, they did. "I'm fine, Harvey; I'm fine," she said, looking up. "See? No tears." She blinked a few times for effect and was thankful when no tears spilled over her cheek.

"You're stronger than you think you are," he said.

"No, I'm not. God is the root of my strength. 'I can do all things through Christ who strengthens me,'"[1] she quoted.

"Philippians," Harvey said, smiling.

Abby smiled back. "Yes, that's right. I know I can make it through this, but I don't know how."

"I know how." She looked at him, unsure. "Does it not say, 'With men this is impossible, but with God all things are possible?'"[2]

"Yes, it sure does," she said and smiled. She loved exchanging Scripture with him. "When will you leave?"

Harvey shifted. "When Christmas is over. Several cadets are leaving from the college, and I'll go with them."

"Will I see you again before you go?" Abby now felt tears in her eyes and didn't bother to hide them.

"I'll come up here the day before we leave, I promise. I'll see you then," he assured her as he kissed her forehead. "But for now, we have this weekend. You have me through Sunday when I have to go back to Clemson."

Abby rested her head on Harvey's shoulder, and he ran his fingers through her hair. One by one, he separated her curls. She felt his breath on her neck, then his lips. She sighed and turned her head up to his. A

---

1 Philippians 4:13
2 Matthew 19:26

sweet, light kiss followed. It made Abby feel happy. She didn't want to think about what was to come. Wanting to savor the moment, she gazed into his eyes to remember this moment forever; then she stood and left him. Harvey was staying on the Walkers' couch that night. Abby went to bed, half-happy he was close by, half-petrified he would be leaving.

The next morning, everyone in the house was rushed. Everyone needed something else done, something that hadn't been done the night before. Breakfast was eaten before it was even on the table, and the guys took off for the church early to get it ready. As she rushed around, Abby found her mother sitting on a chair with a handkerchief over her face. She was crying softly.

"Oh, Momma, everything will be okay," Abby consoled. She knelt next to her mother and held her hand. "Don't worry."

Grace patted her eyes with the handkerchief. "I know, Abigail, I know. But Petey is my baby. I can't believe he's leaving home."

"You'll have five more still at home to keep you busy, Momma."

"But Petey was my first baby," she sniffed. "I wasn't much older than you when he was born. It seems like just yesterday, your father was building this house for us. And now, my first child is leaving the nest."

Abby patted her mother's back as she cried. Grace took a minute to let it out, then got up and went back to work. Abby wondered if all mothers acted this way but didn't have time to dwell on it. There was too much to do.

At the church, Pastor Phillips was waiting on the family. The Madisons were already there, and Emmeline was getting dressed in a Sunday school room. The girls all filed in after her. Wearing her church dress, Eliza sat still; she didn't even fidget. Gabriel cooed over some toys, and Grace was helping Mrs. Madison get Emmeline's dress on over her head.

Abby and Reba were bridesmaids—the first time they had been in a wedding and gotten all dressed up. Their dresses were a soft rose color of Emmeline's choosing. They flowed from the waist to the floor in soft folds of fabric. The sleeves were slightly puffed at the shoulders, and the bodice was fitted. They both wore lace hats of a matching color with fabric roses attached to the back. They were quite attractive, Abby thought. And she was amazed they had managed to finish making them and Emmeline's dress in only a week.

Emmeline was ready, and she looked beautiful. Her dress was white, with long sleeves and a pouf at the shoulder, coming down to a very fashionable point just over her wrist. The neckline showed off her collarbone, and the dress was cinched at the waist and held with a rose-colored sash. The fabric ran down to the floor and pooled at her feet. The train of the dress was not terribly long, but it trailed behind her. In her hair was a simple white hat with lace attached to go over her face. She was wearing a pearl necklace, no doubt handed down from mother to daughter. Emmeline would be carrying a handful of rose-colored carnations, as would Abby and Reba. Mrs. Madison was nearly in tears, but it was obvious she had been crying already.

Reba gushed to Emmeline about how gorgeous she looked, and all eyes were on her. Everyone seemed happy, but Abby could see the pain lurking just under the surface—pain in knowing that the honeymoon would be utterly brief. But she prayed they would get a second chance when Peter came home.

Emmeline came up to Abby with her brow creased. "Abby, are you all right? Don't I look okay?"

Abby quickly smiled and nodded. "Yes, you look fine, Emmeline. I'm just taking it all in. I want to remember this forever. That way, I can tell your children how you looked on your wedding day."

Emmeline blushed at the mention of children. She was clearly nervous. "Thanks," she said quietly. "Now, are we all here? Is Peter here?"

"We're all here," Grace answered. "Come on, girls, let's go out front." She ushered everyone but Emmeline and Mrs. Madison out the door. Before exiting herself, she turned to Emmeline and kissed her on the cheek. "Welcome to the family, dear."

Inside the sanctuary, a few people were seated in the pews. Dottie was in the front row with her parents, speaking with Pastor Phillips. Judy, Grace's other sister, would be playing the organ. Nathan's brother and family were seated a few rows back. The bride's side was dotted with a few of Emmeline's local family. Her uncle Ken offered to use his camera and take a few pictures of the event. It wasn't a great turnout, but it was enough.

Pastor Phillips stood at the podium and announced, "Ladies and gentlemen, I think we'll begin in just a moment, if you'll take your seats."

Peter came out from the side door, followed by Harvey. Abby thrilled that her brother and Harvey had become so close. Peter was dressed in a dark brown suit with pin stripes, an off-white shirt, and brown tie. A rose-colored carnation adorned his lapel. Grace had told Abby that it was an expensive suit, but well worth the money, since Peter would be able to wear it for years to come. He looked so handsome, especially with his hair trimmed and face shaved. Abby thought he shone like a star and looked twice as happy.

The signal from Pastor Phillips came, and Reba marched down the aisle, with Abby shortly behind her. Once they reached the front, all eyes turned back, and Emmeline and her father made their way down the aisle. Abby watched her brother as tears welled in his eyes at the sight of his bride. He was so happy; he loved Emmeline so very much. Abby prayed they would have a long and happy life together.

Pastor Phillips began, "Dearly beloved, we are gathered here today in the sight of God and these witnesses to join this man and this woman in holy matrimony. If there be any person who knows why these two souls may not be joined for eternity, please speak now, or hold your peace forever."

He paused to see if anyone objected. Of course, no one did. The pastor smiled and carried on. "Peter Nathan Walker, do you take this woman before you, Emmeline Louise Madison, to be your wife?"

Peter nodded and said, "I do take this woman."

"Then repeat after me," Pastor Phillips took a breath. "I, Peter Nathan Walker, take you, Emmeline Louise Madison, to be my wedded wife . . ."

Peter smiled and looked at Emmeline. "I, Peter Nathan Walker, take you, Emmeline Louise Madison, to be my wedded wife . . ."

Word for word, Peter repeated the vows of marriage to Emmeline. And when her turn came, she, too, pledged her undying love for Peter. The rings were asked for, and Harvey produced two silver rings and gave them to the pastor. Circles that have no beginning and no end—like the love of a young couple, like the love of Christ for His people—two circles that will show the world these two belong to God first and each other second.

"God has blessed this community with two such wonderful people, and He has blessed Peter with Emmeline and Emmeline with Peter." Pastor Phillips smiled. "I hope all people can know the joy it brings me to marry these two, whom I have known since they were young. It seems Peter and Emmeline have always been together, and now they have the Lord behind them. And now, what God has joined together, let no man put asunder. Peter and Emmeline, I pronounce you husband and wife!"

With those words, Peter grabbed Emmeline into his arms and kissed her. It was a long and beautiful kiss. They hugged after and kissed again. Once they separated, Aunt Judy began to play the organ again, and the pair walked back through the sanctuary as a married couple.

Through all the smiles, however, was apprehension. Each tear of joy was followed by one of sorrow. It was a bittersweet service, and everyone knew it. But they all tried to be as jovial as possible for the new bride and groom.

After the ceremony, Peter and Emmeline posed for a few pictures. Emmeline's uncle took several of them, a few of the entire family, and one of the bridal party. When he was done with that, Harvey asked him for a picture with Abby. They stood side by side, Harvey's arm around the small of Abby's back, and smiled.

"Send me that one, so I have something to show off to the guys," Harvey teased her.

After a filling reception lunch at the Walker home, Peter and Emmeline hopped into the Madisons' car. They would be spending the next two weeks at the Magnolia Inn as husband and wife until Peter left. As the car started, Emmeline tossed her flowers out the window for the single girls to grab. Abby was the lucky winner, and she wondered if she would be the next to get married. She bit her lip as she waved the flowers at Harvey.

When everything was cleaned up, Harvey found Abby sitting outside on the picnic table, still in her dress. He had brought her a blanket to wrap around her and draped it over her arms.

"It was gorgeous," he said.

"Um-hm."

"Emmeline was a pretty bride," he continued. "And Peter looked very happy."

"Yes, they both looked happy," Abby said, but her voice was downcast. She put her head into her hand and sighed. "I just wish they didn't have to get married and then have Peter leave so soon."

"I know; it's tough." Harvey slipped his hand into hers. "But now, Peter has a wife to come home to when all this is over."

Looking up, Abby asked, "It's important to have someone at home waiting, isn't it?"

"Yes," he sighed. "It's what motivates you to get the job done and come home in one piece."

"Well, Harvey, you don't have to worry," she reassured him. "You have me to come home to when this war is over."

"Do I?"

"Of course."

"Will you be waiting at home for me?"

"I'll be right here waiting every day," she said with gusto. *I promise.*

"Do you have to wait here?"

"Where else would I wait?" she laughed, not knowing what he meant.

Harvey looked her right in the eyes. "In Charleston, my home."

Abby giggled again, this time out of nerves. "Harvey, really. Where would I live in Charleston? My home is here; my family is here."

"What if my family was your family?" He was very serious, his eyes dark, his mouth drawn.

"What do you mean, Harvey?"

Harvey ran his hand over his hair and held Abby's hand. He was nervous. "Marry me."

"What?" Alarm bells sounded in Abby's head. *Marry him? Now?*

"Marry me, Abby," he said in a burst of air and excitement. "Marry me after Christmas. Marry me before I leave. I want you to be Mrs. Nicholas before I go."

Stunned, Abby couldn't speak. She didn't know what to say. Everything inside her heart told her to say yes. But in the back of her mind was a little voice that said no. When she had dreamed about a wedding, it was a grand event, not something planned on a whim. It included a honeymoon somewhere exotic—or at least in another city. She didn't want a spur-of-the-moment wedding and then an absent husband for who knew how long.

"Abby?" Harvey searched her for an answer, his green eyes dancing. Abby wished she could stare at his eyes every second of every day. "Abby? What do you say? Don't worry about your father. I asked him about it already, and he's given his full blessings, and your mother thinks it's a wonderful idea."

"Y-You spoke to my father?"

"Yes, Abby, and he gave me his blessing." Harvey's smile faded when Abby didn't give the emphatic yes he was looking for. "Abby?"

"Harvey," she started with a sigh, searching for the right words. "Harvey, I love you and adore you. And I would love nothing more in this world than to spend my days with you . . . "

"Oh, Abby! I knew it! I knew you would agree!" He picked her up and twirled her around in the air.

"Stop, stop!" Abby cried pushing him away. Tears once again ran down her face. "Harvey, I would love to spend my days with you, but I can't fathom spending my days as your wife, waiting for you, wondering when and if I'll ever see you again. What if something happens to you? I don't want to be a widow before I become a wife. I cannot marry you before you leave, Harvey. But I love you, and I will wait for you, and I will marry you as soon as you get home. The very day, if you like."

Sure she had infuriated him, Abby broke free of his grasp and began to walk away. *So much for forever, right? He'll never want me again after this.* But before she reached the steps to go inside, Harvey grabbed her arm and spun her around to face him.

Harvey seethed, "Don't you love me?" He turned and paced in front of her.

"More than anything!"

"Then, let's get married!"

Crying, Abby told him, "Harvey, I do want to marry you, to have your children, to grow old with you. But I need to know that's in my future. I need to wait until you come home. Can't you understand that?"

"No, I can't. Not when we can do this now. Not when we can have our future now." He pleaded, "We can be together for a few nights at least."

Abby blinked. "I love you, but I can't marry you like this. I'm sorry if you think I'd marry you just so we could be intimate." She spoke directly—something she didn't usually do.

Shocked and ashamed, Harvey shook his head. "That's not what I mean, Abigail; you know that. I mean we can have a few nights to just be together, to spend all our time together." He stepped forward and rubbed Abby's shoulders. "I'm sorry that came out all wrong. It's not about sleeping together. It's about being with the person I love before I go off to a world of hate."

As he hugged Abby close, she whispered, "Oh, my love. The day you get home, we'll get married. We'll start a family right away, and we'll have the life we can only dream of. I promise."

He nodded his head in agreement as a tear slid down his own cheek. "As soon as I get home," Harvey repeated. "We won't wait. I want you to have everything ready the minute I get home. I love you."

"And I you. Everything will be ready for when you get back."

Silence filled the cold night air for a few minutes before Harvey jumped up and ran inside the house. Abby wasn't sure what had happened. Was he all right? Did he decide he was still angry with her? Moments later, he came out with a box.

"I almost forgot," he said, handing the box to Abby. "Merry Christmas!"

"It's not Christmas yet." Abby smiled weakly as she turned it in her hands.

"For us, it is; open it."

The box was red and tied with a green ribbon. Abby carefully untied the ribbon and lifted the lid. Inside was a velvet bag. She glanced up at Harvey who was smiling at her. She supposed Harvey thought that an engagement was better than nothing; she surely did. But there wasn't a ring in the bag. Inside were two gorgeous hair combs. They were long—long enough to hold all Abby's curls—and crowned with a gorgeous filigree of silver. Embedded in the silver, along the curves, was something that looked like shiny pearls. In the center top of each comb was a dazzling, light blue stone. Abby had never seen anything so lovely in all her life.

"Oh, Harvey, I love them," she whispered. "Where did you find them?"

"Somewhere special," he said.

"I can't take this, Harvey," Abby said breathlessly. "This is too much."

"Nothing's too much for you," he assured her. "You are worth far more to me than any piece of jewelry or adornment."

"Thank you." Abby hugged him. "Oh, I love you! These are breathtaking!"

"I knew you would love them as soon as I saw them." Harvey picked one comb up and handled it very delicately. "They're actually quite old. The stone is an aquamarine, and these are opals in the sides. I thought the only way these could be prettier is if they were in your hair. You know how I adore your hair." And with that, Harvey pulled Abby's hair back and slid a comb into it and did the same with the other. "I was right, you make them more beautiful."

"Thank you." Abby felt like a princess and straightened her back. "I have your gift finished. But, oh, Harvey, it's nothing like this. No, no, no."

"I'll be the judge of that. Go on," he said. He coaxed her off her perch and shooed her inside. Abby disappeared into the house and came back out with a simple brown box, not even tied up yet.

"I'm so sorry, Harvey. I didn't have time to find a ribbon yet."

"I don't care," he said, taking the box from her hands.

He unveiled the mittens and scarf she made as if they were a treasure. "Abby these are great. They even match my uniform," he said with a laugh, while wrapping the scarf around his neck. He was right; the yarn was a perfect match for the cadet uniform. "Wow, where did you get these?"

Abby laughed. "Get them? I made them, silly!" She giggled as he wiggled his fingers inside the mittens. "I'm sorry they're not fancy like you're used to."

Frowning, Harvey pulled Abby into his lap, and she linked her hands behind her neck. "Never say that," he scolded. "I love them. No one has ever made me anything before."

"No?"

"Nope," he said. "We buy things. My mother or sister would never think to make me something like this. I think these are terrific." He leaned in for a kiss, and Abby obliged.

The night air grew cooler, but neither of them was willing to end their evening. Harvey had to leave the next morning, and they wanted all the time they could get.

"Abigail?"

"Harvey?"

"Are you sure you won't marry me?"

"I will. When you get home."

"But not before I leave?"

"Harvey, I don't want to get married the way Peter and Emmeline just did," Abby explained, her heart aching as she did. "I know they're happy now, but I also saw the pain behind their smiles. They both hate the way this came about. I don't want that. I don't want to smile through pain that you're leaving. I want a big wedding. I want a fancy dress, and I want you looking as smart as ever. I want tons of people to come see us off. I want it done in pure joy, not fear of the future."

There was disappointment in Harvey's face, but he seemed to understand her reasoning. "All I want is you, me, and God. I don't care about the people, or what you wear—although, I admit, the gift was bought in hope you would wear them when we married. I just want you to be Mrs. Nicholas."

"And I will wear these gorgeous combs when we get married," she promised. "I will be Mrs. Nicholas. Just not now. I hope you understand how much pain it gives me to say that. It's tearing me up not to bang down Pastor Phillip's door right now. If you weren't going to the war, I would marry you tomorrow. But I know God is telling me that waiting is the right thing." *Lord, please let him see it, too.*

"Well, we certainly can't go against God, can we?" he asked. "I won't push it any longer. I love you, no matter how long you make me wait."

"I love you, too. And remember, I'll be waiting as well."

They both had pain in their faces. Sadness overcame them, and they clung to each other. Finally, exhausted, they went inside—Harvey to the couch and Abby to her room. She didn't know how Harvey slept, but she knew her sleep was fitful and full of ache.

CHAPTER 8

CHRISTMAS CAME AND WENT; AND like the wedding, it was bittersweet. Everyone was waiting with bated breath for Peter to leave. Abby was doubly worried; and she waited for Harvey to arrive before he and Peter both left, uncertain if they would return alive. Abby hated being so pessimistic, but she had a horrid feeling in the pit of her stomach about the entire thing.

The morning was crisp, but Abby preferred to wait outside anyway, her sweater pulled tight to keep her warm. Harvey would arrive any minute. Reba brought her a cup of hot chocolate to warm her and keep her company.

"They'll both be okay, you know," Reba said, her breath showing in the cold air.

"I hope so," Abby said softly. "Harvey asked me to marry him the day of Peter's wedding."

"I know," Reba replied softly, understanding her sister's decision was tough. "But you don't want to get married?" Abby sighed. "I do, Reba, I do. But not with Harvey leaving. I didn't want to be a bride for a few days and then him leave. What if something happens?"

"Then, I guess you would be happy for the time you had," Reba said. "I know Peter is happy for being married some before he leaves."

Abby looked at her sister in awe. How could her younger sister be so wise? Abby herself hadn't even thought about making the most of the time they had left. "You're very smart for your age. But still, for me, this wasn't right. It was for Peter, but not me."

Reba shrugged and stood, "You gotta do what you gotta do." And with that, she went back into the house.

She must have seen the car coming up behind Abby, because as the door closed behind her, Harvey's car rolled into the driveway. Abby jumped up and ran to him. Harvey barely got the door open before Abby leaped on him and hugged him tight.

"Whoa! I'm happy to see you too, angel," Harvey said, trying to keep his balance.

Abby tilted her head to the side and smiled. "Angel? Where'd that come from?"

"You always look like an angel to me," he explained as he closed the door and picked Abby up. "It's my little nickname for you. All the guys at school know about my angel now. They even tease me."

A giggle escaped Abby's lips. She liked the idea of Harvey having a nickname for just her. She had worn the combs he gave her for Christmas, which made her feel like an angel.

"Come inside; it's cold," Abby begged.

Harvey spent the day with the entire Walker family, including Peter and Emmeline. Abby tried to soak up as much of her brother and Harvey as she could. She kept trying to take mental pictures in her mind, so she would always remember this time and remember it as happy.

Peter and Emmeline had gotten the pictures from their wedding and were sharing them with the group. When she looked at the photos, Abby thought the hurt in everyone's eyes wasn't as noticeable on film. Everyone looked happy. There were photos of Peter and Emmeline, of course. And pictures of Emmeline with Reba and Abby, and Peter with Harvey. Abby said she wanted a copy of that one. And when the page turned in the album, a small gasp escaped her lips. The picture of her and Harvey—it was dazzling. They looked so happy, so well-matched, she thought. Harvey was handsome in his cadet uniform, and Abby looked stunning in her rose-colored dress, even though pictures didn't have color. It was lovely.

"Oh, Abby, I almost forgot to give you these," Peter said, handing Abby an envelope.

"What is this?"

"Open it."

Abby opened the envelope and found two copies of the picture. One for her and one for Harvey. "Oh, Peter. This is so nice."

"I asked Emme's Uncle Ken to give me some extras of that. So, you have one, and Harvey can bring one with him," Peter said. He was the most considerate brother ever. "And I have an extra of my lovely wife here to take with me." Abby hugged her brother, thankful for his thoughtfulness.

"That's not all," Harvey said, smiling. "Peter and I have a surprise for you girls."

Emmeline and Abby giggled; they loved surprises, especially good ones. Peter chimed in, "Yes, we do. Be ready at six o'clock for a dinner out at The Copper Pot."

The girls gasped. The Copper Pot was the nicest restaurant in Clemson, the nicest restaurant for miles around. Abby had only heard of people going there, but didn't actually know anyone who had gone. The only times she ate away from home were to have a sandwich and soda at the local pharmacy. She and Emmeline giggled and thanked the guys profusely.

That night, Abby was dressed up as much as she ever had been before. She wore the dress from Peter's wedding; it was the fanciest she had. She wanted to look nice at the restaurant, but more than that, she wanted to look nice for Harvey. She checked the combs in her hair, making sure they were each in their place. They held her curls back out of her face, while allowing the rest to drape over her back and shoulders. Abby applied a little rouge to her cheeks and lipstick to her lips. She was ready.

At exactly six, Harvey pulled up to the house. He was wearing his cadet uniform, which made Abby both proud and scared. What would his uniform look like after he came back from war? But she tried to put that thought from her mind for the night. Peter and Emmeline were already at the house waiting. When Harvey came in, Nathan took out the family camera, which he rarely used, and snapped a picture of the foursome.

As they went out the door, Harvey whispered to Abby, "One day, our kids and Peter's kids will laugh at that picture." Abby grinned from ear to ear. She hoped his prediction would come true.

Their dinner was wonderful. The gentlemen ordered for the ladies, which made them feel very sophisticated. Abby enjoyed a meal of grilled salmon with asparagus and potatoes. It was absolutely divine, she thought. Harvey extended his fork over to her, allowing her to taste his steak, smothered with a port wine reduction sauce. It was the perfect meal.

Everyone laughed and smiled. Not once was war mentioned at their table. They were just two couples out for a good time. Abby knew that in the future, she would have no idea what she ate, but she was certain she would know every word Harvey uttered.

Before leaving, Abby and Emmeline excused themselves to the restroom to freshen up. While they were reapplying their lipstick, Emmeline commented, "Doesn't this make you feel grown up?"

Abby giggled. "You are grown up, Emmeline. You're a married woman now."

"You know what I mean." She leaned against the countertop. "I love being married, but it feels like when I was a kid playing house."

"Do you really like being married?" Abby hinted with a raised eyebrow.

"It's the most amazing thing in the world." Emmeline turned red. "If you had gotten married like we all thought you would, you would know."

Abby felt a slight panic, wondering if she should have married Harvey, regardless of what she felt was right. "Did I make a mistake? I've been wondering for weeks if I should have accepted. But you and Peter were already engaged; you just moved things up."

Emmeline patted Abby's arm. "I know; I'm sorry. It's just hard to explain. You did the right thing. Sometimes, I wonder if I should have waited as well. But it all happened so fast. The night we got married, I cried all night."

"Oh, Emmeline, why?"

"Because there I was on my wedding night, knowing that when this day came, I would be saying goodbye to my husband without hardly being a wife to him." Emmeline dabbed tears from her eyes. "It is just like playing as a kid. Peter and I live together now—we do what a husband and wife should—but tomorrow, I'll go back to my daddy's house and resume life there as it was before. Without Peter."

Abby hugged her sister-in-law as grief washed over her. "Oh, sweetie, don't cry. You'll go home to your parents, and time will fly. Peter will be home before you know it. And then, you'll find a house of your own. And by this time next year, I bet you'll be settled and expecting your first child."

Emmeline blushed. "You think?"

"Sure. And Harvey and I will be right behind you," Abby promised. "And our children will grow up together and be the best of friends."

The girls laughed and made their way back to the men waiting for them. Emmeline whispered her thanks to Abby as they left the Copper Pot. Abby waved to her brother and sister-in-law as they climbed out of Harvey's car and went into the Magnolia Inn for their last night together before Peter left.

"Harvey, this was all so wonderful," Abby said, forcing a smile. "I just hate that this is their last night together. Emmeline was so upset."

Harvey stroked her hair. "It's temporary; remember that. Besides, this is our last night before I leave as well, angel." Abby nodded, still wondering if she had made the right decision.

Harvey pulled the car into the yard of the Lachlan house, the first place they had ever gone together, the first place they had kissed. Harvey pulled several blankets from the trunk and carried them inside the ruins. Abby followed him. He spread a red wool blanket on the ground and invited her to sit next to him. He had an extra blanket to put around Abby's shoulders.

"I'm sorry it's so cold," he said as he pulled the blanket around her.

"It's December," Abby replied with a wink. "It's supposed to be cold."

Harvey chuckled. He reached a hand out and brushed a stray hair from Abby's face. "I'm so sorry we don't have more time."

"Me too, Harvey." Abby rested her head on his shoulder. "Don't go."

Harvey took her by the shoulders and held her firm. Their eyes met and held fast. "Abigail. I want to make this world a safe place for you. And for the future generations—our future generations. How would you like it if the world were controlled by Nazis?"

"I could endure anything with you," she pleaded.

"Abby, it's a man's job to protect his family. And even if we're not married—yet—I still need to protect you."

Abby sniffed. She knew he was right. She sighed against him in defeat. There was nothing she could do. Harvey stroked her hair, and she closed her eyes. Abby allowed her head to drop into Harvey's lap. She wanted to cry, but no tears came. Harvey slid Abby's head off his lap and onto the blanket, and he curled up behind her. He wrapped his arms around her and smelled her hair. She pulled his hands up to her mouth and kissed them. Abby shifted and turned to face Harvey; she cupped his face in her hands, taking in every feature afforded by the moonlight. They had no knowledge of time, no sense of the cold.

Finally, Harvey whispered her name. Quiet, soft, his voice slipped out on a wisp of air. Then his mouth crushed over hers, forceful and demanding. His hands twisted into her hair, pressing her mouth into his. Abby felt heat radiate off his body, despite the cold. Her body arched under his, becoming malleable to his touch. Harvey's mouth roamed down her neck, and she gasped for air. Abby's own hands ran through Harvey's hair and down his back.

He lifted his head from her, his breath labored, "Abby, I can't. I shouldn't kiss you like this."

"I want you to. Please, Harvey, if this is the last time we see each other . . . "

"Shh, don't," he said. "I'll come home to you. I'll come home, and we'll do everything we want to do right now. I'll love you until time stops, Abigail."

"I know," she said. "But for now, time has stopped. As long as we're here, you're not going anywhere."

She pulled Harvey's head to hers and kissed him. She parted her lips for him, welcomed the warmth of his tongue. She breathed heavily as his kiss returned to her collarbone, sending small shock waves though her body. Abby could feel Harvey's body against hers, and she soaked up the warmth he gave off. The kisses continued down Abby's arm, and she giggled when it tickled her skin. Her skin was moist and dewy from heat, and she could see beads of sweat on Harvey's brow.

Breathless, Harvey pulled himself away from Abby. She could see sweat dot down his face, despite the chilly temperature. Did she really leave him as breathless as he left her? Harvey covered Abby with a blanket and wiped his brow.

"Harvey? What's wrong?" Abby asked, her voice raspy. She sat up, holding the blanket around her.

"We have to stop now," he said. "We have to stop before this goes any further. I made a promise to wait until we were married."

Abby smiled coyly. "But, Harvey, I thought . . ."

He cut her off. "You know that when I get back home to you, we'll get married. And then, we can do this the right way."

Abby blushed, but didn't look away. "I should have married you," she teased.

Harvey shook his head. "Not like this. When we're together for the first time, we'll be in our own house, in a bed with buttery-soft sheets."

Abby could almost feel those sheets against her skin. She imagined what it would be like to live in a house with Harvey, to share a bed with him nightly. "Soon?"

"After this tonight, I'll be back within the week," Harvey smiled. "Hitler won't know what hit him."

Abby let out a small laugh. The sweat on her body was cooling quickly, and she began to shiver in the December night air. Harvey packed up the blankets, and they headed back to Abby's house. She had no idea what time it was and hoped her father wouldn't see how late she was getting home or how disheveled her hair was.

The next day at one o'clock, Peter and Harvey loaded their bags into the car. The tears had already started all around. Doris Newman came to see Harvey off, and the Madisons were also there to support Emmeline and Peter. Abby and Emmeline would be driving the boys to Clemson to drop them off. And return alone.

Doris gave each boy a sack filled with food and a canteen of water. Pain filled her eyes as she watched a second man she loved ship off to war. Her husband had been gone too long already, and he wouldn't be home anytime soon. She left before anyone else, her emotions too much to bear.

The Madisons shook Harvey's hand, and Mrs. Madison gave Peter a hug and told him to come home to Emmeline soon. He said he would be home within a few months, and everyone prayed that would be true. They kissed Emmeline and left for their own house.

Nathan and Grace Walker were another matter, however. Nathan spoke briefly and privately to the new soldiers. Abby watched Peter and Harvey nod their heads solemnly to her father. Harvey stepped away, and Nathan embraced Peter. He was proud of his son, but also scared.

Grace gave Harvey a hug, followed by Reba and Jacob. Eliza and Gabriel were playing on the porch. Before she went to her own son, Grace said to Harvey, "I'm sorry your mother can't be here the day you leave. So, let me speak as a mother. Be careful. Don't be afraid to run away and save yourself. And never forget that God is with you."

"Yes, ma'am."

"And never forget that my daughter's heart is going over there with you as well." She glanced at Abby, as did Harvey.

"No, Mrs. Walker, I won't," he promised solemnly.

Grace patted his arm and went to her own son. Tears were welling up inside Abby's eyes and heart. As they hugged, Abby had to look away. She couldn't stand watching her mother in so much pain.

"He'll be fine," Harvey said. "I'll keep an eye on him."

Abby, Harvey, and Emmeline watched as Peter picked up Gabriel and told him to take care of their mother for him. And he bent down to Eliza and told her to write him letters and send him cookies. Peter tousled Jacob's hair and reminded him that he was the oldest son in the house now and to support their father. As Reba wiped tears away from her cheek, Peter told her to pray for him and to make sure that their mother stayed reassured that he would come home soon.

Nathan told Peter how proud he was. Grace was unable to speak.

"Momma," Peter said, stroking her arm. "I'll be fine. You didn't raise me to be weak. Nothing can stop me; nothing can stop us. We'll finish this battle off and be home."

He put his arms around his mother and held her a few minutes as she sobbed. Abby cried softly into Harvey's shoulder. Emmeline went over to her mother-in-law and husband and joined in their hug.

Soon, the foursome were in the car, driving away. None of them dared look back at the scene they were leaving behind. Abby knew her mother would be miserable for days to come. They went in silence; no sounds could be heard from anyone in the car.

In Clemson, Peter and Harvey put their bags in with the rest of the recruits' luggage. Everyone was saying tearful goodbyes. Some people had cameras and took pictures of their soldiers going off to war. Others pleaded for their sons and husbands not to leave.

Abby turned to Peter to say goodbye. She didn't make any attempt to stop the flow of tears. "Peter, you have a wife now," she started. "So, you have to come home to her. And you have to come home to Momma and Daddy and me."

"I know, Abby," Peter said. Tears brimmed in his eyes as well. "I will do everything I can to come home in one piece and soon."

"I'll take care of Emmeline, if you take care of Harvey for me."

"You know I will. I love you, sis." Brother and sister embraced. They cried. They promised to write often. And when they parted, Abby felt her heart break for her brother, her sister-in-law, her whole family. *God, take care of him. Take care of him please,* she pleaded.

Peter and Emmeline talked quietly for a moment. Married only two weeks, the newlyweds now had to part. The honeymoon was over. Peter whispered promises of love and of the future. Emmeline wept openly, barely speaking.

While they said their goodbyes, Abby turned to Harvey. "Tell me this is a bad dream," she begged, clinging to him as if her life depended on it.

"It is a bad dream, Abby," he told her. "But it will be over soon. You'll wake up, and I'll be beside you forever."

"You promise to write me? Every day?"

Harvey settled against the car. "I'll write you every day and mail the letters at the end of each week, okay?"

Abby sighed, "Okay. But please make sure you write me right away so I know you're okay?"

"Promise," he said as he took her hand. "Abby, I have to ask you something."

"Anything you want, Harvey," she smiled weakly.

He pulled something from his pocket and asked, "Abigail, will you marry me when I get home?"

Abby grinned. "You know I will. We already planned it."

"Then, you'll need this," he said, and he presented a ring to Abby. It was a beautiful gold ring with a marquise-shaped, sparkling ruby in the middle. On either side of the ruby was a small, but brilliant, diamond. The gold was stamped with a braided pattern on the shanks. "It was my grandmother's, and now it's yours. So no one tries to steal you while I'm gone."

Abby couldn't believe her eyes. "I can't take this Harvey. It's beautiful. But won't your mother or sister be upset?"

"No. It's mine to give. Grandmother left it to me to give to my future bride," he told her. "And you're my future bride. So, now it's yours. The ruby was her birthstone, and her family is originally from Ireland; and my grandfather made this himself with the Celtic knot. It's never-ending, as was his love for her. And now my love for you."

Abby sniffed back even more tears. "I love it! I love you!" She kissed Harvey. She had never thought she would get engaged and then watch the love of her life leave her, but now it seemed to be happening. Abby knew she could survive, though, as long as it was official, and they got married as soon as Harvey was home.

Through the tears, Abby watched Harvey pick up her left hand and slide the ring over her third finger. It fit perfectly, surely a sign from God. Abby had never felt happier and more afraid at the same time.

Then, reality came washing back over her. Harvey was leaving, and Abby didn't know for how long. Tears rolled down her cheeks, and she prayed with all her might that he would return home to her. Harvey held her close and a few sniffs escaped from him as well. Wet tears fell onto Abby's curls. Several yards away, men were starting to get on the buses, the engines rumbling. Abby knew it was time to say goodbye. She backed away from Harvey several steps, giving herself space. She looked at him; she memorized every piece of his face. His hair, starting to grow, brushed against his brow. His eyes, bold and green, studied her back. His high cheeks were proud and stern. His mouth was soft and warm.

Peter approached Abby again. "Tell everyone I love them?" he asked. "And keep an eye on Emme for me. I don't have a fancy ring for her, but I think everyone knows she's taken." He smiled at his sister and hugged her. Abby didn't say anything back, but her face spoke volumes.

Harvey again lifted Abby's chin with his hand. "I told you not to look down, Abby," he said. "You're a strong, godly woman, who should always look up."

"I will," she said quietly.

"I love you with everything, Abigail," Harvey told her as he hugged her close. He kissed her sweetly. "I'll be home soon."

"I'm counting on it," she said, twirling the ring on her finger. "I love you, too."

As the men stepped back, Emmeline's hand slipped into Abby's. They each squeezed with all their might as Peter and Harvey finally turned around and headed to the bus, shoulder to shoulder.

Harvey got on first; he turned and waved at the girls. Abby felt hot tears fall down her face and neck. Then he disappeared. Peter stepped up next. He blew his wife a kiss and waved. Emmeline's grip tightened, and she began to wail. The door closed behind Peter, and the bus jerked forward, a puff of smoke billowing out as it rambled down the road. Abby and Emmeline stood motionless, holding hands until the bus was out of sight.

When they could see the bus no longer, Emmeline buckled and fell to the ground. Abby quickly gathered her sister-in-law into her lap, and the pair cried until they had no tears left. It seemed like hours before they got up. Tear-stained and dirty, they got into the car and drove home in silence.

CHAPTER 9

"HOW DO I LOOK?" ABBY asked, twirling for her sister to see her from all sides. She had a new dress to wear for graduation. It was a smart number in navy blue with square shoulders and a wide belt that cinched her waist. Abby even had a matching hat that perched atop her new haircut. When the need for some change had come during the spring, Abby had handed her sister the scissors and a picture of Katharine Hepburn and told her to cut. Reba had done a terrific job, and Abby's hair looked just like Katharine's in *Woman of the Year*. Abby hadn't seen the movie herself, but she saw still pictures from the movie.

"Oh, Abby, you look great," Reba gushed.

Summer had returned, but it was vastly different than it had been just a year before. War had taken over the lives of everyone. Everybody Abby knew had a loved one overseas. Everyone was affected by rationing. And Abby's middle class family felt the pinch. Store-bought clothes were a luxury before the war; now it was even more uncommon. Luckily, before the war started, Grace had gotten a hold of several dress patterns. Old dresses and fabric were given new life.

For Abby, having a new, store-bought dress was a big deal. It was her first new dress since her birthday the summer before. Her parents were thankful that she and Reba were the same size and could easily share clothes. Since foods had been rationed, the older Walker children had an unspoken agreement to save as much food as they could, and because of that, Abby had lost weight and was now nearly as slender as Reba. The girls rushed to finish getting ready and headed to the school for the commencement.

After the ceremony, many people gathered at the Walkers' house to celebrate Abby's graduation. It was partly to celebrate her achievements and partly to help lift spirits. Abby's family had come out for a terrific picnic, and while it wasn't a top-notch menu, it was plenty. No one on the homefront minded doing with less, considering what the boys overseas were dealing with. In fact, Abby's parents had started a victory garden to grow their own vegetables, so they wouldn't be spending their money on food needlessly.

Emmeline and her parents didn't make it to the graduation but came for the party. Emmeline's walk had changed into a bit of a waddle now that she was all belly. She and Peter had only been together two weeks, but it was enough. Both sets of parents were thrilled when they heard the news of her pregnancy. Emmeline was scared to death.

As Abby watched Emmeline rub her middle, she recalled Emmeline first telling her the news. "Abby, can you keep a secret?" she had asked early in the spring.

"Sure."

"You promise not to tell?" Emmeline bit her lip.

Abby, who had grown very close to her sister-in-law, took her hand. "What's wrong, sweetie?"

Emmeline whispered, "Peter's going to be a daddy."

And they had embraced and cried tears of joy for the first time in a long time.

Since then, Emmeline had told her parents and Peter's parents, with Abby by her side. If Peter couldn't be there, she would be, Abby thought. She had promised to take care of Emmeline, and that included their baby. Each week, Emmeline came for dinner on Saturdays, and the family watched her grow. Abby was there when the baby first kicked and wrote to Peter all about the experience. She tried her best to describe it, so he could imagine feeling it.

And Peter, oh, Peter. When Emmeline wrote to him that she was expecting, his letters home were so full of excitement. He said he promised all the men in his outfit real cigars when they could find them. He wrote letters to "Baby Walker." And when he wrote to Abby, he made her promise to share everything she possibly could about the pregnancy. He and Emmeline wrote about baby names that Emmeline and Abby had thought up. And the list was getting shorter the further Emmeline got. Sadly, it was painfully clear that Peter would not make it home for the birth of his first child. But Abby vowed to send him a million pictures and show the baby pictures of Peter, so he would recognize his daddy.

Emmeline interrupted her thoughts and gave Abby a package. "This is for you. For graduation."

"Oh, Emmeline, you shouldn't have gotten me anything," she said.

"It's not from me," Emmeline confessed as a huge smile crept across her face. "Open it."

Abby looked to her sister-in-law with a quizzical glance and tore open the paper. Inside, she found an envelope and a small box. She ripped the letter open and read aloud.

"My Abby," she read. It was from Harvey!

"My Abby,

Congratulations on graduating! I'm so proud of you. I wish I was there with you. Soon, my angel, soon. Now, open the gift. And use it! For heaven's sake, use it often. I will write you soon, Angel.

Love, Harvey."

Abby set the note aside and opened the box. Inside was a camera, a little Kodak Brownie Junior. Abby turned the black box over in her hands. Her own camera. It was something she and Harvey had talked about often while he was at school. She wanted to be able to take pictures and send them. And that desire had doubled when the war started. Abby's family had a camera, but it was used sparingly. Now, she could take pictures all she wanted. The gift meant so much. It warmed her heart that Harvey knew her so well.

"How did you get this, Emmeline?" She had to know.

Emmeline laughed, and her belly jiggled with the movement. "Honestly, Abby? Harvey gave it to me before he and Peter left. He asked me to give it to you today. He really thought ahead." Abby hugged her sister-in-law, amazed at her fiancé's ingenuity.

Abby carefully loaded a roll of film into the camera and immediately took a picture of Emmeline to send to Peter. And she had Emmeline take a picture of her for Harvey. At the end of the party, the entire family gathered, and Mr. Madison took a picture of everyone together, smiling. Abby thought she would send that picture to every soldier, so they knew the people at home were supporting them.

When night fell, Abby put on her nightgown and padded into the living room with pen and stationary. She wished she could have the film developed already to send to Harvey and Peter, but for tonight, just words would have to do.

A letter for her brother came first.

Dear Peter,

Today was graduation. Can you believe I'm a high school grad-
uate? Sometimes I feel like we're still little children, fighting
over ice cream. And other times, I think I'm too old to just
be graduating. Very few girls in my class are engaged, but I
know a handful that are getting married this summer before
their boyfriends leave for some far corner of the world.

What corner are you in, brother dear? Still can't tell me exactly? It's so queer that the government censors your letters
home. Do they really think we're spies?

Oh, you should see my graduation gift from Harvey! Did he
tell you what he got me? A camera! A real one, all my own. I
took lots of pictures today. I took one of Emmeline for you.
I'll send it when I get it developed. She's the one that had the
camera from Harvey. Can you believe them?

Peter, Emmeline is just glowing. It's so hard to believe that
in a few short weeks, your little baby will be here. Emme is
doing great. She's starting to waddle a little, though! But it's
normal, Momma said, and I felt the baby kick again today. Do
you think it's a girl or boy? I know I ask you this each letter,
but I keep changing my mind. I want you to have a son first,
so he can protect his little sisters like you did me and Reba.
But then I think a girl to dress up would be fun, too.

Well, I need to write Harvey before bed, so I'm going to end here.

Much Love,

Abby

Abby was amazed that she could write a letter and send it, not knowing where exactly it was going; but it would get to her brother, and his letters would get back to her. She didn't know how, but she didn't care. As long as she had a steady flow of letters reassuring her and her family that their loved ones were safe, she didn't care.

On another sheet of paper, Abby started again.

My dearest Harvey,

You are very sneaky and very thoughtful. Thank you for the camera. You spoil me! I thanked Emmeline a thousand times for keeping the gift for you. However did you sneak it to her? She said you gave it to her before you left. I took lots of pictures, and Emmeline took one of me today. I'll send it to you when it's developed.

I wish I knew where you were. I hate not knowing. I was just telling Peter that I wanted to know where you were. How can I properly pray for you without knowing your exact location and conditions? In your last letter, you were in France. Are you still there? Are you in Paris? Paris is supposed to be so romantic, but I guess it's not romantic during a war, is it?

Now that school is over, I think I want to get a job. There's no point in me sitting around all day. There are posters everywhere and ads on the radio telling everyone at home to do their part for the war effort. I could sell bonds or work in a factory. I could become a secretary, something. But I wanted to check with you first. If you don't want your future wife to work, tell me, and I won't. But I really want to, at least until you come home.

Summer here is in full swing. Flowers are blooming everywhere, and the days are getting longer and hotter. It's so hard to believe that it was just a year ago we met. Can that be it? Just a year? So much has changed. I went from a naïve girl to the fiancée of a soldier, who's in a war half the world away. And aside from the war part, I wouldn't change a thing.

You said you wanted to know about my dreams for the future? Well, my first dream would be to have you home and the war over. Isn't that everyone's dream? For our boys to be home? After that, we'd have a big wedding with all the family there. And we'd settle into a lovely house. You probably want to go home to Charleston, don't you? You said something before about that. I hadn't really thought about it. I would hate to leave my family behind, but I would do it for you, Harvey. Well, wherever we are, we'll be together. And you'll work, and I'll make you big dinners every night when you get home. Steak and roast chicken and corn on the cob with butter.

Dare I dream further, Harvey? I confess, with Emmeline growing daily, I look in the mirror and imagine myself with child—my waistline growing, my walk changing. Emmeline said that knowing that a part of Peter is in her means everything to her. So, I think we'd have a son first, with your green eyes and your strong chin. He'll be as handsome as you. And then, we'll have another boy, and then a daughter—someone I can dress up and be girly with, someone who will confide in me the way I confide in Momma.

Oh, Harvey, I've made myself homesick for you. Part of me wishes we had gone ahead and married before you left. Emmeline has a part of Peter with her daily, and I'm a little green that I don't have a part of you. I hope I'm not making you too homesick, but fight this war and come home, please.

I should go now; it's late. I anticipate your reply about my working and our future plans.

I love you a million times over,

Abigail Walker

Abby looked at the clock; it was time for her to go to sleep. She hoped Harvey would write back soon about her working. She hoped he would approve and that her parents would approve. She lay in bed and thought of names she would call her own children one day. She shared her parent's affection for biblical names. Two boys and a girl—David Harvey the Third, Daniel, and Ruth, perhaps. She nodded off, dreaming of her perfect future.

***

It was a Thursday, and Abby was left with not much to do. The housework had been done for the day, so she decided to head to the Newmans for a visit. She took Jacob and Eliza with her to play with the Newman boys. She enjoyed visiting with Harvey's aunt. And she felt like it was a way to get to know someone in his family a little better.

Mrs. Newman had received a letter from her husband, Frank, that day. She shared parts with Abby—how Frank was in the Pacific, working with the Marines. Luckily, he was not in the infantry, but a corpsman with a mobile hospital.

"I do miss my Frank," Mrs. Newman said and sighed. "He's been gone so long."

Abby sat next to her. "How long has it been?"

Mrs. Newman pondered a moment before answering. "Freddy is two years old now, so he's been gone almost two years. He left just a few weeks after Freddy was born. He said there wasn't enough work here for him to support all these boys. But Edwin is keeping this farm going now, and we're making a little money . . . "

Mrs. Newman continued to describe her oldest son's duties, but Abby wondered how this woman and Harvey's mother could be sisters. Sure, they looked similar, but they lived worlds apart. Mrs. Nicholas lived in a well-to-do place, in a well-to-do house. She even had a maid, Harvey had told her. And here was Mrs. Newman with five sons, an absent husband, living on a farm that barely operated.

When she finished talking, Abby asked, "Mrs. Newman, tell me about Harvey's mother. I really want to know more about her, and I want her to like me. Can you tell me about her?"

"Please, call me Doris, or Aunt Doris, since you'll soon be married to my sweet nephew," she smiled.

"Okay, Aunt Doris." Abby laughed.

Doris took a deep breath and began, "Jane and I were never much alike. Oh, sure we look alike, not like you and your sister. You don't look anything alike. But Jane and I do. We grew up in a small town not far from Columbia. Columbia is big and bustling, but our little town was small and is still very simple. I was born in 1903, and she is four years older than I am.

"Before the war started, when I was only eleven, and she was fifteen, she fell in love with a man from our church. He was older and from

Charleston. He had just finished school at Clemson College and taken a job in Columbia. He was renting a room from one of our neighbors, actually. He didn't notice Jane for a long time, but before he left to join the army, he had visited her at our house several times. They agreed to write to each other. David came home in 1917, and they were married right away. She was no older than you are now, Abby." Doris sighed.

"Jane loved Charleston right away. I went to visit her for the summer when Susan was born. Their house seemed so huge. David worked in his father's shipping business and was rarely home. They had a maid then, too. It was all so gorgeous. The house was huge, bigger than I ever imagined a house could be. I stayed the summer and then went home.

"About two years later, Jane sent for me and said she was expecting again. That summer, she had Harvey. David Harvey, Junior. He was the light of their lives. Oh, they loved Susan; but when David had a son, that was it. Sadly, Jane couldn't have any more children after that. Very sad, as she wanted more. But it meant that Susan and Harvey got everything they could ever want." Her eyes quickly scanned her meager belongings. Her children would never have everything they could ever want. Doris let out a sigh before continuing.

"They had a wonderful childhood, Susan and Harvey. But still, their parents took them to church and taught them to be humble. I wasn't around much. When I married Frank and moved up here, I saw them less. But Jane and I wrote often; and when they got a camera, she sent pictures of Susie and Harvey as kids. I wish I knew where those pictures were, but they're packed up."

Abby smiled. "That's okay. Thank you for sharing with me."

"Anytime, sweetie, anytime."

July 4, 1942

Dear Abby,

You sure are interested in my childhood lately. I don't mind. I want you to know everything about me. Charleston was great growing up. There's so much history there. And it's beautiful. The ocean stretches out before you, and the trees and flowers are so pretty. It smells like a mix of salty air and hyacinths. It sounds odd, but it's comforting to think of that smell where I am now.

Here, it smells terrible. I can't tell you what I smell, nor would I want to; but suffice it to say, I've smelled war, and I don't like it. I wish I could tell you where I am. But I'm not allowed, since they censor letters home. And to be honest, I'm never sure day-to-day where I am, anyway.

I'm just glad I'm not on the front. I feel safer, even though death and destruction are still all around me. Sadly, I'm used to the weight and feel of a gun strapped across my chest, and I find comfort in it. But now that General Eisenhower is in command, I pray that this war will end soon. We all do.

Keep sending pictures. I really enjoyed the picture of you and Reba sitting in the field of flowers. I can practically smell them—and you. I miss how you smell, angel. It's funny . . . even with a war going on here in Europe, the flowers are still blooming. Apparently, no one told them a war is going on.

Oh, I miss you. I think about you all the time. And it's fine by me if you want to work for now. Find a nice job, though; you're not a Rosie the Riveter type. I want to come home to a woman who still feels like a woman when I hold her. And when I get home, ah, when I get home . . . well, that's for another letter.

Happy Independence Day, Abby. We're all fighting for your freedom.

With Love,

D. Harvey Nicholas, Jr.

29 July 1942

My Dearest Harvey,

I can't imagine the smells where you are now. If I could bottle the scent of the lilacs here, I would send them to you. I wonder if I spritz this paper with perfume if it would still smell when you get it. I'll try.

Can you smell it?

I miss you greatly. Is it horrible that I watch Emmeline and am so jealous at what she has? A part of the man she loves nestled inside her. Each time I see her, I feel an ache in the pit of my stomach. I know jealousy is a sin, and I don't envy that Peter's missing this and will surely miss the birth of his child. Did I tell you they picked out names, finally? Peter Nathan, Junior, for a boy, and Petra Louise for a girl.

I got a job, and I think you'll be happy with it. No Rosies for me. I have a job as a receptionist at Daddy's bank. I answer the phones and greet customers. Daddy said that several of the women had left to take factory jobs, leaving him short-staffed. So, I'm earning a little money and staying busy. Hopefully, in a few weeks, I can sell war bonds. Then, that will really help you.

What is your sister like? Did you like growing up with an older sister? Tell me about her family. Is her husband fighting, too? Do you look like her?

Oh, Harvey, all I can think about is your eyes. Those green eyes. I long for them to stare back at me. I look in the mirror at night and pray for God to show me your face in the mirror. I just want to see you up close, your eyes looking into mine. Just for a second.

It's very late here. I have my nightgown on, and I need to go to bed. Sometimes, at night, I dream that you're with me, your arm draped across me. If my mother saw me writing this, I'd get into a lot of trouble. But she doesn't read my letters to you. And she can't get into my dreams either. Tonight, I'll dream that we're an old couple, with lots of grandchildren, and we're helping each other into bed; and I'll still fall asleep looking into your eyes.

Dream of me, Harvey.

With my Love,

Abby

16 August 1942

Happy Birthday, my Angel,

It's your birthday yet again. I have to admit, I thought we would all be home by now. I long to see you, and Peter longs to see Emmeline before he becomes a papa himself.

Speaking of—I loved growing up with Susie as a big sister. She was like a little momma with me. You'd love her. She looks so much like my mother, nothing like me. She's a typical Charleston wife, I suppose. She has a wonderful house. Her husband, James, owns a factory just outside the city. He's not in the war; he has an injury from childhood that doesn't prevent him from working, but prevents him from fighting—and I don't think he minds. Sue is a great mom to Rachel and Rhett. I'm sure you'll love her. She likes to bake, just like you!

I'm so happy you're working at the bank. It fills me with comfort. And that you're going to sell war bonds makes me a proud man. Maybe they'll put your gorgeous face on a poster for war bonds.

You said in your last letter to dream of you . . . Oh, if you only knew how I dream of you, Abby. You are the whole reason I wake in the mornings. You are the reason I put one foot in front of the other each day. I dream of holding you, of kissing you, and especially of smelling you.

I'm not sure if I could smell your lilacs on the paper for sure; but just knowing the scent was there, I could smell them. And I could smell you. I could swear I could smell you from that night just after Christmas. Has it been that long since I last held you? I miss you.

I'm praying for you daily. I wish I had a birthday gift for you, but no such luck this time. Settle for this letter, okay? I promise next year, I'll have a wonderful gift for you. I pray by your next birthday, we'll be married.

Yours,

Harvey

Abby's birthday had been two weeks before. She was happy she got Harvey's letter so soon. Some letters took longer to get to her. Maybe the shorter mailing time meant Harvey was somewhat closer to home. She could hope at least.

It was a small birthday. Her parents and brothers and sisters gathered around her and sang. There was no cake this year for her eighteenth birthday. No cake and no Harvey. But her family did get her some new paper and pens to write with, and Momma had made her a new dress in secret. Reba had helped her and acted as a model for Momma to sew on. Abby had lost more weight, which concerned her mother, but Abby tried to pretend it made her more glamorous—more like movie stars.

Two weeks after her birthday, the family was sitting on the front porch to stay cool, sipping iced tea, when the Madisons' car came tearing onto their lawn. Mr. Madison leaned out the window and shouted, "It's time! Abby, jump in! Come on, everyone!"

The entire family was on their feet, and instinctively, Abby got into the car where she found Emmeline in the back seat very unhappy and in labor.

"Abby, help me," she panted, sweat pouring down her face.

Abby looked in the front seat. It was just Mr. Madison; Emmeline's mother was not with them. "Where's Mrs. Madison?"

As Mr. Madison peeled out of the yard, he huffed, "Maria left for a few days to visit her sister. Her brother-in-law was killed last week. She thought we had more time."

The car was silent for a moment, everyone now thinking of the father of this child about to enter the world. *Stupid war,* Abby thought. *Keeping my brother away from the birth of his child.*

Mr. Madison broke the silence. "I called, and she's on her way, but it will be a while. I knew I could count on you to help, Abby."

Abby looked at Emmeline. She knew nothing about birthing children. Luckily, she saw her mother driving the car behind her, just as frantic to keep Mr. Madison's pace.

Emmeline let out a low moan that grew into a panicked yell. Beads of sweat rolled down her face and neck. Abby had no idea what to do, so she prayed.

They rolled up to the tiny town hospital and rushed inside. A calm nurse helped Emmeline to a small room. Mr. Madison waited outside in the car. Abby did not think he could handle seeing his daughter in pain. Flanked on either side by Abby and Grace, Emmeline labored to bring her child into the world.

Hours later, little Peter Nathan Walker, Junior made his entrance into the world. Emmeline was assisted by her sister-in-law and her mother-in-law, as her mother had missed the entire thing. The birth of her nephew made Abby happy in a way that she hadn't felt in many months. But when things had calmed down, a wave of sadness covered the family. Once Mrs. Madison arrived at the hospital, Emmeline broke down in tears.

Out in the hall, Abby turned to her mother full of anger. "Peter should be here, Momma. He should be here, at home, with his wife and his new son."

"I know, Abby."

"It's not fair," Abby cried. She took off down the hallway to seek solitude.

She made her way to the nursery, where little Peter was the only baby in the room. The small town hospital didn't see many births. She peered at him through the window. So tiny and helpless. She had promised Peter she would take care of Emmeline and the baby. But now that the baby was here, she wanted her brother home to do it himself. But she had promised, and she would uphold that promise until Peter could care for them himself.

Footsteps behind her made Abby take a deep breath and wipe her face clean with her hands. She turned to see Reba and Eliza coming toward her, beaming.

"Is the baby in there, Abby?"

Smiling, she replied, "He sure is, Eliza. Come on, and I'll lift you up to see him." She hoisted her youngest sister up to gaze through the window. The three sisters all looked in on the sleeping baby, freshly washed and swaddled. Reba took Abby's hand and rested her head on her sister's shoulder. On the other side, Eliza also rested her head on Abby's cheek. Abby finally felt some peace.

After a few moments, Reba spoke up. "I brought your camera." She handed it to Abby, who quickly snapped a picture of the baby for her brother.

After several pictures of the new mother and baby, as well as pictures of all the grandparents with P.J.—as he would be called—the Walkers made their way home.

That night, Abby wrote to Peter and to Harvey. She had already asked Emmeline if she could share that he was the proud papa of a boy. Emmeline said it was fine. She promised to send pictures the moment they were developed. It was getting harder to get pictures in print, but she always did her best to send pictures quickly.

She wrote about the miraculous birth she witnessed herself. How she held Emmeline's hand and told her how Peter was proud of her. That she had watched P.J. enter the world as his mother gasped for breath. She congratulated her brother and berated him for not being there. Then she apologized, knowing he had no control over the war.

In her letter to Harvey, Abby poured her heart out. Her joy at the day's events and her anger toward a war she knew practically nothing about consuming her days, yet she tried to stay as far removed from it as possible. She told Harvey how proud she was of Emmeline and how she didn't know if she could ever do the same. But she promised to try if Harvey would just come home.

She fell asleep that night exhausted, angry, and overjoyed at the same time. She slept hard and barely dreamed at all. All she remembered the next morning was seeing Peter over and over in her head and praying he would come home soon.

1 October 1942

My Dearest Sister,

I can't believe I'm a father! Can you believe it? How is little P.J.? I got your picture. He looks like Emmeline, I think. I'm ready to come home and hold my son and kiss my wife. Will you do that for me? Maybe just hug Emme, though. How is she? I'm sure she's a great mom, but how is she holding up alone? I'm sure she's not alone, though, is she? I hope you're helping out as much as you can. Just watch out for those diapers! Oh! Diapers! When I get home, Emme won't ever change another diaper. I'll do it all for her. She deserves it. Don't tell her, but I'm saving up some of my pay to get her a ring. Maybe not as fancy as yours from Harvey, but still, a ring. Tell my son I'll be home soon!

Your Brother,

Peter "Papa" Walker

P.S. Tell Momma and Dad and the kids "Hi" for me!

2 October 1941

Abigail Angel,

I don't have much time to write today. Things are getting serious over here. I won't go into detail, but know that Pete and I are safe for now. I love you desperately. I keep your picture over my heart. I will always love you.

Harvey

That last letter from Harvey scared Abby. She showed the letter to her father, something she had never done before. Nathan read over the letter several times, shaking his head and scowling.

"Daddy?" Abby was petrified. She didn't know what to think and her stomach did flips.

"Well, honey," her father said, raking his hands through his thinning hair, "I can't tell you for sure, but I do know that things are escalating in Europe. It sounds like Harvey and Peter are in the middle of that. I can't tell you what will happen, but God knows, and He will protect them."

Tears welled in Abby's eyes. "Daddy, they have to come home."

"We will pray that God will spare them, and they'll both be home soon, Abigail. That's all we can do."

Abby studied her father's face. In the months since Peter had been gone, Nathan seemed to have aged ten years. His hair was thinning; he had lines around his eyes and mouth. Maybe they had been there all along, and she had never noticed. Abby wasn't sure.

She wrote to Peter and Harvey daily—about work, about P.J., and about life in general. She wrote nothing but happiness and how things would be when they came home, how the flowers were waiting to bloom just for them. She sent pictures whenever she could. If life was hard for them, she would be a light. A beacon to call them home. Even Reba, Jake, and Eliza had started writing to other men in their unit to cheer them up. They were all a part of the effort to keep their boys going day to day.

Each night, Abby prayed the same thing over and over until she fell asleep. *Lord, please bring our boys home. Especially my boys. I need Harvey; Emmeline needs Peter. P.J. needs Peter. We need them home, Lord. Please. Why do You allow war to happen? What purpose does it serve? Young men killing other young men. And I know that innocent children are getting killed as well in crossfire; I hear it on the radio. Why do You allow this? Please bring them home, Lord. Please. Can't You hear all of us praying?*

CHAPTER 10

THANKSGIVING PREPARATIONS HAD BEGUN A week ahead of time, and Abby was in the kitchen the night before, getting the final things ready alongside her mother. Things had been calm for a while, with no more eerie letters from either Harvey or Peter. It had been nearly a year since the war began, nearly a year since Abby last saw her brother or fiancé. Life went on, though—a new, adjusted life—and she prayed it would go back to the way it was before quickly.

Abby glanced at the ring on her left hand. The ruby shone bright; the diamonds sparkled. It made her smile. She wondered what her wedding ring would look like next to it. The more time that passed, the more she thought about her wedding. She longed to plan a great party for it, but without knowing when Harvey would be home, there was no use. But all her ideas were filed away in her head, saved for when one day became now.

Emmeline was at the house with P.J., who was growing so fast. Already three months old, and everyone was convinced he was the smartest baby ever. His eyes followed Gabriel around the room as he toddled to and fro. Gabe, in turn, would pick up little items and bring them to Emmeline and P.J.

The back door sprung open, startling the ladies in the kitchen. They all jumped a little as Nathan strode in, his face stone.

"Nathan, what are you doing home at this hour?" Grace asked, setting the food down. She got no reply as Nathan motioned that they follow him to the living room. The children were scooped up, and the ladies nervously followed.

Grace, Abby, and Emmeline filed into the living room like school children. They sat, the babies between them. Nathan held his arms out for P.J., and Emmeline handed the infant to his grandfather, fear on her face. Nathan cuddled the baby and spoke softly to him.

Grace could take the silence no longer. "Nathan, what is going on?"

He looked up from the baby and looked at each of the women before him, his eyes red. "They tried to find you and came to the bank when they couldn't," he said, looking down. Abby didn't know what her father was talking about, but she didn't like it. "They . . . they came to the bank and pulled me aside," he stammered, the grief welling up in his voice. "I'm afraid it's bad news."

Abby, in the middle of her mother and sister-in-law, held both their hands. No one spoke for a moment. Everyone held their breath.

Nathan looked from his wife to his daughter-in-law several times, and Abby knew. She felt it in her heart; and when her father knelt down next to Emmeline, she held her breath. Nathan couldn't meet Emmeline's gaze, but whispered, "I'm so sorry; he's gone."

Emmeline sucked in her breath and held a silent howl. The silence was deafening. Then the sobs began. Tears flowed freely, and Abby now understood why her father had taken the baby. Emmeline's body went limp, and she slumped into Abby, who caught her and held her tight.

On her other side, her father and mother cried as they cradled P.J. between them—their only link to their son. A son who would never meet his sweet baby. A life gone before it began. They cried for their loss, but more for the loss P.J. would experience not knowing his father, the loss of a husband for Emmeline.

Within minutes, Emmeline's parents arrived. Nathan had called them before he came home. Grace gathered herself enough to leave the room and speak with the Madisons in private. Abby didn't know how her mother managed to get up and walk again, as she wasn't sure she would be able to. They left Abby and Emmeline alone for a few minutes in the living room.

Emmeline's head rested in Abby's lap, her hands drawn up near her face, her legs curled behind her. Abby smoothed Emmeline's hair over and over, comforting both her sister-in-law and herself. Emmeline's tears had dried for the time being, but she lay motionless. Abby's tears were still flowing, silently, down her cheeks and dripping into Emmeline's hair.

How could Peter be gone? What had happened? She had just gotten a letter from him the day before. What did it say again? It was dated nearly three weeks before. Something about doing lots of walking, and he was imagining they were walking home. He said the people were nice, and he was suddenly aware of all the young children around him—young children affected by the war. And he hoped P.J. wouldn't ever know such a side effect.

Except now, P.J.'s entire world was affected by the war. Not just a side effect—a total effect. No father to teach him to ride a bike or tie his shoe. No Daddy to play catch with. No one to give him a stern talking to when he disobeyed his mother. Peter never met his son, except through pictures, and now P.J.'s knowledge of his father would be the same.

Finally, Emmeline stirred. Reaching her hand up and taking Abby's, she asked, "What do I do now?"

Abby cleared her throat and tried to sound strong. She didn't know where the words came from; she could only guess from God Himself. "I don't know, Emme. But we'll do it together, okay? I will always be here for you. I will help you. And you'll have your parents and my parents to help you. We'll all make it through this."

Abby felt terrible for lying because she didn't think they would make it though this. But she couldn't let Emmeline give up completely.

"Okay," Emmeline said, sitting up. Her hair was matted to her head, her cheeks stained with tears. "You'll help me?"

"I will do anything I can. You know that," Abby replied, and she attempted a half-smile. The act of putting a smile on her face hurt every fiber of her being. "I'll be right here for you and P.J. as long as you need me."

"P.J.!" Emmeline stood in complete panic as her eyes raced around the room searching for him. "Where's P.J.? Where's my son?"

"He's in the other room with my parents and your parents. Let's go get him, okay?" Abby combed Emmeline's hair with her fingers and helped to steady her. She led her sister-in-law out of the room to find her son.

That night, Nathan and Grace had the terrible duty of telling Reba, Jake, and Eliza what happened. Eliza didn't seem to understand just yet what it meant. Peter had been gone a long time, so she didn't see how things would be too different. Reba cried and cried. She allowed the grief to cover her, and she ran to her room to escape. But Jake was a different story. He asked questions. He wanted to know why Peter was gone. How had he died? A land mine, apparently. Would they bring him back home? Yes, they would. And then there would be a funeral. Jake wanted to know lots of details that his father refused to give. Some answers he didn't know, and some he didn't think a young boy should know.

When the entire story came out, the family learned that Peter's unit was walking through a field in North Africa, moving from town to town after an invasion. Land mines hadn't been an issue, but a few were found to be scattered throughout the fields. Someone in the unit stepped on one, sending him and others around him flying through the air. That soldier was killed instantly. Other men were thrown by the blast and sustained a few injuries. Peter, who was next to the one who stepped on the mine, flew back about ten yards, his left leg and arm ripped to shreds. Others in his unit tried to help him, but the bleeding was too much. Peter bled to death on a North African field.

Abby wished she hadn't found out the details. Not only did it paint a gruesome death for her brother, but it made her anxious about Harvey. They were in the same unit. Was Harvey okay? Was he there? Did he try to save Peter? Or was he injured himself? She thought losing her brother was tragic enough; losing them both would surely kill her.

***

The funeral was held on a Friday. Peter's body had been cremated at Nathan's request. Emmeline didn't care; she hadn't seemed to care about anything since receiving the news. The past few weeks had been a blur. The entire town came out to Mount Olive Baptist Church for the service. Pastor Phillips, who had married Aunt Dottie several weeks before, delivered a moving sermon about duty to family and to country. He commended the Walkers for allowing their son to make the most awesome sacrifice. He lamented for Emmeline and P.J. over the loss of husband and father.

It was two weeks till Christmas and just days before Peter and Emmeline's first wedding anniversary. Everyone was agonizingly aware that just a year ago, they sat in the same place and celebrated the union of the pair. And now, they helped a woman, widowed at a young age, bury her husband. Peter was just twenty years old. Emmeline, only nineteen.

A box of Peter's things had arrived at the Walker house a few days before. Pictures of the family, Peter and Emmeline, and little P.J. The pictures of P.J. were the most worn, and they guessed he had shown them off regularly. His clothes arrived, still dirty, caked in North African dirt and grime. Emmeline held them close and breathed them in, hoping to smell Peter on them. She vowed never to wash them and preserve them just as they were, so they would always carry her beloved's scent. Also in the package were a few books, Peter's Bible, and a small box.

When Emmeline opened the box, she gasped. Inside was a ring and a note. The note, which Abby had to read to Emmeline, said that their unit helped a French woman in passing, and she gave him that ring after seeing Emmeline and P.J.'s picture. She said it was payment for helping her; and Peter was to give it to Emmeline, so she would always know that her husband was a hero. He had tried to refuse the ring, saying it was too valuable, but the woman insisted. She said she could tell Peter needed it more than she did. Peter planned to give her the ring when he returned home.

The ring was stunning—a thin, silver band supported a simply elegant opal stone. The opal shone pink and blue in the light. Inside the ring was an engraving, "Toi et moi," Peter's note said it meant "you and me" in French. It fit Emmeline perfectly. She put it on her finger above her wedding band. The light reflected off the stone onto her band, and her wedding ring lit up a brilliant light blue color. Emmeline smiled as she looked at the ring, then fresh tears began to stream down her face. Abby, who had become her righthand in this time, was by her side—holding her and keeping her strong, so she didn't have to be.

But the strength was all a lie as far as Abby was concerned. She wasn't strong. She was only strong for Emmeline and P.J., so she could be weak for herself. She hadn't received a single note from Harvey since before news of Peter's death. And it scared her tremendously. At night, when the lights were out and she no longer had to be Emmeline's life support, Abby cried. She didn't care if anyone heard her. It had become habit now for Reba to crawl into bed with her. Reba would hold Abby's hand and hum softly to her. They would fall asleep that way and wake that way. Still tired, still hurting, but comforted for the time being.

The day before Christmas, Doris Newman pounded on the door furiously. "Mrs. Walker!" She beckoned from outside. "Abby! Quickly! I heard from Jane! I have news about Harvey!"

Grace ran to open the door, and Abby rushed into the kitchen steps behind her. "Harvey? Where is he? Is he okay?" Abby held her mother's hand as Doris sat, breathless, at the table. Her hands were trembling, her lip quivering.

"He is injured, but he's alive. Praise God, he's alive!" Doris began to cry as she told the account of what she knew.

Her sister, Jane, had called her, saying that the army had contacted her. Harvey had been hit in the blast that killed Peter. Abby's breath caught at hearing this, and tears stung her eyes. Doris continued, saying that Harvey was thrown, but luckily, only suffered some broken bones and shrapnel in his skin. His mother said that Harvey had crawled over to a wounded man—a friend, apparently—to help him, embedding the shrapnel deeper into his flesh. That friend had been Peter. Harvey was taken to a field hospital in Northern Africa and then flown to Algiers, France, where his wounds were treated, and he was recovering. But his arm and hand were too injured to write, and he had spent several weeks going through surgeries and being moved throughout Africa and Europe.

"So, he's okay? He's all right?" Abby asked through tears. She brushed them away and smiled. Harvey was alive, and he had been with Peter to comfort him in the end. Abby's heart soared.

Then Doris smiled and laid a hand on Abby's. "Abby, he's coming home."

Harvey had been in the French hospital for a while, but his arm and leg would never be the same. The shrapnel had done enough damage, the doctors said. He would walk with a cane for some time, if not forever, and was of no more use to the army. He would be home right after New Year's.

Abby jumped up and hugged her mother and then hugged Doris. "He's coming home! And soon! Soon!"

Grace spoke up, wiping her own tears from her face, "That's wonderful news. I'm so relieved Harvey is okay." While she was relieved, the pain in her voice was obvious. Harvey would come home, but Peter would not. He may be hobbling, but at least he would be breathing. "Abby, you have to realize, Harvey may not be the same. If he has to walk with a cane . . . "

"I don't care if he never walks again, Momma! He's coming home! Thank you, God!"

"Now, Abby," Doris reminded, "keep in mind, he'll need a lot of help recovering. He'll be going home to his parents in Charleston. It may be a while before he can travel back up here."

Abby was quiet for a moment. She hadn't thought about him going back home to Charleston. She thought he would come straight to her. How would he come get her? Or how could she get to him? Would he go back to Clemson to finish school? She had so many questions, but they were all overshadowed by the fact that Harvey would be back in South Carolina soon. And across the state was a hundred times better than across the world.

"I don't care," she gushed. "I'll get to Charleston and nurse him back to health myself. As long as he's home!" Abby danced around the kitchen, bliss finally replacing heartache, even if for a short time.

***

Christmas joy was eclipsed by family grief that year. It seemed colder than it ever had before. Abby was torn between grieving for her brother and rejoicing over Harvey's return. Before the gifts were opened, Nathan settled his family down to pray. He prayed for all the troops still overseas fighting. He prayed for the families on the homefront, waiting for them. He prayed for each family member by name, adding extra prayer when it came to Grace, Emmeline, and P.J. He even prayed for Harvey to return safely, which Abby appreciated. While her father prayed, Abby started her own prayer but stopped short. She was angry with God and just didn't know what to say to Him at that moment.

Her father finished praying, and the family began to open their meager gifts. New socks, a handmade scarf—all small but handy gifts for the Walkers this year. Three boxes stayed under the tree when they finished. A gift for Emmeline and two for P.J. They expected them after supper.

The entire family watched a nearly-four-month-old P.J. open his gifts with the help of his mother. Each person in the room wore a plastered-on smile and had red-rimmed eyes as P.J. delighted to play with the crinkly paper and not the gifts themselves.

While Abby was so thankful to be present for the baby's first Christmas, she couldn't help but think back to the Christmas before when his father was strong and energetic. Newly wed, Peter was certain he could take on every Nazi and win the war singlehandedly to come back to Emmeline. He should have been there. He should have been holding P.J. as Emmeline snapped pictures of their first Christmas as a family. She hated to fake being happy and excused herself the minute P.J. lost interest in the wrapping paper.

Abby went to her room and wrote another letter to Harvey, just as she had every day. She didn't know where to send it. She knew the address for the army by heart, but had no idea what his address in Charleston was. If she sent it to Clemson, would they forward it to Charleston? She decided she would just have to wait and get the address from Doris the next day.

25 December 1942

My dear Harvey,

I got word from Aunt Doris yesterday that you're coming home! Injured, but coming home! She also said you were with Peter before he died. I wish I had known. It has given the family comfort to know he was with you during his last breaths. His funeral was two weeks ago now.

It's been nearly six weeks since your last letter. I tried not to imagine the worst, especially after news of Peter arrived. But now that I know you were in a hospital, I completely understand what's going on. Your aunt said your legs were hurt, and your hands not much better. I imagine writing just isn't a possibility right now, is it?

Aunt Doris said you would be coming home to Charleston. I'm so glad you'll be back in the States; I don't mind if I can't see you right away. But now that you'll be back, we can plan our wedding, right? Maybe for the first of spring? By then, you should be as good as new. But we can talk about that later.

Oh, Harvey, I have missed you so much, and the last month has tripled that. Emmeline is so bad off. I wish I could do something for her. I wish I could make the hurt stop for her. And Momma. Momma's putting on a brave face, but I can see the pain in her eyes. I wonder if it will ever go away.

But that's enough of that. I just want to focus on your return. When can I see you? I'll come to Charleston if I have to. Just let me know when you're home.

Until then, I will wait. I love you.

Love,

Abigail

CHAPTER 11

3 January 1943

Miss Walker,

I thought you would like to know that Harvey is home. He can't write—he hasn't the strength or capability right now—but he asked me to write to you. I, of course, obliged.

He said he doesn't want to see you again and that he was mistaken about you. He was just using you, you know—something to pass the time until he and I could be together. You know our parents have had Harvey and I matched up for years now.

I thought you would like to know that Mr. and Mrs. Nicholas knew nothing of your supposed engagement. They have decided to throw us an engagement party the second Harvey is up to it. He asked me to marry him the very day he came home, after realizing how much he missed me. He said I was the love of his life. I do like your letter's suggestion, though; a spring wedding sounds lovely.

Now, one last order of business. There's a certain ruby ring that needs to be returned to the family. Any idea where that might be? I'll expect it shortly.

Sincerely,

The Future Mrs. Harvey Nicholas

Clarice Renard

Abby was shocked and dumbfounded. Words escaped her. He was just using her? What about his promises? Why would he have asked her father's permission to marry her? Why would he have given her the ring? Did he even read the Christmas letter she sent to his parent's house? What about all the other letters she had sent, promising her love, begging him to return? Maybe he couldn't write, but surely he could still read.

I need to call Harvey. I have to talk to him. I can't believe that he would want this! Abby ran to the phone and fumbled with the receiver. She dialed each number as tears rolled down her cheeks.

After two rings, someone picked up on the other end. "Hello?"

With a deep sigh, Abby said, "Hello? This is Abigail Walker. I need to speak with Harvey, please."

"Abigail," came the cold reply. "This is Mrs. Nicholas. I'm afraid I can't let you speak with Harvey."

"Please, I need him to know that I—"

"I know, Miss Walker. You better bet I know," Harvey's mother interrupted. Her voice was low and dark. "I know how you weaseled your way into Harvey's life. Harvey wants nothing to do with you. Not now, not ever. Please respect his privacy, and leave him alone."

Tears flooded Abby's cheeks. "But, I don't understand what happened. Please, Mrs. Nicholas . . . " But she received no response. Jane Nicholas had hung up the phone, and Abby was left holding a dead receiver. She hung it up and stepped away.

Hurt and bruised, Abby slipped her ring off. She examined the stones carefully. Despite the ache she felt, the stones still sparkled magnificently. They had sustained her for a year, like magic. They had comforted her when she cried, held her up when she was weak, and made her smile when all she wanted to do was cry. Apparently, the magic had been fake. An illusion.

Didn't he love her? Didn't he promise to love her forever? What had changed? Abby thought she should fight for the man she loved. But her fight was gone, used up. She had fought for a year to will him home. She had fought tooth and nail for her sister-in-law and nephew to survive tragedy. Harvey didn't love her; apparently, he never had. He had used her in the worst possible way. Why would she fight for that?

How could I have been so naïve? Did I honestly think such a sophisticated, wonderful man would want to marry me? I should have known better. I'm just a stupid girl. So stupid. I feel so ashamed and disgusted. Why me? Why me? At least, I know now; at least, I didn't give myself to him. What a horrible person, that Harvey Nicholas. I can't believe he would want such a nasty, vicious girl over me, but she can have him. Good riddance.

Without a word to anybody, Abby walked out of the house and toward the post office in town. It was windy, and the gusts stung at her face; but she could barely feel a thing. Along the way, she stumbled and fell, the ring tumbling out of her pocket and landing in the dirt. She picked it up and studied it again. Particles of dirt were now caught inside the setting, spoiling the shine. Now, the ring looked like she felt. Dirty and blighted. Her hair whipping around her face, Abby stood. She didn't bother to dust it off, or herself for that matter, and continued on her way.

At the post office, Abby asked for a small box. She dropped the ring into it, gave the clerk the address, and told him to send it postage due. She watched him tape the package and toss it onto a pile of outgoing mail. She stood still for a moment, thinking she should take it back. Maybe she should fight back. But between Clarice's letter and Mrs. Nicholas on the phone, it was painfully clear. Clarice would wear the ring and marry the love of Abby's life. Harvey wanted nothing to do with her.

With the deed done, she turned and went back to her parent's house. Abby did her best to convince herself that she was now better off, but the thought was fleeting. She was heartbroken, devastated, and drained. Her insides screamed in agony, but on the outside, she was a shell, numb to everything.

At home, she sought her mother, curling up in her lap and sobbing the entire affair to her until her heart and tears felt like the rest of her body—empty.

***

April 1943 was the coldest on record, or at least Abby thought so. It seemed colder that month than it had in January, especially in the constant sheets of rain. She pulled her coat collar up closer to protect her from the wind and wet. She slipped and struggled to hold onto her grocery bag. She hassled with the door and finally made it up the stairs to the apartment she now shared with Emmeline and P.J.

After receiving Clarice's letter and taking some time to recover, she talked to Emmeline and all of their parents about getting an apartment together. Both young ladies agreed it was best to get out of their parent's houses and be responsible together. The Walkers and Madisons agreed reluctantly. They helped the girls get set up in a small apartment in town, just across from the grocery store. Abby had gotten a driver's license, and she still drove Harvey's car to and from work. He had never asked for it back, and she had no way to return it, so she made use of it. Emmeline was trying to find a job herself; her mother had volunteered to keep P.J. for her during the days.

The apartment was on the bottom floor of a three-story building. It was sparsely furnished. An old couch sat in the living room. Behind it was a small, round table with four chairs. The kitchen was just an extension of the living room. A nook, really, with a small stove and oven, an ice box, and a sink. The apartment had only one bedroom, so P.J.'s crib was in the very back of the living room, along with a few toys. Abby and Emmeline shared the bedroom—two small cots on either side, between them a desk nobody wrote at, and a chair nobody sat in. A mirror was opposite the desk, but neither girl paid much attention to their appearances. There was a common bathroom down the hall, which they shared with an older widow, who lived next door. They were the only tenants on that hall.

When Abby got into the apartment, Emmeline was preparing dinner, and P.J. was trying to reach a toy just out of his grasp. The girls tried to take turns cooking, but since Emmeline was home, she usually cooked. P.J. was growing by leaps and bounds and could now sit on his own. He attempted crawling, but was, so far, unsuccessful. Abby set the sack on the counter and began to empty the contents—what fruit she could find, vegetables, milk, and some chicken. It would last them several days. They usually ate at the Walkers' house one night a week and at the Madisons' one night as well.

But Abby and Emmeline barely ate, anyway. Both were mourning and cared nothing for food. They both lived their lives to raise P.J. the way they felt Peter would have wanted. Abby's paycheck paid their rent and bought their groceries; the rest was put away until needed. They mended what clothes they had, letting P.J.'s out for his growing body and taking theirs in as they whittled away.

Once the grocery items were put away, Abby's right hand instinctively felt her left hand. Her ring was still gone—a vacant reminder that not only was her brother gone, but Harvey also. Living his life happily in Charleston with Clarice. How could she have been so stupid? How could she not realize that her happily ever after would never happen?

Emmeline noticed Abby's blank stare and spoke up. "It's okay. We're stronger than that, right?" She squeezed her sister-in-law's shoulder. Emmeline had managed to rise up out of her depression, for the most part. Abby was jealous of her for that. "Look at P.J. How big he's getting."

Abby glanced at the infant as he rolled himself over to get to a toy. He looked so much like Peter. The same big, dark eyes, the sandy-colored hair. But P.J.'s hair curled just like Abby's. He looked nothing like Emmeline, but she said she didn't mind at all. She said P.J. was his father all over again, and that was more important. P.J. wasn't chunky like most babies, but Abby chalked that up to how much he moved; the child was never content to be still.

She stooped to pick him up. "Come on, P.J. Let's sit over here, and I'll tell you a story about your papa."

Abby enjoyed telling stories about Peter to his son. They were often stories about Peter tormenting her when they were children. Sometimes, they were stories about when they were older.

"What shall we tell today?" she asked. "I know, how about the time your papa chased a pig around Uncle Jed's place?"

She told the story by rote as it was one of her favorites. Peter had accidentally let the hog free from its pen when he was about ten years old and had to chase it all over the yard to get it back for Uncle Jed. Abby had tried to help, but she was scared of the pig herself. And the other kids were too small to jump in. As she told the story, she could see Emmeline stop and listen. Eyes closed, she leaned against the counter and imagined her husband strong and running around. Even as a boy, he was very strong. When Abby finished, Emmeline wiped a tear or two away and set dinner on the table for the threesome.

Once P.J. was in bed, Abby and Emmeline retreated to their room as they usually did. They had no radio to listen to, no men to write to, so they frequently talked or read books. Some nights, Reba came over and brought games. But this night was too cold and wet for visitors. And neither Abby nor Emmeline felt like talking much. So both ladies retreated to their beds and fell into restless sleep. Both dreamed of what life would have been like if it hadn't been for the war.

Abby's dream was so full of color. Pearl Harbor had never happened. There was no talk from anyone she knew about going off to war. In her dream, Peter was alive and well. He and Emmeline lived in the apartment together. He worked hard and drove a nice, new car. Emmeline was dressed in a gorgeous pink outfit, and P.J. had mountains of toys to play with. But he always preferred to play with his papa. In the dream, Abby and Harvey were married, and Abby could feel a flutter in her abdomen. She was expecting. A girl perhaps. Harvey was standing so strong; his muscles pulled the sleeves of his shirt taut. Everyone was glowing, despite the cold outside.

But suddenly the dream turned dark. There was screaming and crying. Emmeline's dress was torn. The men vanished from the scene. And then something started pounding louder and louder. More crying and more pounding. She could hear her name over and over, "Abby! Abby!"

She woke with a start, her body covered in sweat. Her chest heaved as she realized she was safe in her bed. Emmeline was standing over her, holding a crying P.J. "Abby?" she said softly. "I'm sorry to wake you, but Mrs. Newman is at the door."

Abby rubbed her eyes. Mrs. Newman? Here to see her? She hadn't spoken to Doris Newman since before Christmas. Abby put her robe on and padded softly to the living room. "Aunt Doris? Sorry, I mean, Mrs. Newman," Abby corrected herself. "What's wrong?"

Doris scooted around the table, waving a piece of paper. "I'm sorry to have woken the baby; truly I am. But when this came last night, I could barely wait till now to come over." Doris shoved the paper into Abby's hand and folded her arms across her chest.

"What is it?" Emmeline asked, curious as to what was so important.

Abby unfolded the paper and read it carefully. Tears welled up in her eyes. "Why did you bring me this? To upset me?"

"What is it?" Emmeline asked again, taking the paper from Abby's trembling hand. "The marriage of Harvey and Clarice? Mrs. Newman, how could you bring this for her to see? Don't you know how much she's hurting?"

"That just shows you how serious Harvey really was, doesn't it?" Abby cried. "He never wanted me. It was all lies."

"That's not true!" Doris exclaimed. "He loved you, and I bet he still loves you. He asked me for that ring for you. I had been holding it all these years for him. I called Jane after I got this last night, asking for an explanation. She said she was told you had run off to marry some local boy. I told her that wasn't true and that you were still here, waiting for Harvey. Jane said it didn't matter now because Harvey was going to marry this Ranid girl."

"Renard," Abby corrected with a sniff. "It's French."

"Whatever, honey, you have got to do something about it!" Doris shook Abby's shoulders.

"He doesn't want me anymore, Mrs. Newman."

"I'm Aunt Doris, hear? I'm not going to sit idly by while he marries some ninny! You've got to go down there. You have got to go down there and tell Harvey that you didn't run off. He's been lied to, and he's heartbroken."

Abby shook her head, her curls springing all over. "No, he's not. He would have come here himself if he really cared. It's been months; he could have checked to see if her story was true. But he didn't come, he didn't even call. Would he really think I would marry someone else? Why would he believe such a thing?"

"Abigail, he can't come up here," Doris pleaded. "He can barely walk. He has to use a cane to move around. Jane says he's getting better, but he still needs help. And his hands are messed up; he's having to learn to write all over again. She said this ninny girl is doing everything for Harvey these days."

"So, Clarice told him I married somebody else." A lightbulb went off in Abby's mind, and she felt like she was woken after months of hibernation. Abby could see Clarice in her head. She probably showed Harvey the ring, saying it was sent back. Harvey believed her and instead asked to marry her. It all made sense.

Doris stood swiftly. "That's what Jane said. Get yourself dressed, and get to Charleston. You've got to stop Harvey from making a fool of himself."

Abby hesitated. "I can't do that. You see the invitation; they're getting married!"

Emmeline spoke up. "I'll go with you. P.J. and I will go with you."

Abby hesitated. She realized now why Harvey didn't write or call. He had been lied to, cheated. Clarice had it all planned. But could she be sure Harvey wanted her and not Clarice?

"Well, it is his birthday this week. Wouldn't that be a surprise?" She giggled a little. "But I don't know. Is this a good idea?"

"God will be with you, honey." Doris took Abby's hand in her own. "The wedding's not far off, so get moving."

All three women began packing as if it were their life's mission, tossing any clean garment they could find into the bags. Then, they stuffed them into the back seat of the car. Abby packed all her clothes but nearly forgot her shoes. She gave all the food they had to Doris, who still had five boys at home to feed.

When the car was loaded up, the girls both hugged Doris and got into the car. "I'll call you soon!" Abby called after her, smiling for the first time since Christmas. But the smile didn't last.

The pair stopped at the Madisons' house to tell Emmeline's parents they would be going to Charleston. Mr. Madison was irate. "What do you mean you're packing up and leaving for Charleston? Where will you stay? How will you pay for things down there?"

"We need to go, Daddy. If I can't be happy, Abby deserves to be."

Mrs. Madison piped up. "What about P.J.? You can't take a baby with you."

"People do it all the time, Mom."

"I'm sorry, Emmeline, you can't go." Mr. Madison put his foot down.

Emmeline's chin quivered as she fought tears. "I'm a married, and now widowed, woman, not a little girl. I'm sorry if you think this is a bad idea, but we're going."

She took P.J. from her mother and then left. Getting into the car, Mrs. Madison ran out after them. "Wait, Emmeline. At least, take some money with you." She shoved some cash into Emmeline's pocket. "I love you; be careful with my grandbaby." Mother and daughter hugged, and Abby drove over to her own parent's house.

They exchanged glances as they walked up the porch steps to the Walker household. Abby wasn't sure how her parents would react. On one hand, they knew about the letter from Clarice claiming Harvey had just used her and lied to her. But on the other hand, they knew how badly she was hurt; and once they realized Harvey was lied to as well, Abby hoped they wouldn't oppose.

Much like the Madisons, Nathan and Grace were none too happy about Abby's brash decision to travel across the state to chase after a man who broke her heart.

"Abby, if he's getting married to someone else . . . " Nathan started, shaking his head.

"She lied to him and me, splitting us up. She's a . . . a . . . ninny!"

"Abby, don't talk like that," her mother said. "But I have to agree; she was a bit of a snob. But your father's right. Taking off on such a trip so suddenly is not a good idea. And so out of character for you, dear."

Nathan laid a hand on his daughter's shoulder. "Your mother is right. This behavior is not like you. Are you sure this girl lied about everything?"

"She told Harvey I ran off and married someone else! In fact, Mrs. Newman about broke our door off this morning because Mrs. Nicholas had been told the same thing by Clarice. I have to go."

Grace hugged her eldest daughter and brushed the tears off her cheeks. She looked beyond her daughter to Emmeline. "What about you, Emmeline? You and P.J. are going as well?"

"Yes, ma'am. We are."

Grace looked at her husband. "Nathan?"

Abby's father looked at all three women. "What if it doesn't go the way you expect?"

Abby hung her head. "I don't expect anything at this point. But I have to at least see him. I've spent all this time praying and waiting for him. I need to see that he's okay and let him know the truth. He can decide who he wants then."

Nathan looked at his wife and raised an eyebrow. Grace lowered her head. Abby looked nervously from her mother to Emmeline.

"Give me just a minute," Nathan said. He walked out of the kitchen. The women were silent; only P.J. cooed. They all looked at each other until Nathan came back. He handed Abby a billfold. "This is what I have tucked away. Take it."

Abby hugged her father tight. "Thank you, Daddy. We'll call you as soon as we get to Charleston."

"Do you even know where you're going?" Grace asked. "Do you need a map?"

"We guessed the roads would be marked. We'll figure the rest out once we're in Charleston," Abby confessed.

"Nathan, get her the map from the car. Now, girls, do you need some sandwiches for the road? It's a long drive." Grace began to move in the kitchen, gathering up some snacks for the girls.

While Nathan found the map, Abby and Emmeline prepared food to take with them. Grace held onto P.J. and cuddled him. When the sandwiches were packed and the map folded, Nathan prayed over the travelers. He prayed for safety and for ease of trip. He prayed for them to accomplish their mission, whatever that may be. Grace clung to Abby, tears flowing.

"We'll be home soon, Momma. Don't worry. Tell the rest of the kids we love them."

Emmeline chimed in, "We will call as soon as we arrive in Charleston."

Abby and Emmeline got into the front seat. Nathan and Grace gave P.J. one last hug and handed him to his mother. As Abby backed the car down the driveway, her parents waved, her mother crying. She hoped they understood that she would be right back, within the week most likely. She just needed to make sure Harvey was okay and that he knew she hadn't run off with someone else. Then she would leave him to marry Clarice if that was truly what he wanted. Abby wasn't sure what parts of Clarice's letter was a lie. Maybe Harvey had just used her. It hurt, but she felt it was better to know the truth now. In time, she would recover. And this was the first step to that recovery.

As P.J. slept in Emmeline's arms, the two friends—now sisters—glanced at each other and smiled. "Here we go."

She looked behind her and got onto the highway that took her from her sleepy little town, in the middle of nowhere, across the state to Charleston. It might as well have been another country as far as Abby was concerned. She knew the place she called home was considered very rural and unsophisticated compared to other parts of the country. And she knew that Charleston was one of the most bustling cities on the East Coast. It was modern and high class—nothing that she would consider herself to be.

Neither Abby nor Emmeline had ever left the foothills of the Blue Ridge Mountains. As they took turns driving, they marveled at the flatness the road took. As they drove through the state capital of Columbia, tall buildings surrounded them. They were amazed and a little scared. If Charleston was anywhere near as big as Columbia, they would never find the Nicholas house.

It was nearing nightfall when Abby spotted signs announcing Charleston. Emmeline and P.J. were asleep on the passenger side of the car. Was it just that morning she was being woken by Doris banging on the door? She recalled her dream. The crying had been P.J.; the pounding was Doris. But in her head, it was Peter and Harvey in the war. So far away, but at least still a part of their lives.

Near the heart of downtown, Abby found a small motel and paid for a room. She pulled two bags out of the car and helped Emmeline with P.J. Abby made a few quick calls from the office to let the family know they had arrived safely, and they slept soundly that night with P.J. nestled between them. Abby dreamed, but when she awoke, she couldn't remember if her dreams were good or bad.

Before getting out of bed the next day, Abby thought to herself, *Why am I here? Am I crazy? I'm in a strange city, dragging Emme and the baby with me. Harvey is marrying someone else in just a few weeks' time. I don't know where I'm going. What do I do now?*

And since she didn't know the answer, she asked out loud, "What do I do now?"

Emmeline, who was awake and feeding P.J. a banana in bed, said, "We pray."

"Pray?"

"You haven't stopped praying, have you, Abby?"

Abby thought. She couldn't remember the last time she had prayed on her own. Certainly not since Peter had died. She knew she hadn't prayed much since the boys left them that cold December day over a year ago. And she knew she hadn't prayed at all since she received the letter from Clarice. She was angry with God, and like a bitter child, she showed that by ignoring Him. But would praying help now? In her anger with God, was He now angry with her? Maybe He wouldn't help her now. Abby felt ashamed for turning a cold shoulder to the ever-present God, but didn't know how to make the move to turn back to Him.

Emmeline looked closely at Abby and knew what the silence meant. "Go on, then. Pray now."

A hot tear burned down Abby's cheek. "I don't know if I remember how."

"God is here with us. Talk to Him. I pray all the time. I don't know how I would survive otherwise," Emmeline told her. "I'm sorry I didn't realize this before. It might have helped weeks ago."

Emmeline and P.J. turned from Abby, giving her as much privacy as they could in the small room. Abby rolled over in the bed and put her face into the pillow. *God? Are You there? I know it's been a long time. I didn't even realize it, and I'm sorry. Let me turn back to You, Lord; bring me back into Your graces. I've made such a mess of things. Harvey is going to marry Clarice, and I didn't even fight for him. Now I've got Emmeline and P.J. with me, and we're hours away from home. Help me, Lord! What do I do now?*

Feeling somewhat more at peace, Abby got up. She pulled out an old dress and sturdy shoes. She ran her comb through her hair and was thankful for the jackets they remembered to bring with them. As they headed back to their car, Abby rummaged through her bag for something. She had the letter from Clarice in it somewhere. She pulled it out and ran back into the motel office.

"Sir, do you know where Elizabeth Street is?"

"Of course, everyone knows where Elizabeth Street is. Let me draw it out for you," came the reply. The man behind the desk took his time drawing out a map for Abby to get from where they were to Elizabeth Street. It was just about two miles away. Abby thought they could drive along the road until she hit the right street number and know exactly where Harvey was.

It was what to do after finding the address that Abby wasn't too sure about now.

They loaded into the car and took off, following the directions they were given. Soon enough, they came to a corner and found a building with the right street number on it.

The house was more than a house, Abby thought. It was massive. Nearly three of her parent's house could have fit into this one building. It was the color of sand, with white trim and shutters. Three stories high, each level had its own white-washed porch. Palmetto trees were lined along the front of the house, flanking the front doors. Abby could see more trees in the backyard. Every inch of the property was landscaped and impeccable.

"Is this just one house? It's so swanky," Emmeline marveled, straining to see the top of the building through the car window.

"I have no idea. I suppose so," Abby guessed. "And now I realize just why Harvey didn't come after me. This life is too comfortable, too lavish. He could never leave this for me. He probably got home and realized he couldn't give this up."

"Abby, stop. He wanted you to come here. He wanted to share this with you." Emmeline rested her hand on Abby's arm. "I think he still does."

Abby said nothing, but instead put the car into drive and continued down the road. She and Emmeline drove down Rainbow Row and tried to enjoy the scenery while Abby decided what to do. It was the most crowded place she had ever seen. Abby thought Charleston must be much like New York, where people everywhere was commonplace. People were walking down the sidewalk; couples ate lunch at street-side cafés; and it was bursting with life.

Back at the motel, Emmeline and P.J. napped. Abby took the chance to get out on her own and think. She headed east on foot, but didn't pay attention to what she was passing. She was lost in thought, deep in prayer. As she walked, she argued with God, and her thoughts went round and round.

Lord, I'm here, and I'm just not sure what You want me to do. Why am I here? I feel so foolish, chasing after Harvey like this. Why didn't he come for me? If he really loved me, he would have come after me himself. He would have never believed Clarice's lies, and he would have come home and found me. Waiting. Just like I promised. He promised to love me forever, God. Forever. Forever didn't last so long, did it? A few months until he could come back to Charleston and his cushy life and his pretty, Hollywood-style Clarice.

Why is it that I can be so independent at home, but so dependent on Harvey at the same time? I live on my own; I work; and I'm helping raise P.J. Yet, it all means nothing without someone to share it with, Lord. But You know that, don't You? You know we all need someone to share life with. But Emmeline had Peter, and now he's gone. I thought I would have Harvey, and now he's gone. Duped and lied to. Both of us.

So I'm still wondering, God, why I'm here. Am I supposed to find Harvey? Do I knock on his door and expose Clarice? Do I even speak to him? I said I just wanted to see that he was okay. Seeing him is not the same as talking to him.

Lord, guide me. Guide me down the path You have chosen for me. I know I haven't been seeking you recently, and I'm truly sorry. I want to follow You. Just show me the way.

Abby looked up, unsure of where she was. As she looked around, she realized she was at the Battery, a historical Charleston landmark, flanked by the Ashley and Cooper Rivers. The vast Atlantic Ocean stretched out before her. She had never seen the ocean before this; it was calm, yet untamed. It spread on forever, but she could reach out and touch it if she wanted. Abby had always wanted to see the ocean, but she wasn't as excited as she always imagined she would be. Instead, she wrapped her arms around her middle, chilled by the cold breeze as she stared out into the blue water. She spotted a bench nearby and sat down, still wondering what to do next.

Abby asked quietly, "Lord, how can I follow You if You won't show me where to go?" Tears welled up in her eyes. The hot tears stung as they rolled down her cold cheeks. She didn't bother to wipe them away, opting instead to let them fall freely and land where they may. Her hair twirled around her face, and a few strands stuck to the tears.

Abby thought back over the past two years. Two winters ago, life was simple; Abby was still a girl. Life revolved around school and family. Then, she met Harvey, and everything turned upside down. The girl who couldn't even imagine having a boyfriend suddenly became a woman in love. Her eyes closed, and Abby thought back to the brief time she was with Harvey. It seemed like forever ago, and indeed, she hadn't seen him in over a year. How different was he now? And was she different, too? Not just physically, Abby wondered, but inside as well.

Images of Harvey during their months together filled her head. Memories of his hand on her arm or in her hair. Memories of his infectious smile and laugh. And most of all, memories of his kisses and how he smelled. He smelled divine, like sophistication and hard work all at the same time. Abby wondered if he smelled the same now as he did last she saw him.

With her hair blowing around her, Abby didn't see a figure approaching her from behind. But she felt a presence around her, a sudden warmth, and knew she wasn't alone. Of course, the park was public, but she really didn't want other people around her. A few seconds later, Abby heard footsteps. Footsteps with an extra *tap*, it sounded like. Maybe two people? No, she thought, just one. The footsteps were coming toward her, but she didn't feel friendly. She thought if she ignored the intruder, he would pass by without speaking to or looking at her.

"Excuse me," a gruff and muffled voice said to Abby. "Do you have the time?"

Without turning, Abby shook her head. "No."

The man with the brusque voice didn't walk on. "Are you looking for someone? Waiting for your husband, maybe?"

Abby sighed. "I'm not married," she said.

The voice sighed in return. "Not married? That's not what I was told."

"Excuse me?" Abby fumed and turned to see who would have the gall to speak that way to her. "How dare you!" As Abby turned, she saw a man wrapped up in a scarf and coat. His hands were gloved to compensate for the unseasonably cold weather, and he leaned one hand on a cane.

All she could see of the man's face were his eyes. Deep green eyes. Abby gasped.

CHAPTER 12

IT WAS HARVEY. SHE FELT excitement and nerves and anger all at the same time. Abby drew in a deep breath; she was frozen in position. Had he known it was her all along?

"So it is you, Abby," he said, unraveling the scarf from around his head. Then his voice was clear, just as she remembered it. "So, you're not here with a husband. Does that mean you came here to get married? Are you eloping with him? Did you intend to scorn me first? I know all about your secret love affair. It was Jack, wasn't it?" His eyes were slits, his mouth turned down.

Abby studied Harvey's face. It looked a little more weathered, sadder than before. But he was still Harvey. Gorgeous green eyes, solid chin, amazing mouth—it was him.

There was no time for relief over seeing him, though. Fresh tears fell down Abby's cheeks, and she refused to meet Harvey's stare.

"I think you've been misinformed. There is nobody else, least of all Jack. Last I heard, he had joined the navy. I spent a year waiting for you to return to me, and then I got word from Clarice that you two lovebirds were getting married. I just had to see for myself."

"Why was I told you had run off with someone else then?" Harvey accused.

Abby turned her back to Harvey, angry. "And who told you that?"

"My mother did, actually," he said. "She even had your engagement ring."

"And do you know why she had that ring? Because Clarice wrote me a letter saying that you two were getting married and to send it back."

"She wouldn't do that," Harvey said, slowly walking in front of Abby to be face-to-face with her.

"Wouldn't she?" Abby laughed. "I have the letter she wrote. She said you just used me until you could go back to her. She told me to send back the ring. I could show the letter to you; I brought it with me."

Harvey looked uneasy, realizing his trust might have been misplaced. "That can't be true. When Peter died, all I wanted was you. And then, I get back here, and I'm told you gave up on me. That you had sent the ring back and married someone else instead."

"Never, Harvey."

He winced. Abby wasn't sure if it was from pain or the cold or the recognition that Clarice had lied. "I'm getting married in two weeks. Why are you here?"

Abby stood and looked into Harvey's eyes—the eyes that had hypnotized her so long before. "I came to see for myself that you were alive and recovering. I came to see if it was true that you believed her lies over my love. Emmeline, P.J., and I drove all the way down here, but it was obviously a bad idea."

His expression changed instantly. "Emmeline and the baby are here? Where? I want to see them. I have to give Emmeline a message from Peter."

Abby sighed and shifted on her feet. "They don't want to see you. And if my brother had a message for her, I should be the one to give it to her."

Harvey stepped closer. Abby stepped back. "I'm sure you'd understand that I promised Peter I would do it myself," he told her.

"You also promised to love me forever. You broke that promise easily enough."

Harvey shook his head. His eyes softened; now he looked more like the Harvey she remembered. "No, Abby. Never. I will always love you. But I am admittedly very confused about what you're telling me Clarice did. Yes, she's crafty, but I don't think she would lie to me like that."

"You're marrying into that lie, Harvey."

He was quiet. He flexed his hand over his cane. It hurt Abby to see him in pain. She wanted to reach out to him, to hold him. She longed to kiss him, but she restrained herself. He was not hers to hold.

After an awkward minute, Harvey finally spoke. "Bring Emme and P.J. to the house. Please. Come for dinner. I do need to speak with Emmeline. And I need to speak with you further, but somewhere warmer. I can't be out in this weather for too long. And I need to speak with Clarice first."

Abby wanted to protest; but if Harvey had a message from Peter, Emmeline needed to hear it. She had no right to keep that from them. "Fine, but only so Emmeline can get your message, nothing more. We'll head back home tomorrow."

Against every yearning in Abby's body, she walked away. She wanted Harvey to come after her, to call her name, but that didn't happen. She wanted to run back to him, but she didn't. She gulped back sobs as she walked, aching to turn back and at least look at Harvey again. When she turned the corner, she started to run as fast as she could back to the motel where Emmeline and P.J. waited.

Back in her rented room, Abby broke through the door and fell onto the bed in sobs. Thankfully, both Emmeline and the baby were awake, as she shocked them when she ran into the room. Aside from her cries, there was no noise; Emmeline waited until she stopped to approach her.

"You saw him," she guessed. Abby nodded, her head still buried in the bed. "What happened, Abby?" Emmeline sat next to her on the bed, and Abby turned and told her sister-in-law of the encounter with Harvey.

When she finished, Emmeline looked at Abby with pain in her eyes. "So he knows he was lied to, right? Maybe he'll fix it. Maybe he'll call off the wedding to Clarice." When Abby said nothing, Emmeline continued, "Well, do you want to see him again or just go home?"

"Oh, Emme, he said he had a message for you," Abby said, her breath still heavy.

"For me?"

"From Peter, he said. We're to go over there for supper," Abby added. "At first, I told him no; but if it's from Peter, you need to hear it. I can't be selfish about that. We'll go tonight and then head back home tomorrow."

Emmeline smiled. "I'm sorry, Abby. I know I shouldn't smile at this situation, but to hear anything about Peter makes me happy."

"Me, too, Emme. Me, too."

The girls hugged for a long time. A few tears were shed, but more as stress relief than grief. When P.J. started grunting and trying to pull on Emmeline's skirts, they laughed and picked him up, hugging him between them.

CHAPTER 13

AT A FEW MINUTES TO six that evening, Abby pulled the car up in front of the oversized house on Elizabeth Street. She and Emmeline got out of the car and gave the house a look over. Both ladies stood still for a few moments, just taking the scenery in while P.J. wriggled in his mother's arms. They were a little nervous over the circumstances before them; but they knew they were together, and that made all the difference.

As they went up the walkway, Emmeline squeezed Abby's hand. Abby was so thankful to have a sister-in-law like Emmeline. Regardless of what happened between her and Harvey, Emmeline really needed closure about Peter's passing. And if Harvey could provide that, Abby would endure an evening at his house.

Before she could raise a hand to knock on the door, it burst open. Clarice was startled to see Abby standing before her and took a step back.

"You!" she screamed. "What are you doing here?" She was wearing a royal blue dress with a wide, black belt and black pumps. Her yellow hair shook in rhythm with her head.

Abby was so taken aback by seeing Clarice that she could hardly speak. Emmeline pulled P.J. close as if to protect him from the vile woman.

Thankfully, Abby didn't have to answer, as Harvey appeared in the doorway just then. "I told you, Clarice, I invited Emmeline and Abby here. I need to talk to them about Abby's brother."

Clarice's eyes turned to slits; her cheeks grew red. It was obvious she didn't believe Harvey. "Humph. What else do you need to know? He's dead, isn't he?"

Tears immediately leapt to Emmeline's eyes, and Abby's jaw dropped momentarily before she found her voice. "Excuse me? Could you be ruder? My brother, this woman's husband, died in battle. He died, and Harvey could have died with him! Don't you have any compassion?"

Abby felt her anger rise up in her belly as she stepped closer to Clarice. Clarice, in turn, backed away. "How dare you be so callous, so cruel, so cold? Don't you ever speak about my brother again!"

Despite her step back, Clarice wasn't done yet. "You're just jealous because I have Harvey, and you don't. Where's your hillbilly husband, Abigail?"

Harvey spoke up from behind them. "Stop it, Clarice. Stop the lying. I told you inside I knew all about your lies."

So Harvey had confronted her about the lies. Abby felt relieved that the truth was now out.

"You know there was never anyone else. You're the one who told me to send back the ring. You're the one who told me Harvey had never loved me. How can you live with yourself?"

Harvey spun Clarice around to look at him. "You lied to me, Clarice. You lied to both of us. Why?"

"Argh! I did this for your own good, Harvey Nicholas," she shouted for the whole world to hear. "So what if I lied? She's not good enough for you, anyway. She's just a stupid hillbilly, country girl."

"Don't you dare say a negative word about her, Clarice. How could you do this? Did you expect to never be exposed after all these months of deception? I can't believe I was going to marry you, of all people." He was angry, but he spoke with calmness.

Abby watched the exchange between them. Harvey tightened his grip on his cane, but he didn't put more weight on it. Clarice pushed a loose curl from her face and did her best to maintain her aloof appearance.

"I'm the best thing you could ever get. Especially now that you're a cripple. You can't even walk straight. I don't know that I want to marry a man who can't even walk, anyway. To top all this off, you tell me you want to give up your father's business and become a minister? I think that war did something to you, Harvey. And I don't just mean to your legs."

She was shouting, and her face was as red as a beet. Abby was completely shocked that anyone would ever put on such a display in public.

Harvey's mouth turned down, and his eyes swam with fury. "Leave now, Clarice. Right now."

With that, Clarice was down the steps and walking toward the street. But before she got ten steps down the path, she turned back and set her eyes on Abby. Abby wasn't sure what was going to happen. Did Clarice intend to strike her? She stood her ground, expecting the worst.

Clarice sauntered up to Abby and said, "If you want that stupid cripple, take him." She grabbed Abby's hand and thrust something into it. Before Abby could speak, Clarice took off down the road and out of sight. The click clack of her shoes hitting the sidewalk faded.

In Abby's hand was the engagement ring Harvey had given her over a year ago. She studied it for a moment, then held her hand out to Harvey and dropped it into his open palm.

Harvey didn't say a word about the ring; instead he apologized. "I'm sorry you had to see that. I'm sorry I didn't believe you. My family is waiting. Please come in."

Still shaking from anger, Abby laid her hand on Emmeline's arm and looked her in the eyes. Emmeline nodded that she was okay and released her stronghold on P.J. Abby followed Harvey into the house, with Emmeline and P.J. on his heels.

The house was opulent. A staircase stretched in front of them with red carpeted steps and a pure white handrail. The eggshell walls were decorated with gorgeous paintings and pictures of beautiful men and women. Vases filled with flowers were on every corner. They walked through the main foyer and down a hallway.

In the hall, a beautiful woman met them. Susan, Harvey's sister, stood outside the dining room, waiting for their guests. She was tall, nearly as tall as Harvey. Her light brown hair was tied in a bun at the nape of her neck. Susan wore a burgundy dress, and Abby noticed a diamond bracelet as they shook hands.

"I'm sorry there's no time for a tour before dinner. But perhaps after? Of course," Susan said, smiling. She seemed so happy, completely unaware of what had just happened outside. Directing her attention to Emmeline, she asked, "Do you need anything for the baby?"

Emmeline stammered, "No, no thank you."

"Very well, this way to the dining room," Susan said. Harvey followed his sister, with Abby and Emmeline trailing behind them.

The dining room was large, but cozy. A grand fireplace with a crackling fire stood on the end opposite the door. The walls were deep green, and a large mahogany buffet stood against the back wall. In the middle of the room was the biggest dining table Abby had ever seen. It was also made of mahogany and had ornate carving around the sides. The chairs were upholstered a deep green to match the walls. On the table were place settings for seven people, with room for plenty more.

Seated at the end of the table was David Nicholas, Harvey's father. His hair was gray at the temples, but still dark otherwise. His blue eyes twinkled. To his left was Jane Nicholas, Doris' sister. She was dressed in a smart red dress with matching heels. A pearl necklace draped around her neck. Next to her was a man Abby didn't recognize, but she assumed he was Susan's husband, James.

Across from his mother, at Mr. Nicholas' right side, were three empty place settings for Harvey, Abby, and Emmeline.

When they walked inside, the others all stood. Susan made introductions, "Father, Mother, I believe you've met our guests—Miss Abigail Walker and her sister-in-law, Mrs. Emmeline Walker. And what was the baby's name again?"

"P.J.," Emmeline whispered.

"And Mrs. Walker's son, P.J. Abigail, Emmeline, you recall my parents Mr. and Mrs. Nicholas?" Susan was very good at playing hostess. "And this is my husband, Mr. James Andrews. We have seats for you over here."

Now that she had a moment to study Harvey, Abby's heart beat faster as she looked at him. He was wearing a brown suit with a starched white shirt and green tie. Abby loved it when Harvey wore green. His hair had grown from his cadet haircut and looked very much like it did when Abby first met him. She fought the urge to touch him. She wasn't sure if she would hug him or slap him. But no matter what, he was still as handsome as ever, and Abby could never deny that.

As the trio made their way across the room to their seats, Mrs. Nicholas said, "It's so very nice to see you girls again. Mrs. Walker, if you like, our grandchildren's nanny is here, and she can care for your baby while we dine."

As if on cue, a woman dressed in black and white came forward. Emmeline handed P.J. over to her, unsure if she were okay with that arrangement, but too scared to say otherwise.

The women sat, and the three men waited until they were all seated before descending themselves. Everyone waited a few extra seconds for Harvey to get situated. Abby could see how Harvey strained to take his seat as gracefully as possible. The politeness and quietness of the room made Abby want to scream. She wanted to let Emmeline and Harvey talk and then leave the awkward situation as quickly as possible.

Without speaking, the hosts bowed their heads. Abby and Emmeline did the same. Mr. Nicholas said a brief prayer, nothing like what Abby's father would have said, but a prayer all the same. At the word "amen," all heads were raised, and dinner was served.

"You traveled a long way, ladies," Mr. Nicholas observed.

"Yes, sir, we did," Abby said quietly.

"How did the baby do on the trip?" Mrs. Nicholas asked. It was as if nothing was amiss, though Abby thought she could have cut the tension with a knife.

"Fine, thank you," Emmeline answered.

This time, Susan spoke up. "We were very sorry to hear of your family's loss."

Abby and Emmeline nodded thanks in unison.

The rest of the conversation was just as curt and polite. Abby wondered if the discussion was normally livelier at dinner, or if they were always so terse. She presumed it was the recent outburst from Clarice and her own presence that made the table seem colder than it should have been. From another room, she could hear the happy chatter of Susan's children playing with P.J.

Dinner wrapped up after three courses, and Mr. and Mrs. Nicholas stood. The rest of the table followed suit. Abby and Emmeline followed the group as they walked into another room. It matched the rest of the house in lavish style and decoration. A burgundy couch sat in front of another fireplace, crackling red and orange like its dining room mate. It was paired with two gold chairs and a mahogany coffee table. Behind the set was a rocking chair, a settee, and a wall full of books. Abby had never seen so many books in one room before.

"If you'll excuse us," Susan started. "But we do need to get home."

Again, on cue, the nanny entered, holding P.J. She was followed by two flaxen-haired children, a little girl about three and a young boy who was perhaps two years old.

"Rachel, Rhett, say hello to our guests." The children giggled a greeting.

The nanny handed P.J. back to his mother and said he had eaten heartily. Abby and Emmeline shook hands with Susan and her husband as they departed.

"We've had some excitement here today; I hope you will forgive us if Jane and I part ways with you here. We have some business to take care of, and we understand you do as well," Mr. Nicholas explained, eyeing Harvey. "But we had a lovely time seeing you this evening. We hope you'll both return soon."

Abby was relieved that they would be able to get things done quickly and leave. She nodded to Harvey's parents. "Thank you for inviting us, Mr. Nicholas. We appreciate your hospitality. Dinner was delicious, Mrs. Nicholas."

"Please, call me Jane." Mrs. Nicholas smiled. "It was good to see you again. Please give my sister Doris a hug for me when you see her again."

Abby nodded to Harvey's mother, and the elder pair exited the room, closing the door behind them. Abby and Emmeline were now alone with Harvey. She wanted to get this over with and leave as quickly as possible.

Harvey remained silent. His eyes were brooding, angry. Abby wondered if he was upset with her or Clarice. He was possibly cross with the both of them. Or maybe his legs hurt. She turned to face him. As he rested his hands on the back of a gold chair for support, his dour expression was exchanged for a softer one. Emmeline and P.J. were perched on the couch, Emmeline's eyes looking down at her son. Silence and awkwardness filled the room. The only thing Abby could hear was the sound of rain outside, and she thought it was the perfect expression of her mood at the moment.

After an agonizing minute of quiet, Harvey took his cane and walked around to the couch. He slowly lowered himself onto the coffee table in front of Emmeline and took P.J.'s hand. P.J. cooed in response and reached for Harvey. He scooped the baby up and smiled. Abby held her breath, and she saw a tear slip down Emmeline's cheek.

Lord, how could I be so selfish? Here's my beautiful sister-in-law, grieving for her husband. And she has the chance to hear the account of Peter's death firsthand, to hear his dying message to her. This is the chance to let the last person to see Peter alive speak to her and hold Peter's son. And all I can think of is getting out of here. Shame on me, Lord.

"Hi, big guy," Harvey finally said, his voice choked up. "Abby, you'll want to hear this as well. Come sit down."

Abby sat next to Emmeline and held her hand. Harvey's eyes were red-rimmed, and he only looked at P.J. In turn, P.J. smiled at Harvey.

With a big sigh, Harvey started. He retold the story of their unit. Their main purpose was to clean up after battles, something that had relieved both he and Peter. They did not see the main action, just the effects of it. They travelled across Europe, aiding civilians and helping other units clear out. Their unit was in France for a long time before they transferred to North Africa.

During a routine march across the fields, someone named Smith stepped on a land mine. Peter was right next to him, Harvey there as well. They were in the back of their unit. Smith was gone; Peter was screaming in pain. Harvey couldn't get up to walk, so he crawled on his stomach over to him.

Harvey took a break in his story, his breath labored as if he had just finished that agonizing crawl. Abby wiped her cheek and found it wet with tears. Emmeline was holding her hand so tight, her knuckles were white. Even Harvey had tears in his eyes. It was obvious to Abby that recalling the events of that day was very painful for him. Harvey rubbed his knee without thinking.

"Peter knew right away that he wouldn't make it," Harvey continued. "And he wanted to. I promise you, he tried to stay with me."

Emmeline began to cry, and Harvey paused again, setting P.J. on the floor.

"Should I stop?"

"No, please continue," Emmeline said. Harvey handed her a hand-kerchief from his pocket, and she wiped her eyes.

"Peter said he had to come home to you, to P.J. He said he had to meet his son. But when he realized he wouldn't make it out alive, he asked me to tell you this. He said to tell you that he loves you very much. That all his life, he loved you. That he carried your pictures with him everywhere, which he did. He showed them off often. In fact, a widow in France gave him a ring for you. Which I see you got," he commented, pointing to Emmeline's ring.

"Peter said he wanted you to know that he hopes your grief is short and that soon you and P.J. will lead full, happy lives. He wants you to grow and change. And he said he was fine with the idea of you finding love again one day. But he said he would be watching over you from heaven. He said he knew he would be in heaven because God was watching over him, and he could actually see a white light calling him home.

"He wanted me to tell you specifically that even though he wasn't going home to you, that he would always be with you. He would always be with P.J. That your lives would be blessed in his absence," Harvey said.

Then he looked at Abby for the first time all night. "Abby, he said to ask you to always watch over Emme and P.J., but to also live your life to its fullest. He wanted your parents and siblings to know that they were on his mind as he went home to be with God.

"I pulled his head to my chest as he spoke, and we prayed. Peter prayed for protection over me and our unit. He prayed for our relationship, Abby. He also prayed for P.J. to always know that his papa fought for him and his mother above all else, and for none of us to be bitter about his passing.

"Then I prayed. I prayed first for Peter to stay with us and return home alive, but that wasn't in God's plan. I prayed for understanding for your entire family about the situation. I prayed for Peter to pass safely. When I finished, he gave me something and asked me to give it to you personally, Emmeline." Harvey reached into his pocked and pulled something out.

It was a silver necklace, and dangling from it was Peter's wedding ring. Abby hadn't realized it never came home with Peter's things. Harvey handed it to Emmeline, who pulled it over her head and slipped the ring over her own wedding ring. She leaned her head onto Abby's shoulder and sobbed.

While she cried, Abby looked at Harvey, tears swimming in her own eyes. "Thank you, Harvey, very much. This means so much to her and to me."

"Now you know why I wanted to see her myself," Harvey said, looking down at P.J.

"I understand," Abby said. She looked at Emmeline and smoothed her hair. "Are you okay?" Emmeline mutely nodded. "I need to get her out of here. I'm sorry; we need to leave."

"Abby, it's late and cold. And it's raining terribly out there. Don't you hear it? Spring storms are much worse here than they are where you're from," Harvey replied. "We have plenty of room; please stay here tonight. She's in no condition to go back out, and the weather is not suitable for people who don't know their way around the city."

Abby stammered, "I don't know, Harvey."

She looked at Emmeline and then P.J. Emmeline's face was tear-stained, and she was shaking. Abby could hear the rain pound on the windows. It did sound particularly dreadful. And Harvey was right—she would have a hard time getting back to their motel with the dark and the weather combined.

With a shaky voice, Emmeline spoke quietly, "I think we may be here for the night if you don't mind. I'm very tired."

Defeated, Abby agreed. "All right. We'll stay. But our clothes are back at the motel . . . "

"Don't worry about it," Harvey said. "We have extra nightgowns here for guests. I'll send the housekeeper, Helen, over to your room in the morning for your things. They'll be here before you wake up. I'll just write the address down for her . . . " Harvey's voice trailed off, and he looked at his hands.

Abby had not looked at them before now. His left hand didn't look too bad, but his right hand was covered in scars, his fingers set at odd angles. "I keep forgetting. They plan to do another surgery soon to reset the bones. Hopefully, things will be better after that." His voice was low and raw. He looked to Abby, ashamed.

"I'll write it for you, Harvey," Abby whispered. She moved out from under Emmeline and stood. Curiosity overcame her, and she had to ask, "So, you really can't write?"

"Not legibly. I'm working on it, but right now, it's just not an option. I can barely feed myself," he admitted. He instinctively flexed his hands.

Abby found paper and pen and wrote the motel address down. She left the note out for Helen. Harvey pulled himself up with his cane, while Emmeline stood up and hugged P.J. close. They followed Harvey out to the stairs.

"Do you need separate rooms?" The girls shook their heads. "Forgive me for not leading you up the stairs. It's been a long day, and I don't have much energy left. Go up to the second floor, down the hall to the third door on the left. You'll find a large enough bed for you all, and in the dresser are nightclothes. The bathroom is across the hall. It's all yours," Harvey told them. "My parent's room is on the third floor, so you won't disturb anyone. My room used to be on the second floor, but I've moved down here, since I don't handle stairs well. The kitchen is always open; help yourselves."

Harvey stood at the base of the stairs while the girls started up. Abby turned back toward him. He stood as tall as he could while leaning on his cane. He looked like her Harvey, but she just wasn't sure. His green eyes sparkled when she looked at him.

"Thank you, Harvey," Abby said, and turned back up the stairs. Harvey was quiet and retreated to his own corner of the house.

Abby went to the third door on the left and opened it. She found her way to a lamp on a table and switched it on. The room glowed a soft yellow. This room was nowhere near as elaborate as those downstairs, but perhaps the Nicholases didn't want to offend any guests with opulent décor. Two simply shaded lamps sat upon nightstands on either side of a large bed. The bed itself was covered with a blue goose down comforter. It looked divine after sleeping in a motel. Across the room was a small tan couch and a bookshelf with several selections for guests to choose.

The girls went to the walnut dresser and found several nightgowns to wear. P.J. was changed quickly, followed by Emmeline; Abby wasn't ready to settle down yet. She thought they would be giggling about sleeping in such a luxurious bed in such a grand house under other circumstances. Instead, they smiled half-heartedly at each other.

Emmeline chose the right side of the bed and snuggled in with P.J. She opened the top of her gown and positioned P.J. to nurse. She closed her eyes and relaxed at the now-familiar feeling. Abby didn't shy away, as she was used to the scene.

"Abby?" Emmeline called softly, her eyes still closed.

"Yes, Emme?"

"Can I bother you for a glass of water?"

"Of course, Emme," she said. "I'll be back in a minute." Abby opened the door quietly and padded barefoot down the hall and stairs. She found the kitchen without too much trouble and saw that the light was still on. She opened the door a little and slipped inside, only to find Harvey sitting at a small table with a glass of water of his own. He was holding a pen to paper and practicing writing.

"I'm sorry, Harvey," Abby stammered as he looked up to her. "Emmeline wanted a drink. I'll get out of your way in a minute." She walked to the cabinet, but wasn't sure where to find a glass.

"Look to your left," Harvey told her without looking up.

"Thank you," she replied softly. Abby took a glass and filled it in the sink with cool water. "Goodnight."

"Abby, please sit with me for a few minutes. I would like to talk with you." Harvey motioned to a chair across from him.

Abby hesitated. Should she sit with him? She wanted to, but wasn't sure it was a good idea. Determined that they would be leaving Charleston the next morning, she gave in, telling herself this would finalize their relationship once and for all, and she could move on. She gave in and sat.

"It's so good to see you, Abby." Harvey sighed. He closed his eyes and was quiet a moment, composing his thoughts. When he opened them again, he gave her a sad smile. "I've dreamed for a year of seeing you walking through my house with your hair loose and your feet bare."

"Stop, Harvey," Abby insisted, holding up a hand. "You lost your right to talk to me like that."

Harvey didn't respond to that comment but instead asked, "Will Emme be okay?"

"Some days are harder than others. Peter's birthday was in January, and that was very tough." Abby sighed. "But many days, we just look at P.J., and we smile. He's what makes our world go around these days."

"I'm sorry, Abby," Harvey said, shaking his head.

"For what, Harvey? For Peter? Don't be. We're all comforted to know you were with him, even with what happened between us," Abby admitted. "If you mean what happened between us . . . "

"What happened seems to have been a huge mistake of Clarice's doing," Harvey said. He reached a shaky hand across the table to Abby's, but she pulled hers away.

"And you believed her, Harvey. How could you believe her?"

"I was in a tremendous amount of pain when I got back stateside. I asked for you daily. I asked Mother and Father to send for you and bring you to me. Apparently, Clarice told them immediately that you had gone off with another man. When I finally demanded to know why you weren't brought to me, Mother said you had married someone else. She even showed me the ring I had given you."

"And you believed it? After everything we went through? After all the letters? All the promises?"

"Abby, she had your engagement ring. Why did you send it back? How could you have believed Clarice?"

Abby sighed and looked down at her empty hand. "I wrote you a letter and sent it here after I learned that you would be coming home. Clarice responded to that letter and told me that you had just used me while you were at Clemson. The letter said you wanted the ring back because you two were getting married. She even stole my idea for a spring wedding! I didn't want to believe her, so I called and spoke with your mother. She told me to never look for you again after what I had done. She fell for the lies, too. I felt so used and so upset, I sent the ring back as requested. I ran right to the post office and sent it that day. I thought you were done with me. I was hurt and already grieving for Peter; it was too much."

"You didn't fight for me either, then," Harvey alleged.

"I didn't think there was anything left to fight for. You and Clarice were suddenly engaged. It sure seemed that I was nothing more than a brief romance. Something to pass the time."

Harvey looked her in the eyes. "No. When she said you were gone, I was so upset. She said she would take care of me from then on, and she would help me walk again. Before I knew what was happening, she was planning a wedding and had your ring on. I don't even recall asking her to marry me, though she insisted I did. Of course, I questioned her today about it. I didn't tell her I had seen you, but she admitted openly to lying about your marrying someone else," he revealed. His voice was unsteady, but his gaze was solid as a rock. He stared Abby down into the depths of her soul. "So, what did make you come now? Why didn't you come months ago?"

"Your Aunt Doris, actually." Abby laughed. "She brought me your wedding invitation and told me to go after you. We—Emmeline, Doris, and I—finally figured out that Clarice had lied to us all. I figured I had lost my chance, but I just had to see for myself. I had to see that you were actually home and all right." Harvey started laughing, and Abby stopped and frowned. "Why are you laughing?"

"You came all this way just to see if I was actually marrying Clarice."

Abby felt slighted that he found it all so funny. "Are you?"

"No. Never." He licked his lips and slowly took a drink from the water in front of him. "Can I tell you something?"

"What is it?" Abby shifted and tucked her curls behind her ears.

"You still love me," Harvey said with a twinkle in his eye. He leaned into the table toward her, a wide smile across his face.

Abby didn't return the smile. Her voice got quiet, but she kept her gaze steady. "You know I do."

"Yes, I do know," he said. Then he added, "You didn't look down when I said that."

"Someone once told me not to look down anymore."

"I'm so glad you learned that what you have to say is important."

Abby instinctively wanted to look down as she would have before, but she didn't. Instead, she held her head high to show that she was a new woman and that she had grown in their year apart. Her self-confidence had matured in the last year, but she hadn't realized how much.

Harvey spoke again. "You've changed. You're still the same, but you're also a very different woman."

"Perhaps," was all Abby said on that matter. "Your hand is shaking."

"I try to hold a pen, and half the time, I just can't. It didn't help that Clarice started writing everything for me, so I got out of practice." He flexed his hand.

"She had no right to lie to you and to speak to you the way she did this afternoon."

"I was disillusioned by her. Cheated," Harvey said, his eyes glowering. "And she had no reason to speak to you as she did, either. I can't believe the nerve she has. She was a jealous brat of a girl, not even half the woman you are. I should have come to you, Abby. I'm so sorry."

"I was so fearful when Peter died," Abby said softly after a minute. "I didn't know what happened to you, if you were okay." She fought back tears.

"I survived. After Peter, I was afraid maybe I wouldn't, which is why I didn't send anything to you. I just wasn't sure, and I didn't want to worry you unnecessarily. I wasn't even sure what you were told about Peter, and I didn't want to upset your family. I spent a long time in an army hospital in France. Once I could be moved, they transported me back home with my discharge papers," Harvey told her. "All I wanted was to see you, to hold you. But I was immediately put in physical therapy; I was told I couldn't travel. I spent a lot of time in pain and spent days at a time sleeping. And, well, you know the rest there."

Abby gulped. "And your legs?" She looked at Harvey intently, and she knew he wouldn't lie to her.

"Still there, for the most part. Shrapnel was embedded in my left leg for two days before I got to a hospital for them to get it out. My right leg is a little beat up, but the left is much worse," Harvey said as he instinctively reached down to rub his leg. "They did a lot of work on it. And with the therapy, I can walk with a cane. I spent a month in a wheelchair. My doctors don't know if I'll ever walk unassisted again or be pain-free, but I'm fine with that. I'm just happy to be alive and still have my legs."

"I'm so sorry you had to go through that," Abby whispered. She ran her finger around the glass of water she held. "I'm so sorry about everything."

Tears swam in her eyes. No matter how upset she was at him, she loved him and hated to see him in so much pain. But she wasn't sure if she could trust him again. She wasn't sure if he was still the man she had fallen in love with so many nights before. Not wanting to cry in front of Harvey, Abby stood.

"I need to get this to Emmeline. We'll be gone in the morning, so I'll thank you now for your hospitality."

"You're just going to leave? Just like that?"

Abby stopped, anger welling up inside her. She raised her voice louder than she had meant to, but she couldn't help herself. "You left. You left me to fight in the war. You and Peter just left." Tears fell, but Abby didn't hide them. "And look what happened. Peter is gone, leaving Emmeline to raise P.J. on her own. My brother is dead. My mother is without her oldest son. And you! You got injured and might never walk on your own again. You said yourself just how much pain you were in and may never live pain-free again. We all lost a lot because you left. And to top it all off, I lost you," she practically shouted. And then, quieter, she said, "And you lost me, too."

Harvey grimaced and stood. Leaving his cane behind, he moved slowly closer to Abby and leaned on the table.

"Listen to me," he demanded, pounding his fist into his other hand. "We left for *you,* Abby. We left to protect you and the rest of the country. I fought each and every day so I could come home to you. I carried a gun, ready to shoot, just to make it home to you." He grabbed her hand in his, and even though Abby tried to wrestle free, he was still much stronger. "You don't get to just walk away from me now. I love you, and I may have messed up, but I'm going to make it right."

Through tears, Abby asked, "How? How will you make it right after all this? Can you bring my brother back? Can you fix your leg? Can you give me back the last year of my life?"

"Abby, I know you love me. You know I love you. We can fix it all right now," he said as his face got closer to hers.

He let go of her wrist and put his hand to her cheek. Abby didn't shy away. She took a deep breath as Harvey's lips caressed her own. Lightly, slowly, he kissed her and then backed away. Harvey looked at Abby, his eyes fixated on hers.

"Why did you do that?" Abby said, her breath still caught between them. She held her gaze on his.

"I'm sorry, Abby, but I've been waiting a long time to kiss you again."

Then she smiled and whispered in his ear, "No, Harvey. Why did you stop?"

With that, Abby wrapped her arms around his shoulders and held him tight. She kissed him, giving everything she had into that kiss. Harvey's hands weaved into Abby's hair, pulling her even closer. Abby could feel the muscles under his shirt flex and bend, and she finally felt safe again after so much time. This time, the tears that fell were of joy and not sorrow.

Abby sobbed as she kissed Harvey's lips. She pressed her body into him as his lips devoured her neck. Harvey's hands ran down her back, giving her chills. When his mouth found hers again, they both tasted her salty tears. Harvey's calloused hands grazed along the delicate skin of Abby's neck, and he buried his head into her collarbone. Abby moaned and arched her back, allowing him better access to her. Harvey stopped abruptly, his breathing labored. Abby took a step back, her own chest heaving, her hair mussed.

"What's wrong?" she asked.

Harvey shook his head and waited a moment to catch his breath before speaking. "It has been a long time since I kissed you. Oh, has it been a long time, and I don't want to go overboard."

This time, Abby did blush. "Surely, you and Clarice kissed . . . "

Harvey hushed her. "Don't ever say that name again. I never laid a hand on her; I swear to you. I never even kissed her."

Taming her hair, Abby replied, "I believe you. Don't worry."

Harvey put his hands out for her, and Abby came close to him again. He linked his hands behind her back and squeezed. "Boy, you've gotten skinny. I don't think I like this. Your body feels like a stick."

"Thanks a lot," she said sarcastically. "A year of worry and rationing will do that to a girl. I thought you might like me thinner; I was so plump before."

He shook his head. "No, you were perfect before. Full hips, generous breasts, my perfect angel."

Abby buried her head in his shoulder, inhaling his scent. "Call me that again."

Harvey smoothed her hair. "Angel. My Abby Angel. Oh, I missed you for too long. And don't worry, we'll put some meat back on you soon enough. Once we're married, and you're expecting our first little one." He put his right hand on her stomach as he said it.

Abby drew back and looked Harvey in the eyes. "You still want to get married?"

"Abby, I want nothing more," he said with a smile. "And as it happens, your engagement ring seems to be waiting for you." Harvey pulled the ruby ring out of his pocket and allowed the light to dance off the stones. He took her left hand in his and slipped the ring back on her finger. "Let's put this back where it belongs, shall we? Marry me, Abigail Walker."

"Of course, Harvey Nicholas," she beamed, the ruby ring glittering on her hand. "You already asked me once, and I said yes already, too. I'd say yes a hundred times over." And with that, Harvey kissed her.

Thank you, Lord, Abby prayed. *Thank You for sending me down this path. It turned out I did know how to follow You after all. And only You, Father, could make all my dreams come true like this. I am so grateful. And thank Peter for me; I know he had his hand in this as well. I love You.*

CHAPTER 14

AT THE TRAIN STATION, ABBY hugged Emmeline tight. "Are you sure you're okay to go back home by yourself?"

"Of course, Abby. You stay here with Harvey. I'll see you in a week, right?" Emmeline brushed a tear off her cheek.

"Yes, one week, I promise," Abby vowed. "Harvey wants to show me more of Charleston before we head back up."

Emmeline and P.J. had stayed two additional days at the Nicholas house, but felt they were in Abby and Harvey's way. When Mr. Nicholas offered to pay for her and the baby to take the train back home, she jumped at the chance, saying it was time to go back.

"I'm so glad you're back together. I knew you would be. And I can't believe he's going into seminary," Emmeline said.

"It's all working out. I'm so happy, Emme." Abby beamed as she looked at Harvey holding P.J.

"And I'm happy for you," Emmeline replied with a smile. "And I know Peter's happy for the both of you. I know he's smiling down from heaven."

The whistle blew a warning for all passengers to climb aboard. Abby took P.J. and hugged him close. She had never been away from him a week before, and she prayed protection over him. Harvey and Emmeline hugged, and Emmeline thanked him for Peter's wedding band. Abby handed a happy P.J. over to his mother, and Emmeline climbed the steps of the train. The pair watched as mother and son took their seat next to the window. P.J. clapped, and Emmeline waved as the train shook into motion and pulled out of the station. Abby waved back, sad to see them go, but happy for the private, extra time in Charleston.

She wove her arm around Harvey's back and hugged him close. He placed his arm on her shoulder, releasing some of the pressure off his cane. Despite his handicap, Harvey was still strong and lean. Abby never felt safer or more at home than when Harvey's muscular arms were wrapped around her.

And he smelled divine. Abby had always been intoxicated by the aroma around him, but now she found herself always inhaling just to breathe him in. She especially loved his scent after they had been kissing, or after he had been doing something strenuous. There was something wonderful about the combination of his aftershave and perspiration that made Abby's heart beat faster.

They headed back to the car, driven by the family's driver, Giles. Harvey had said he preferred to drive himself; but since that wasn't possible for the time being, Giles took him wherever he needed to go.

"The next stop is physical therapy, Giles," Harvey said without taking his eyes off Abby. The car started and took off, but the love birds didn't seem to notice. "Are you okay with Emme leaving?"

Abby sighed. "I'm sad to see her go. And I haven't been away from P.J. for so long before. But she decided to move back in with her parents for now, so I think they'll be okay." She thought before adding, "Besides, I think a week with just you sounds heavenly. I can't wait for you to show me around Charleston!"

"Well, sadly, the first place I have to show you is my doctor's office. But maybe we'll see if I can't get to driving again after this week."

Abby leaned her head on Harvey's chest. "I want to go to your doctor's office. I want to learn to help however I can."

Within minutes, Giles stopped in front of a hospital. He opened the door for Abby, who in turn assisted Harvey out of the car. Harvey held his cane in one hand, Abby on the other, and led her into the building and down a hallway.

He greeted the nurse at the desk by name. "Bess, this is my fiancée, Abigail."

Bess raised an eyebrow and waved the two back into another room.

The therapy room was stark white. The floor was covered with tan mats to pad knees. A medicine ball sat in one corner, a table off to one side. Aside from that, the room was empty. Harvey excused himself to change into suitable attire, so Abby leaned against the table while she waited.

The door she had just come through opened, and a doctor in a white lab coat came through. He startled Abby, and she jumped.

"Who are you?" he asked with a slight accent.

"M-my name is Abigail Walker, sir," she stammered. "I'm here with Harvey Nicholas."

"Are you his aide?" he questioned, his face uncertain of her.

"No, sir."

Harvey's voice came from behind them. "This is Abby, my fiancée. Abby, this is Dr. Levi Simon."

The doctor looked Abby over. "I thought . . . "

Harvey held his hand up to stop the doctor. "Think no more. This is the one I told you about—the one who kept me going that long year in Europe."

The doctor shrugged. "Miss Walker. Charmed." He turned his attention to Harvey. "Now, Mr. Nicholas, I understand you desire to get back behind the wheel of a car."

First, the doctor wanted to take a look at Harvey's legs, and he instructed Harvey to climb up on the table. With pant legs pulled up, Abby got her first glimpse of Harvey's mangled legs. She was horrified by what she saw. His once-superb legs were now lumpy and distorted. Pieces of flesh and muscle were missing, scars in their place. Abby's stomach churned, and she had to look away.

Her aversion couldn't be masked, and Harvey frowned. "I'm sorry, Abby. I should have told you what to expect."

"No, I'm sorry, Harvey," she choked. "I knew your legs were wounded, but I had no idea." She moved next to Harvey and sat close to him. "How can I help him, Dr. Simon?"

Dr. Simon was noticeably surprised. "Many women run from the room when they see damaged legs like these. The last, er, lady, Mr. Nicholas brought in refused to even look. I'm impressed."

Abby smiled, as did Harvey. Dr. Simon instructed Harvey to sit on one of the floor mats. Abby helped him move off the table, but Dr. Simon pointed out that if Harvey wanted to move independently again, he needed to do for himself. They all sat on the floor. Abby paid close attention to everything Dr. Simon did, from leg lifts to tossing the medicine ball.

After a round of tasks that had Harvey sweating and grimacing in pain, Dr. Simon said to take a break. "After this, we'll work on relearning to drive."

"Do you think I'll be ready in a week?" Harvey asked.

"A week? Well, you haven't lost your license, I assume." Dr. Simon tapped his forefinger to his chin. "I think you can maybe do some light driving in a week's time. Just around town. No more than, say, ten minutes at a time."

"That's it? Dr. Simon, we'll be leaving in a week and heading across state. It's a long drive."

Abby patted Harvey's arm. "I drove all the way down here; I can drive back."

"Or you can take the train, even," Dr. Simon suggested. "You have to build up slowly. Driving for long periods is not good for the legs. Just know when your legs tell you it's time to stop."

"Yes, sir," Harvey said. "Thank you. We'll see you in a few days."

The men shook hands, and Dr. Simon turned to shake Abby's hand. "Nice to meet you, Miss," he said, then exited the room.

Harvey kissed Abby on the cheek and said he would be right back after changing his clothes. He disappeared behind the dressing room door again, and Abby perched herself on the table. She thought back to how Harvey's legs looked. They had nearly sickened her. But she loved him and wanted to help him regain full use of his legs—whatever that took. Now she understood just how much pain Harvey was in day to day, and she vowed to work with him however she could. Abby prayed for guidance, for a way to help Harvey. And she prayed for God to bring him complete healing. She understood that his legs would never look the same again, but she prayed that they would be of full use soon.

Harvey emerged from the dressing room looking crisp and clean. His hair was damp from a quick rinse in the shower, and he was wearing a beige button down shirt and dark blue slacks. His matching tie was undone, his blazer slung over his shoulder. Abby's heart swelled at the sight, and she straightened her back. With the help of his cane, Harvey ambled over toward her and lifted his chin, so she could fix his tie.

Abby touched his throat first, stroking it with her fingers. It made Harvey swallow hard. She lifted the ends of the tie and began knotting the fabric. When she finished, she patted Harvey's chest. He brought himself close and positioned himself between her knees. He held her and kissed her forehead.

"Harvey," Abby breathed. "Harvey, anyone could walk in here."

"Let them," he murmured, his lips tickling her ear. "Seeing you sitting there . . . " he trailed off. "You were gorgeous when I met you, but still a girl. And now, there's an even more gorgeous woman before me now. And you're not only a looker, but your mind, your compassion, your faith just make me want you all the more."

Abby's body began to respond to Harvey's touch, but she resisted. "Ah, and my mind and my faith say we better stop here."

She pushed him away and slid off the table, straightening her skirt back over her knees. "Let's go."

Back at the Nicholas' house, Abby and Harvey had dinner with his parents. It was their first meal as a foursome, and it made Abby a little nervous. Things had calmed a little since she first arrived at the house, but she wasn't sure that Mrs. Nicholas trusted her. Although, after things with Clarice, Abby didn't blame her. And Mr. Nicholas seemed out of sorts as well. Harvey said his father was cross because he had chosen not to follow him in the family shipping business.

The housekeeper, Helen, had prepared a simple, yet delicious, meal. Food rationing seemed to have not affected this household. Generous portions of steamed vegetables, fresh sea bass, and greens over rice filled Abby. She ate heartily and still had plenty of food left on her plate.

Conversation at the dinner table was sparse. Abby had learned that dinner was meant for eating, not talking, in this house. She spoke when spoken to, but otherwise stayed quiet.

After the meal, Mrs. Nicholas invited everyone into the parlor for dessert. Abby thought it was so high-class to be having dessert in the parlor, but didn't say so aloud. Crisp apple turnovers were waiting for them as they settled into their seats. Mr. Nicholas sat on the gold chair to the left. Mrs. Nicholas sat to his right on the couch. Harvey assumed his position on the other gold chair, leaving Abby to sit next to Mrs. Nicholas.

Before picking up her plate, Mrs. Nicholas turned and addressed Abby. "Abigail," she began, "we really hope to get to know you better if you'll be joining our family soon. I seem to recall you telling us when we first met that you had aspirations to become a chef."

Abby gulped when she realized this was not intended to be a family dessert, but instead, an interview by her future in-laws. "Yes, ma'am, that was my original plan and something I would still like to do. I love to bake and would love to take classes," she said. "But now, I'm not so sure. With Harvey going to seminary, he'll one day become a minister, and I'm sure that will keep me busy enough."

Mrs. Nicholas nodded approval, and Mr. Nicholas spoke. "And you're fine with him becoming a minister, a civil servant of sorts? You know the needs of the church will come before yours."

"I'm not a demanding person. And if he's meeting the church's needs, then that means he's also meeting mine as well." Abby looked to Harvey and smiled. He returned the smile as he took a bite of his dessert, enjoying the show.

"Abby, I want you to realize something." Mr. Nicholas got serious. "I want you to realize that Harvey's not the same person you knew up in Clemson. War changes people. You can see the physical side effects of that immediately. That doesn't deter you?"

"Father . . . " Harvey began to protest.

"No, son, I don't want her to run off when things don't go her way."

Abby spoke up. "I'm not Clarice. I'm thrilled Harvey wants to become a minister. And his physical limitations don't deter me at all. In fact, they make me want to be with him all the more," she said, glancing his way. "You met my father, sir, and you'll recall he's a deacon at our church. He approved wholeheartedly of my marrying Harvey. I hope you won't put other people's problems and flaws on me."

"Well said, Abby," Harvey beamed.

Mrs. Nicholas put her hand on Abby's arm. "No, dear, of course not. We're just very protective of our children. I hope you can understand that. Truth be told, I thought Clarice had become a little mad and controlling these past few months. Your experiences have made you wise beyond your years. You know, I was only fifteen when I married David, but I knew he was the one God had chosen for me right from the start." Mrs. Nicholas looked at her husband lovingly.

"We do support your marriage," Mr. Nicholas said. "And speaking of, when will this event take place? Could we convince you to do it in two weeks' time? We have the church already booked."

Harvey shook his head. "Sorry, Father. I'm afraid not. We'll be getting married at Mount Olive Baptist Church, where Abby grew up. How does June tenth sound to you all?"

Abby and Harvey hadn't discussed a date yet, but when Harvey suggested June tenth, Abby's heart leapt. That was two years to the day that they had first met. It was the perfect day. Not only that, but the flowers would be in full bloom, the air warm. Abby thought it was just right, and Harvey's parents quickly agreed.

Once initial plans were set, Mr. Nicholas departed to call Abby's father and discuss their children's marriage. Mrs. Nicholas went into party-planning mode.

"Well, dear, that doesn't give us much time. We'll go this week and get you fitted for a wedding dress. We'll need to decide on what flowers and decorations . . . "

"Actually, Mrs. Nicholas, I already have a dress I want to wear." Abby smiled, thinking of her mother's own wedding dress. "But I would love help picking out flowers. I don't know much about what's in season when."

"Please, Abigail, call me Jane. I already know you call my sister Aunt Doris."

"You do?" Abby grinned. She felt a little embarrassed at Harvey's mother knowing she called Doris "aunt" already.

"Of course. She is my sister, Abigail."

Abby bit her lip. "Jane, please call me Abby."

"Abby. Well, then. We'll get started tomorrow looking at floral arrangements. I'm going to call it a night," she said, standing. "Goodnight, son. And goodnight, Abby." Jane walked to the door, turned and smiled, and strode out.

Abby let out a big sigh of relief. "Goodness! I thought I was on the firing range for a minute there," she laughed. "But I think your parents like me."

"I told you before that they do, Abby," Harvey said, sliding next to her on the couch. "Now, how long is it until June tenth?"

Harvey leaned in and kissed Abby. It was quick and sweet to begin. The kisses grew more intense, more passionate. Harvey wrapped his arms around Abby, and Abby's hands cupped his face as she kissed him. His fingers tickled her neck as his lips caressed her collarbone, sending shocks through Abby that she didn't know were possible. Their breathing was heavy, their kisses hot.

Abby wasn't sure what to think. Days ago, she had never felt more alone, more desperate. And now, here she was a world away from home, engaged again to Harvey. His hands touching her, his lips tenderly moving over her body. Was all this real? With the bursts of emotion and excitement that came from her body, she knew it had to be real.

They broke apart, gasping for breath. Harvey ran his hand over her shoulders and gazed into Abby's eyes, his chest heaving. Knowing she needed to leave lest she compromise herself further, Abby stood and blew Harvey a kiss before running up the stairs to the guestroom for the night.

She changed into her night clothes and braided her hair. As she fell into the big, soft bed, Abby thought she could get used to this lifestyle. But she missed her family. She missed the hustle and bustle of her parent's busy home. But at least she wasn't missing Harvey any more. Abby fell asleep imagining what it would feel like to be married to Harvey.

By the next morning, Mrs. Nicholas—Jane—had scheduled out the rest of the week. "Now, I know you want to see Charleston, and you will, Abby," she started, peering at Abby over the top of her glasses. "You and Harvey can have lunch on your own, since it's his birthday today; but at two, I have us scheduled to speak with a florist. Certainly,

I can get some arrangements done and bring them with me when we come in June. And then, we will have supper with Susie and her family.

"Tomorrow, Harvey has another therapy appointment in the morning, and I'm assuming you'll go with him," Jane continued, "so that's out for shopping. How about you and I have lunch together tomorrow? We can eat at the club. And that will leave your afternoon free to sightsee . . . "

Jane continued rattling off the week's schedule, which was all written in a large ledger book. She spoke of food, cakes, decorations, and even a honeymoon. It was all too much for Abby. Peter and Emmeline's wedding had been so simple to plan. She knew she wanted a big wedding before, but now she just wanted to be married. Besides, she always assumed her family would be cooking and making a cake and arranging everything else.

"Mrs. Nicholas? Sorry, Jane?" interrupted Abby. "May I call my mother before we go further? I miss her terribly, and I'm sure she may have some ideas as well."

Jane looked surprised. "Yes, of course! We don't want to exclude your mother. Go on in the sitting room and give her a ring."

Abby excused herself and smoothed her lavender sweater as she walked into the sitting room. It looked just like the parlor, and she wasn't sure how it was different, but it had a different name. She sat at a small desk, where the phone rested, and dialed her parent's number.

"Hello?" a small voice answered.

"Eliza! Eliza, it's Abby!" Oh, it was so good to hear her little sister's voice. Abby hadn't realized just how much she missed her family—not just her parents, but her littlest sister as well.

"Abby! Abby! Momma! It's Abby calling all the way from Charleston!" Abby heard some commotion on the line, and then her mother picked up.

Breathless, Grace picked up. "Abby! Oh, honey, how are you?"

"Oh, Momma! It's better than I ever expected. Harvey and I are back together, as I'm sure you guessed. We're going to get married in June, Momma! Can you believe it?" Abby's voice shone through the phone.

"So I heard!" Grace exclaimed. "Mr. Nicholas called last night and talked with your father at length. It seems the beginning of June will show some wedding bells up this way. The entire family is excited. When Emmeline called us to let us know she was home, I told her, and she wasn't surprised at all."

"Oh, she and P.J. got home all right? Good, I'm so glad. I miss them already," Abby said.

"They're just fine back at the Madisons' house. When will you be home?"

"This weekend." Abby sighed. "Listen, Momma, Mrs. Nicholas—Jane—wants to do a lot of planning for this wedding, but I wanted to call you first and get your thoughts. I don't want to miss planning with you."

"You let her do whatever she wants to, sweetie." Grace laughed. "Will you be shopping for a dress down there, where all the high-class shops are?"

"Actually, Momma, I thought I could wear your dress." Abby slowed down and smiled.

Overcome with emotion, Grace replied, "Of course, Abby. We'll alter it when you come home."

"Okay, Momma. I'll talk to you soon. Give my love to everyone," Abby replied.

They said their goodbyes, and Abby hung up the phone. She really did love her mother, and she stopped to thank God for such a wonderful family.

She looked around the room and spotted a large mirror on the far wall. Stepping in front of it, Abby inspected herself. Her hair was swept out of her face and pinned back, but the rest hung loose over her shoulders, cascading in soft curls. She wore a lavender V-neck sweater fitted to her body. She was too thin, she admitted. Her body was suited to be a few pounds heavier. Even her skirt, which had been taken in not too long ago, was loose on her waist. The gray skirt had been modified from frilly to fashionable with a new military-style cut. Abby and her mother really were handy with a sewing machine, and she was thankful.

"I hope I look all right," she said to herself. "I feel so self-conscious and out of place here."

"You shouldn't," Harvey said from the doorway. "You look just fine." He stepped behind her, so she could see him in the mirror.

"Thank you." Abby sighed.

She turned to face him. Each time she saw Harvey, she felt butterflies in her stomach, just like she did when they first met. He was dressed in a dark blue suit, tailored to fit his tall, lean frame. A blue fedora-style hat was upon his head. He looked amazingly dapper.

"Speaking of looking fine," Abby teased, "I look like a ragamuffin next to you."

"Never," Harvey said. "Are you ready for a morning of sightseeing?"

"Oh, yes, I am. And happy birthday, too!" Abby linked arms with Harvey, and they made their way out of the house to enjoy their morning together. *Thank you, God,* she thought, *for everything You've given me.*

After a whirlwind morning of museums and sights, Harvey took Abby to his favorite place for lunch. It was a little French bistro called Chateau de Degas with an overlook of the Cooper River. As soon as they walked in the door, Harvey was recognized by the staff.

"Monsieur Nicholas, right this way," a man with a heavy accent gushed, ushering Harvey and Abby into the restaurant. "We have not seen you since before the war began. We are so happy you returned home. Shall I take you upstairs to your favorite table?"

Abby looked at Harvey, unsure if he would manage the stairs, especially after such an exhausting morning. But Harvey just smiled and replied in French, "Ouí!" Harvey took his time going up the stairs, and the maître d' did not rush them.

The bistro was quaint; Abby imagined it would fit right in if it were actually in France. Small iron tables with two chairs each were perched in the front of the main dining room. Behind them were a few larger tables for those dining with groups. Up the stairs were several more small tables with just two seats. The black ironwork was exquisite, the chairs cushioned under bright red fabrics. The room was also bright red, with beautiful impressionist paintings on the walls.

Harvey pulled Abby's chair out for her, and she thanked him as she sat. The maître d' then held Harvey's chair for him. A waiter brought out glasses of water and a basket with warm baguette bread in it. The maître d' gave Harvey a wine list and waited for him to select a bottle.

"Do you drink wine, Abby?" Harvey asked after realizing she probably didn't.

"I've never had it before," Abby admitted.

"Hmm, then let me choose the perfect starter wine. One of my favorites," he said. "Veuve Cliquot Brut, s'il vous plait." The maître d' nodded and left them alone.

"What did you say?" Abby wondered, her eyebrows raised.

"Oh, it's a type of champagne. Straight from France. I think you'll like it. And 's'il vous plait' means 'please.'"

"Oh," Abby said, scowling. "I can't speak French. I can't speak anything but plain, old, American English."

"That's okay, angel," laughed Harvey. "I only speak French because it was forced on me by our nanny, Annette, when I was a child."

Soon, the waiter returned with the bottle of champagne and popped the cork for the pair. He poured Abby a glass first, then Harvey. "Are you ready to place your order, Mousier Nicholas?"

"Ouí, Ramon," Harvey answered, calling the waiter by name. "We'll start with le plateau de fromages. The lady will have la gratinée d'oignon and la salade niçoise au thon poëlé. I believe I'll also have la gratinée d'oignon along with l'omelette aux crevettes."

"Merci." The waiter bowed and walked away.

"What did you say that time?" Abby whispered.

"I ordered some wonderful cheeses to begin, followed by French onion soup for us both. I ordered a shrimp plate and got you a salad with yellow fin tuna. Doesn't that sound wonderful?"

"I'm amazed," was all Abby could say. She truly was amazed. Harvey was fluent in French? She had no idea.

Harvey lifted his wine glass and raised it to toast Abby. She followed his example. They clinked glasses, and Harvey toasted "the future Mrs. Nicholas." Abby blushed for the first time since she had been in Charleston.

"Thank you, and happy birthday to you, Mr. Nicholas."

"It's the best birthday I've ever had," he added.

While they ate, Abby noticed that everyone in the restaurant seemed to know Harvey. "Why is it that everybody is scurrying to help you here?"

"My father is part owner of this restaurant," he said, taking a sip of champagne.

"Part owner?" Abby asked, not sure she wanted to know who the other owner was. She had an idea with it being a French restaurant.

Harvey knew what she was thinking, "Yes, the other owner is Mousier Renard. I'm sorry, Abby, I should have told you. Maybe we shouldn't have come here." He took her hand to comfort her.

"No, that's okay, really. I should have known." She shrugged. "No wonder they had you and . . . well. Never mind."

Harvey gave her hand a squeeze. "Never mind is right. Let's just enjoy the scenery."

"Oh, yes, the river is lovely. Look at all the boats coming and going," Abby said, peering out over the balcony.

"I meant you." Harvey smiled.

CHAPTER 15

"I CAN'T BELIEVE THE WEEK is over. I'll be sad to leave here. And you," Abby said taking one last look through the house, but her gaze landed on the man she loved. "This house is so big and wonderful. I really love it. I love you."

"And I love you. I miss your house, actually. Bustling with excitement and people," Harvey noted. "It's so cozy, like a whole other world."

Abby smiled, then frowned. "It's been very empty without Peter. I bet Momma thinks it's even emptier without me, too."

Harvey kissed her on the forehead. "I'm sorry, angel. We'll be back there by nightfall."

"I'm really glad I'm keeping the apartment, though," Abby sighed. "Especially if we'll be getting our own place after we get married."

"That's right. I'll finish my last class at Clemson this month, and then we'll be moving to Greenville for me to start seminary in the fall." Harvey smiled. "I guess once we're married, we should just stay in the apartment until August. That will give us time to find a place in Greenville, anyway."

They had said their goodbyes to Harvey's parents over breakfast. A whirlwind of hugs and kisses were exchanged before they exited, promising to send up soon a car full of items for the wedding. The Nicholases kept a very busy social calendar and had already left the house by the time Abby and Harvey were ready to go.

As Abby got into the passenger seat—Harvey insisted on driving them out of the city—she looked again at the house Harvey grew up in. It amazed her that such a humble, godly man could have grown up having everything. It was a home of extravagance, but nobody inside let it get to their heads. And for that, Abby had a newfound respect for her future in-laws. They had done a wonderful job raising Harvey.

"Ready?" Harvey asked, his hand on the wheel.

"I'm ready," Abby said and smiled. "I can't wait to see everyone. And they'll be so glad to see you."

"Are you sure?" Harvey wondered as he put the car into gear. "After everything that happened, will they be glad to see me?"

"If you mean our brief split, I don't think they believed it from the beginning. They gave me money to come down here, didn't they? And if you mean with Peter gone . . . " Abby trailed off and paused a moment. She laid her hand on her arm and stared into his eyes. "You were with him. You are a part of Momma's last image of him. All of us—we last saw my brother with you. And we know you were the last person he saw before going home to Jesus." She smiled through tears. "So, I think that will be a comfort to everyone. I expect Momma to hug you tight and not let go for a while. So, be prepared."

Harvey took Abby's hand as he turned on the road out of Charleston. "I wouldn't have it any other way. Now, tell me about these wedding plans my mother is making. Is she driving you batty yet?"

Abby laughed. "No, not at all. We do things so simply at home. I am amazed by how much planning other people put into a wedding. But what I wonder is if she realizes the wedding is just a day. It's the marriage we all should prepare for."

"Well said, Abby. I'm sure Pastor Phillips would be happy to hear a member of his flock say that."

"Oh!" Abby squealed. "Did you get that letter? Aunt Dottie and Pastor Phillips got married this past October." Abby laughed as she retold the story of the wedding and how it took so long for the pastor to propose to Abby's aunt, but it took her only a few weeks to get the bachelor down the aisle.

Harvey and Abby talked throughout the entire car ride about their childhood, about their plans for the future, and about everything else in between. They stopped frequently for Harvey to stretch his legs. Abby did most of the driving, but Harvey maneuvered the city streets when they came upon them. It seemed like no time had passed at all when Abby pulled the car into her parent's driveway.

She honked the horn, and her family came pouring out of the house, including Aunt Dottie and Pastor Phillips. As she opened the door to the car, her mother called out, "You're just in time for supper. Come on!"

Jacob came running down the stairs and opened Harvey's door for him. "Harvey! You're back; you're back!"

Harvey put his cane into the dirt and pulled himself up. "I'm back; that's right, Jake."

Jake gave Harvey a big hug, which Harvey returned emphatically. Abby was happy that her little brother didn't seem put off by the cane.

"Let me see you; let me see you!" Grace exclaimed at seeing Harvey. She rounded the car and squeezed Harvey tight. When the sobs began, Harvey didn't hesitate—he wrapped his arms around her and let her cry. Everyone watched as a mother finally had peace about losing her son. Abby brushed tears off her cheeks as she mourned her family's loss.

"I'm so sorry," Grace said with a slight laugh. "How embarrassing."

"Not at all, Mrs. Walker," Harvey said, keeping his arm around her. Abby could see light glisten off his moist cheeks as well. "Maybe after dinner, we can talk if you like." Grace merely nodded as they walked toward the house.

Abby went up to her sister. "Reba, I missed you!"

Her sister glared. "You left without saying goodbye to me." The scowl on her face told Abby that her departure had been rough on her sister.

"I'm so sorry, Reba," Abby offered. She hadn't thought it would be such a big deal, but it was to Reba. "You were in school, and Emmeline and I were rushing. It was so last minute. But I brought you a gift. I'll get it out later." Still hurt, Reba offered Abby a half-hearted hug, glad she was home.

Once inside, Abby took a deep breath and looked around. The house was modest, compared to the one they had just left. No opulent decorations, no gold upholstered chairs. The kitchen was sparse. The once-yellow walls were faded to off-white; the dishes were gifts her parents had gotten for their wedding so long before. The dining table was almost as large as the Nicholases' but not nearly as elegant. Plain-backed white chairs encircled it, no padding or red fabric in sight. Until now, she didn't know there was another option in the world. Abby smiled, though, happy she grew up with what she did.

Dinner was boisterous, to say the least. Everyone wanted to know about Charleston and what it was like. Everyone wanted to hear what happened to Clarice and how Abby had gotten the ring back. Laughter was offered up to heaven in spades, and Abby prayed that Peter could hear it and be happy with her.

After everyone had eaten, Harvey, Nathan, and Pastor Phillips—now Uncle John—went into the living room to talk. Abby wondered what they would discuss, but she was fairly sure Peter would be the first topic. She felt sorry for Harvey having to relive that day over and over, and she made a mental note to thank him profusely for it later.

The ladies all sat around the table, talking excitedly about the upcoming wedding, while Eliza and Gabriel ran through the house. Before they got too far into the conversation, the door opened, and Emmeline came in carrying P.J.

Abby leaped out of her seat. "Emme! P.J.! Oh, big boy! You've grown a foot in the last week," she said, taking the baby into her arms.

They sat back down, Abby happy to see her sister-in-law and nephew again. The table grew quiet as everybody watched Emmeline as she fought to catch her breath.

"Are you okay, Emmeline, dear?" Grace asked as she got Emmeline a glass of water.

Emmeline waved her hand around her face. "I'm fine. Just need to catch my breath after carrying P.J. over here is all. He's getting heavy."

Everyone nodded, but Abby didn't like how pale Emmeline was looking. It worried her. But this was not the time to bring it up. After all, P.J. was getting bigger, and Emmeline was still quite thin.

After an evening of hustle and bustle, Abby admitted she was exhausted. She and Harvey gave a round of hugs to everybody, and they left. It was a quick drive to Abby's apartment. Harvey would be spending the next several weeks staying with an old friend from Clemson, Walter McBie, who was also back in Clemson after being discharged from the army.

When she pulled the car into the parking lot, Abby smiled at Harvey. "Do you want to come up and see it?" Abby asked, half-afraid he would say yes and what it would mean to have him in a room where there was no chance of interruption. Before the question was completely out of her mouth though, Harvey had gotten out of the car and was waiting for her to join him. It made Abby smile, and she bit her lip to hide her grin.

Once Abby found her key, she flung the door open. She flipped the light switch, and a dim light came on overhead, illuminating the meager furniture.

"So, this is where we'll be spending our first few months as a married couple?" Harvey asked, wrinkling his nose.

"Trust me, it looked a lot more appealing before I saw your parent's house," she chuckled, tossing her jacket onto a hook next to the door.

Harvey inspected the small apartment. It had been emptied of Emmeline and P.J.'s clothes and belongings during the week, so it was even more vacant than before. He poked his head into the bedroom and small closet.

"Two little beds, huh?"

"It was perfect for two single gals," Abby said, leaning against the wall. She watched Harvey search around.

"Where's the bathroom?"

Abby squinted and sucked in a breath between her teeth. "Down the hall. It's a shared bathroom . . . "

Harvey's eyes grew to the size of saucers. "Are you serious? Maybe we'll need somewhere else before we move to Greenville."

"You're spoiled rotten," Abby accused jokingly.

"Nah, this is just fine. It's a hundred times better than our living conditions in Europe and Africa," he said, moving to the couch. He sat and rubbed his leg.

Moving to his side, Abby asked with concern, "Are you okay? Put your foot up on the coffee table."

"I guess Dr. Simon was right—being in the car all day did make my leg feel a little lousy. Nothing a good night's sleep won't fix."

"I'm sorry, sweetheart," Abby said, tucking her feet up under her. "Can I get you anything?"

"Just this," Harvey said as he kissed Abby. As their lips parted, Abby smiled and giggled uneasily. Harvey took a deep breath. "Are you nervous?"

Abby sighed. "A little, I guess. There's no chance of interruption here, like there is in one of our parents' houses. It makes being alone with you feel a little more dangerous, I guess."

Harvey laughed. "We were alone when we went to the Lachlan house all those times," he pointed out.

"True." Abby thought on it. "But I never thought about that then. We weren't the people we are now."

Harvey brushed Abby's hair behind her ear. "Don't be nervous. We can hold out a few more weeks. Should I stop kissing you?"

"Good heavens, no!" Abby squealed as she leaned into Harvey again and kissed him long and deep. She toyed with the buttons on his shirt, tempted to undo a few, but unsure how she would stop herself if she did.

Lord, give me strength. The wedding is in eight weeks; give us patience for eight more weeks.

When the kiss ended, Harvey let out a low moan and changed the subject. "You know, you're absolutely right, we're not the people we were before the war," he teased. "You've gotten so much more self-confident since I've been gone."

Abby picked herself up off Harvey's shoulder. "Have I?"

"Yes, you don't blush nearly as much; you don't hide your face or look down anymore. You're a woman full of pride, and rightly so," Harvey stated. "When I left, you were still very much a girl. Strong and loving, but a girl. Suddenly, you're a woman. I like it."

Abby beamed. "I don't know what to say. I feel like a woman around you. You make me feel . . . I don't know. Like I've never felt before."

Running his fingers through her hair, Harvey smiled. "I feel the same way. God certainly brought you to me when I least expected it and gave me feelings I didn't know existed."

Abby closed her eyes, recalling the way her heart skipped a beat when they had first met at the church almost two years before. It amazed her that God gave Harvey the same feeling. They sat still, without moving or talking, for what seemed like hours.

Finally, Harvey left Abby in her apartment. She headed to bed, her body weary, her mind exhausted. She fell into a deep slumber.

When Abby woke, she couldn't recall where she was. It was cold, and she was alone. It took her a few minutes to remember that she was back in the apartment. She rose and dressed, picking out a blue blouse and brown skirt from her wardrobe. Putting on slippers, she made her way down the hall to the bathroom and scrubbed her face clean.

With a kerchief on her head, she ran across the street to the grocery store to get a few essentials. She chose some canned fruit and vegetables, along with bread and milk. Abby had gotten accustomed to the large meals in Charleston, but now she was back to the real world. She bought only what she needed to survive.

After a glass of milk and a few bites of canned peaches, Abby walked down the street to her parent's house. It was nice to be back home, Abby thought as she nodded to people she passed on the street. Her week in Charleston seemed like a dream; it had been slightly warmer, and there was no shortage of food. The war was a distant thought for her down there. The wind gusting through Abby's kerchief told her she was back from her fairy tale.

Abby made her way up the steps and into the house she grew up in. She sat at her parent's dining room table for a few minutes once she got inside. The room was still warm from breakfast, and Abby felt the need to thaw out. Reba came into the kitchen and sat with her.

"I'm still mad you left without telling me," Reba said. She pouted a little for effect.

Abby touched her sister's arm. "I'm sorry, Reba. It wasn't planned. Otherwise, I would have told you. You know that."

Reba smiled half-heartedly. "I know. But I wanted to go, too."

"I'll take you one day, I promise," Abby said with a smile.

"I know you will. But I am a little jealous. For now. Tell me all about it."

Abby laughed and told Reba all about the Nicholases' house, how big it was and how extravagant the décor was. She told her sister all about the French bistro and the museums and the clubs. Reba took it all in, longing to go herself.

The door opened, and Emmeline came in carrying P.J. "I thought you would be here," she said to Abby. "Where's Harvey?"

"He'll be staying with his friend Walter until the wedding. I'm sure I'll see him today," responded Abby.

"Ah, okay," Emmeline said, sitting with a huff. "Oh, Reba, take P.J. for me." She passed the baby over. "He's getting so heavy."

"Not really," Reba commented, tossing P.J. up and down, making him laugh.

Abby furrowed her brow. "Emme, you're not looking good these days. I noticed before we went to Charleston that you have been sleeping much more."

Emmeline became defensive. "My mother said that, too. I'm fine. I'm raising a baby by myself with no husband. I'm tired and worn out."

"I'm sorry, Emme," Abby said, concerned. "I love you and don't want to see you run down is all."

"I know, Abby," Emmeline said, rubbing her temples. "But I am run down. I'm so tired all the time, and I can barely eat."

"Maybe you need to see a doctor," Reba suggested. She was also concerned. "Just to be sure." Abby nodded in agreement.

They were disrupted by Eliza running into the room, followed by Gabriel and Grace. Grace was carrying an old white box under her arm.

"There you are. All my girls," Grace said with a smile. "Come on; I have something to show you."

They all stood and followed her out of the room and into her bedroom. Reba and Abby sat on the bed, Emmeline in a chair. Grace laid the box on the bed and opened it. She unveiled a white lace dress and fluffed it up for them to see. It was her wedding dress.

"I wore this nearly twenty-five years ago," Grace said. "Your daddy and I were married by Pastor Mills, who was at Mount Olive until he retired. It was September 25, 1918. Your father looked wonderful. Almost as good as he looks now," Grace smiled. "Well, Abby, you're welcome to it if you want it."

Abby's smile stretched from ear to ear as she stood. Her mother held the dress out for her. "I was all of sixteen when I got married. Your father was twenty. Not too much younger than you two. Go, try it on."

"Thank you, Momma," she said as she took the dress from her mother.

She ran from the room to the bathroom and tried the dress on. A few zips and snaps later, and Abby had the dress on. Everyone gasped when she slipped back into the room. Grace's eyes filled with tears when Abby stepped in front of her mother's mirror to see how the dress looked in full length. She took a deep breath and gazed into the mirror.

The dress was a perfect fit. It was stunning. Typical of Edwardian style, it employed a lot of lacework. The V-neck collar lay across her chest and was made of beautiful lace roses; the sleeves were nearly sheer and contained hundreds of little eyelets. The dress came to the floor, and the skirt had matching roses and eyelets, the waist gathered in all the right places.

"I love it," she whispered.

"We can update it if you would like," Grace offered.

"No, Momma, this is perfect. Just like this." Abby turned and hugged her mother.

"What about your hair?" Reba asked.

"Oh yes, by next month the flowers should be blooming, and you can wear flowers in your hair," Emmeline chimed in.

"Some daisies should be in bloom by then; those are your favorites," Reba added.

Abby laughed. "Funny you mention that. Mrs. Nicholas and I went to a florist and ordered Shasta Daisies for the bouquets—and even some extra for my hair!"

All the ladies smiled and giggled. Abby took a deep breath and tried to take a picture in her mind of each person in the room. This was a time to remember.

Back in her regular clothes, with her wedding dress tucked away, Abby helped her mother prepare lunch for the group. Hot tomato soup sprinkled with rationed cheese was set at each chair around the table. Nathan and Jake appeared from doing some yard work as the ladies were sitting down.

Abby held P.J. and spoon-fed him sips of her soup. He was such a happy baby, and growing so much. But he wasn't getting especially heavy, as Emmeline claimed. Abby glanced at her sister-in-law, who sat quietly in her chair. Emmeline took one sip of her soup and pushed the bowl away, looking green. *No wonder Emmeline can't lift P.J.,* Abby thought. *She's getting especially thin herself; she's lost all her strength. I'll have to help her find her appetite again.*

After lunch, Emmeline and P.J. went back to her parent's house. Abby cornered her mother, determined to talk to her about Emmeline's health.

"Momma, I'm worried about Emme. She's lost a lot of weight; she can barely hold P.J.," Abby said. "She's not eating."

"She's depressed, Abby," Grace acknowledged. "Maybe she needs a pick-me-up. I tell you what, why don't I watch P.J. one day this week, and you two go out on the town. Eat lunch out; go shopping. Maybe you can drive your car up to Greenville and start househunting."

Abby jumped up and hugged her mother. "What a great idea! Emmeline will love it." Abby hoped that a small break and a day of treating themselves would help Emmeline come out of her funk.

***

Emmeline's mood did pick up in the weeks leading up to Abby and Harvey's wedding. She lived vicariously through Abby as they planned what they considered to be a lavish wedding.

With the big day a mere week away, the Walker women had started getting the menu together. They planned to have roasted chickens, courtesy of Aunt Dottie and Uncle John, who were now raising them. Grace had pulled several cans of preserved carrots, squash, and beans out of the cellar, along with several fruits. Bread would be freshly baked by Aunt Judy. Abby had been bartering family and friends for sugar rations to make a cake and even sweetened iced tea for Harvey. It wouldn't be the grand soirée Abby had dreamed of, but it would be wonderful, nonetheless.

As they chose vegetables for the wedding meal, Emmeline and Reba had retreated to try on bridesmaid dresses. They were reusing the dresses from Emmeline's wedding, with Emmeline wearing Abby's dress.

Abby had made sure to craft changes on the dresses, so they weren't exactly like Peter and Emmeline's wedding. That was partly to give them new life and partly to keep everyone from feeling sorrow at seeing them. The rose-colored sleeves had been shortened to caps, the flowers removed. The hemlines were taken up to mid-calf. Abby had found some lovely yellow sashes to tie around the waist of the dresses. She also had taken the time to modify their old hats and decorate them with yellow ribbon and lace. Daisies would be added to the dresses and hats the day before the wedding.

When the girls emerged, they looked wonderful. The dresses looked totally different, which gave Abby a sigh of relief to know that Emmeline wouldn't be reminded too much of her own wedding.

Both girls were thin as rails, the yellow sash accentuating their tiny waists. The hats looked smart atop their heads.

"Oh, you both look wonderful!" Abby exclaimed. Grace and Dottie also gave their approval. Reba twirled and posed for effect, but Emmeline stayed still. Abby hoped the dress wasn't too grim a reminder for her sister-in-law. The girls quickly retreated to change back, so they could help with the rest of the preparations.

Abby, Grace, and Dottie sorted through jars of canned fruit to find the right ones for the wedding day. As Dottie opened a jar of spiced apples for a whiff, her face turned green, and she ran from the room.

"Is she okay?" Abby asked with concern. "Are the apples bad?" Abby took the jar off the table and cautiously sniffed. "No, they seem okay."

Grace merely laughed at Abby's concern. When Dottie came back into the room, Grace scolded her. "You know better than to do that, Dottie. And you had better clue Abby in."

"Clue me in?"

Dottie smiled radiantly. "Abby, I'm pregnant."

Abby rushed to her aunt and hugged her tight. "Why didn't you tell me? When are you due?"

Through laughter, Dottie said, "I'm sorry, Abby, I should have told you. I'm due in November."

"How exciting, Aunt Dottie! That's wonderful."

Dottie beamed. When Reba and Emmeline came back into the room, she shared the news with them, and everybody gave out hugs again. Abby was so glad for more happy news. Maybe this war would be over soon, and happiness would be back all over the place.

The following days were a whirlwind. Harvey's parents had arrived, as it was the Friday before the wedding. They got a room at the

Magnolia Inn and reserved rooms for Susan and her family as well. They were scheduled to be in the next day. David and Jane had brought several decorations for the church, as well as for the Walker home for the reception. Susan planned to bring fresh flowers with her for the wedding party.

Abby was desperate for some time alone with Harvey in the midst of all the preparations. They planned a private date for Friday evening to get away from the chaos of wedding planning. Harvey picked Abby up at the apartment and said he was willing to drive if she was willing to trust him.

"Trust you? Of course!"

Harvey smiled and pulled a black cloth out of his back pocket. "Then you'll need this." When Abby raised her eyebrow to question him, Harvey added, "You said you trust me. Put this on."

"Right now? Can I wait till we get into the car?" They laughed, and Abby looped her arm around Harvey's. She couldn't believe in a matter of days they would be husband and wife.

At the car, Abby slid into the passenger side. Over the last several weeks, Harvey had been driving more and more, getting stronger and stronger. His leg still bothered him, but driving was becoming easier for him, as was walking. As Harvey fell in behind the wheel, he handed Abby the blindfold once more. She obliged, tying it around her eyes with a sigh.

"Where are we going, Harvey?" She felt around for Harvey's hand and grasped it when she found it.

Giving her hand a squeeze, Harvey chuckled. "That defeats the purpose of the blindfold now, doesn't it? Just sit back and relax. It will take a little while to get there, but it will be worth it. I promise."

Abby smiled and wanted to look at Harvey, but she left the cloth over her eyes. "Okay then, let's go."

Harvey drove off, making turns and going over hills. Abby knew the roads for several turns, but then was lost, unsure exactly where they were heading. With her eyes covered, Abby's other senses took over. She could hear the faint sound of a train whistle, a familiar and comforting sound. She could hear the car's soft hum as they drove. She took a deep breath and could smell the leather of the seats. She could also smell Harvey, the intoxicating aroma that made her heart beat faster. Abby licked her lips, trying to get some sense of the mysterious place Harvey was carrying her off to.

They rode mostly in silence. Abby wished she could look at Harvey. She found all his mystery to be very silly, but she indulged him. She appreciated a little silly now and then. She started to giggle.

"What's so funny?"

"I don't know. All of this," she said, waving her hands around her face. "I just love that you want to surprise me with something. And I know it's a surprise because we're way out of town now."

Harvey chuckled. "Well, we're almost there. Just hang tight a few more minutes."

She moved toward Harvey and smiled.

A few turns later, and the car lurched to a stop. "We're here." Abby heard the excitement in Harvey's voice as he spoke.

The car door opened and then shut. She waited in silence, her eyes still covered. She was too excited to keep the blindfold over her eyes. She quickly pulled it off and squinted in the bright sunlight. After a few blinks, her eyes adjusted, and she found that the car was sitting in a driveway. A shadow crossed in front of her, and then Harvey opened her door. He held out his hand for her. She stood, but the sun was still in her eyes. When she could see properly, Harvey was smiling from ear to ear.

"Where are we?"

"Take a look." Harvey turned Abby in front of him.

Before her, she saw a quaint little house, white with green shutters. On the windows were small, yellow box planters with little, green shoots pushing up through the dirt. The front door matched the shutters perfectly. The front yard had small shrubs and two saplings reaching for the sun's nourishment. It was a darling little house, but Abby had no idea why they were there.

"Whose house is this?"

Harvey took her hand and started pulling her up the driveway. "It's your house, Abby."

She stopped. "My house? What do you mean?" Abby's heart pounded, unsure she heard exactly what Harvey said.

"Our house. I bought it," Harvey said.

Dumbfounded, Abby couldn't speak. Their house? He bought it? *Dear Lord, can it be true? He bought us a house?*

"Abby?"

She started quietly, "This, this is our house? For us?" She could feel her heart beat faster, and her hands began to shake. She looked to Harvey who had the silliest and most endearing grin on his face. He nodded, yes, this would be their house. "Really?"

"Well, we're going to be moving up here this summer for seminary. And since we'll be here a few years, I thought why not?" He beamed. "This is your wedding present!" Harvey stretched both hands out wide, his cane hanging off his wrist. "Let's go in and look."

He grabbed Abby's arm and pulled her inside. The house was still being completed. In fact, he bought it and was able to make a few requests about the wall colors and other small details. They crossed the threshold and were standing in a small living room. The walls were a cheery yellow, and Abby could still smell fresh paint. A modest fireplace sat off to the side; a large window looked out into the front yard. Behind that was a charming little kitchen with a brand new refrigerator and range. The floor was wooden throughout, and matching cabinets lined the wall. Beside that was a small dining room with white walls, just big enough for a four-person table and chairs. Abby thought it was perfect.

"I love it," she whispered. "Harvey, I love it." She turned to him and hugged him tight, nearly knocking him over.

"I knew you would," he said. "Come on; look at the rest."

Between the living and dining rooms was a small hallway. To the left was a bathroom, to the right a bedroom. Abby peeked into the bedroom. More fresh paint, this time a soft baby blue, and Abby knew right away it would be the perfect nursery. She turned to Harvey and beamed. She knew he had chosen that color for a reason. Beside that was another small room, which Harvey called a study. Harvey said it could be used for books, reading, writing, or anything else.

Across from that room was the largest bedroom. Abby entered it fully and turned completely around. The walls were a soft peach color on the top with a chair rail and then a muted green below. Two windows allowed views of both the back and side yards. A closet already full of hangers sat waiting for their clothing to fill it up. She stood in the center of the room, her eyes taking it all in, her mouth hanging open in awe.

Abby couldn't believe this would be her bedroom. Her and Harvey's bedroom. She felt her face grow hot and red, and she knew she was blushing, but she didn't hide it. She looked at Harvey, and he held one arm out and rested it on the wall as he watched her take it all in. His face broke into a smile, and Abby's did the same.

She bounded over to her future husband and hugged him close, thanking him over and over.

"Welcome home, Mrs. Nicholas."

CHAPTER 16

ABBY HATED RUNNING LATE; HER whole family did. It was her wedding day; it was pouring rain; and they were running late. Aunt Dottie said it was supposed to be good luck to have rain on your wedding day, but Abby was sure that was just something people said to make a bride feel better about the whole mess. Nathan was running around, trying to find socks for him and the boys. Reba had accidentally sat on her hat and was trying to fluff it. Both Gabriel and P.J. needed to eat before they could leave.

The only one ready was Abby. She wished she could talk to Harvey. Why was it bad luck to see each other anyway? Hadn't they had their share of bad luck as it was? Between Peter's death, their breakup, and the war . . . surely nothing else could go wrong if they saw each other for just a minute.

Standing in front of a full-length mirror, Abby studied herself. Two years before, when she had met Harvey, she had judged herself to be too plump with wild hair that called too much attention. She thought her chest was too large and her nose too small. She was young and naïve and had never imagined this day arriving so soon.

Her hair was still wild and unruly, but now Abby appreciated that feature and considered it her best. She had thinned out way too much and longed to put a few pounds back on. Abby had always wanted to be thinner, but now she wished she looked like she had before—fuller and healthier-looking. And Harvey liked her fuller. She was older now, more mature. She appreciated the little things in life now more than she ever had years before. How she had changed in two years' time. Harvey was right; she had grown up a lot.

Her mother's dress poured over her body like it was made for her. The lace hugged and flared at all the right places. The sash at the waist was drawn tight, accentuating her trim waist. The eyelet sleeves stopped just above her elbows, and the skirt ran down her legs, barely sweeping the floor. Abby had new white shoes for the occasion, with small heels and ankle straps that made her feel very much like a woman.

The combs Harvey had given her two Christmases before were now secured into her hair. One was fastened on each side, with her hair tumbling down her back between them. Abby admired the blue and opal stones; they looked marvelous with the dress. Her ringlets hadn't been cut in quite some time, and they spilled down her back with a select few over her shoulder and down her chest.

Abby thought to the clothing she had waiting for her in her suitcase. Aunt Dottie, ever the romantic, had bought her some lingerie for the honeymoon—a destination still unknown to Abby. Pure white satin and lace expertly sewn together to make a gorgeous nightgown were tucked away in tissue paper at the bottom of her suitcase. It even had marabou feathers across the top and along the bottom hem. Abby had been so embarrassed when she opened the box, but in truth, she couldn't wait to put it on.

Abby had spent a lot of time talking to Emmeline about marital relations in the past several weeks. She didn't feel comfortable talking to her mother or even her aunt. Emmeline was the only person she trusted to tell her the truth.

"It's kind of painful," Emmeline admitted one day over lunch.

"Painful?" Abby's eyes had gotten wide with concern. If it was painful, how did so many women go through with it?

"Just at first." Emmeline tried to ease her fears through smiles. "Then it's . . . it's . . . well, it's very nice. I promise. Now childbirth . . . that hurts like the dickens!"

Abby flushed just thinking about their conversation and suddenly felt very warm. She fanned herself with her hands and snapped out of the memory right as her mother came into the room.

"Nervous?"

Flustered and embarrassed, Abby agreed. "Yes, a little."

"Don't worry. People get married every day. And God really knew what He was doing putting you and Harvey together."

Abby sighed. "Do you think so, Momma?"

"Of course, Abigail. I wouldn't tell you if I didn't believe it." And Abby knew her mother was telling the truth. "Let's get going. There's a very fetching groom waiting for his bride!" Grace squeezed her daughter's arm and gave her another moment alone.

Lord? It's me, Abby. I'm ready for this if You are. I love Harvey so much. I can't believe the day is here that I'm actually going to get married in front of everybody we know. I am so blessed, Father. All blessings from Your hands. Please continue to bless us and our love. Bless us with a happy home and family. Bless us with children, as many as You see fit! Lord, see over Harvey as he goes into seminary to do Your work. Thank You, Lord, thank You. Amen.

With one last look in the mirror, Abby took a deep breath and headed for the car. With a jacket and umbrella covering her, she ran outside and slipped into the passenger seat next to her father. They were in Harvey's car while the rest of the family rode in the Walker family car.

It took only minutes to get to Mount Olive Baptist Church. Abby wasn't sure if it seemed like an eternity or if they appeared there without the car actually moving. Her father didn't speak until he turned the car off.

Nathan turned toward his eldest daughter. "Abigail," he started with a sigh. Abby blushed and looked down, waiting for her father's words of wisdom. But instead of insight, Nathan shed a tear. "You look so much like your mother did when we got married in this very church. The same curly hair, the same quiet strength. You've done so very much for this family since the day you were born."

Tears slipped out of the corners of Abby's eyes. "Daddy . . . "

"Oh, Abby. I am the proudest father ever. I may not show it much, but I am. And I want you to know that your momma and all the family is proud of you." Abby heard a sob catch in her father's throat. "And Peter . . . he would . . . "

"I know, Daddy," Abby whispered as tears washed freshly over her. "I know. I miss him, too."

"I love you, Abigail."

"I love you, too, Daddy."

Nathan took a handkerchief and handed it to his daughter. She dabbed it at her eyes and pressed it to her cheeks. She smiled at her father, who nodded in turn that she looked fine. Abby glanced out the window and saw that the rain had stopped. *Thank the Lord.* She kissed her father on the cheek and opened the door.

She sneaked into the back room to wait for the pastor to signal her around to the front. She stood in the middle of the room, surrounded by the women of her family. Reba and Emmeline were in their refurbished bridesmaid's gowns, Eliza in a beautiful, frilly blue dress. Grace wore the same dress she wore for Peter's wedding—a peach frock with pearl buttons down the front.

Jane Nicholas also joined them, wearing a striking yellow dress that complimented her every feature. Abby had helped her pick it out in Charleston, choosing a dress that wouldn't upstage her own mother, as she knew was quite possible given the Nicholases' panache for fancy clothing. Doris also joined them, wearing her finest Sunday dress in a beautiful teal color.

"Abby, are you ready?" her sister asked.

"Oh, Reba, am I ever," she smiled. "You know, I met Harvey in this very room."

Her mind was taken back to what seemed like decades ago but, in reality, was just two years ago that very day. She stood in the same room, hot and overwhelmed by young children when a stranger walked in. Tall with dark hair, Harvey strode into her life. Abby recalled his green eyes. She had been captured by them from the beginning, and she knew they would hold her for a lifetime. He had been warm and open. Harvey helped her care for the children without complaint, and she had known he would be a great father one day. Her stomach flipped like it had on that very first meeting.

Abby received a kiss from each of the ladies in the room, and she held onto her mother for an extra long hug. John brought Nathan into the room and shooed them all out. They exited the building and walked to the front of the church for the grand entrance.

Jane went first, escorted by David. Next was Grace. It would have been Peter's job to escort her down the center aisle, but Jacob did the job very well, doing his best to look serious and mature. Emmeline and Reba marched down the aisle together, Emmeline doing her best to hold back tears. Eliza, who was the flower girl, tossed daisy petals in front of her with a big smile across her face.

Harvey stood at the front of the church, to the left of the pastor. On his right was an empty chair holding a large picture of Peter and a boutonnière propped against the picture. It had been Harvey's idea, as he had asked Peter to be his best man a long time before. Not wanting to replace him, he thought to have Peter hold his position, even if from heaven. On the other side of the chair was Jacob, still serious and doing his best to fill his brother's shoes. Jacob held both wedding rings on his thumb and knew to wait for the word from John. Everybody thought the memorial was touching, and Emmeline cried silently as she stared at the empty chair across from her.

Aunt Judy played the introduction to the wedding march, and the doors opened before Abby and Nathan. Abby took a deep breath and looked toward her groom. Although he was discharged from the army, Harvey wore his dress uniform, and he wore it proudly. The dark green color set off his eyes; Abby could tell from across the church. His jacket fastened with brass buttons and a leather belt cinched his waist, making him look very handsome. His black hair had grown and hung over his forehead in the same way Abby remembered from the day they first met.

When Harvey saw Abby, a smile slowly spread across his face. His chest puffed a little, and he cleared his throat. His eyes sparkled as his bride made her way toward him. Neither of them saw anybody else as she approached; their gaze never shifted. Next to him, Abby had to use every ounce of willpower she had to not jump into Harvey's arms. She smiled nervously, and Harvey smiled in return.

"Family and friends, we are gathered here this day, in the sight of God, to join Harvey and Abigail in holy matrimony. This is an important step for two young people. They have come today to seek God's blessing and yours, as well, in their marriage. No marriage is a joining of just two. It is a joining of three—the bride, the groom, and our Holy Father. And so I ask, who presents this woman to this man for marriage?" John asked.

Nathan stood stoic. "I do." He kissed Abby on the cheek and then the forehead. His touch was light and warm. He then shook Harvey's hand and joined it with the hand of his daughter.

John continued with his booming pastoral voice. "Harvey and Abigail, we read in Genesis, 'Therefore shall a man leave his father and mother and shall cleave unto his wife,'[1] and in Proverbs 'Whoso findeth a wife findeth a good thing.'[2] He has ordained that the husband be the head of the wife. He instructs the man to love his wife as Christ loves the Church. It should be your desire and delight to follow this Scriptural teaching. Harvey, please repeat after me." John recited a line of the vows, and Harvey repeated it word for word.

"I, David Harvey Nicholas, Junior, take you, Abigail Rachel Walker, to be my wedded wife as ordained by God. To have and to hold . . . " Harvey said. Abby took each word in. She watched as his mouth formed each word carefully and with thought. She loved how his eyes sparkled as he spoke.

Then it was her turn. John asked her to repeat after him. "I, Abigail Rachel Walker, take you, David Harvey Nicholas, Junior, to be my wedded husband as ordained by God . . . " She spoke each word with as

---

1 Genesis 2:24
2 Proverbs 18:22

much love and certainty as she could muster, willing Harvey to feel just how much she meant it.

Then John smiled. "May I have the rings?"

Jacob suddenly burst into action. "I have them! I have them, Uncle John!" He jumped up and down excitedly, waving the rings in the air. The entire congregation chuckled at his enthusiasm. John leaned toward Jacob and took the rings from him.

"Thank you, Jake," he said with a laugh. "Now, the ring is a perfect symbol of Christ's love for us. It has no beginning and no end. The gold is pure, like Christ Himself. Harvey, please place this ring on Abby's left hand."

Harvey obeyed the pastor and said, "Abigail, I give you this ring as a sign of my love. My pledge of never-ending devotion to you and our family. Wear it each day as a reminder of our faith and our union together."

Abby did her best not to cry as Harvey easily slipped the ring onto her finger. The gold band had an inlaid Celtic knot, just like her engagement ring. In the center of the knot work was a traditional Irish Claddagh—two hands holding a crowned heart. Abby was thrilled and knew that her face shone as brilliantly as the band on her finger. She never felt as blessed as she did in that moment.

John handed Abby the ring for Harvey and instructed her to place it on his hand.

"Harvey." She sighed. "Harvey, I give you this ring as a sign of my love, my devotion, and my faith to God and to you. Wear this each day as a reminder of our pledge to one another this day."

The ring glided onto Harvey's finger. His ring matched Abby's with the same Celtic knotting and Claddagh in the center. Harvey was very proud of his Irish heritage, and Abby loved the symbolism of the Claddagh. He smiled as the weight of the ring settled onto his finger. Abby felt giddy with excitement as Harvey winked at her.

"Harvey, Abigail, you have endured much in the time that you have known each other. You have witnessed the effects of war firsthand. You have had your hearts broken in many ways. But broken hearts can mend, as you well know. Your hearts have mended together, thanks be to God.

"You have promised before God and these witnesses to love each other, to lift each other up, and to follow God all the days of your lives. May you go forth and show Christ's love to all you meet, and may you raise your children to be good, solid Christians. What God has joined, let no man separate. It is my pleasure to pronounce you husband and wife." John sighed and smiled. "Harvey, you may kiss your bride!"

As clapping and cheering broke out from the congregation, Harvey pulled Abby into his arms and held her close, pressing his lips onto hers. Abby felt her heart melt as her lips caressed Harvey's.

When they parted, John announced, "Ladies and gentlemen, Mr. and Mrs. David Harvey Nicholas, Junior!" Applause began again as Aunt Judy fired up the piano for the recessional. Harvey and Abby retreated down the aisle, laughing and smiling the entire way.

Outside, the sun was shining through the trees, and the air was warm. It was a perfect day. The rain water had absorbed into the ground, making everything Abby could see lush and green. Harvey took her into his arms again and kissed her long and hard. It left Abby feeling dizzy and light, and she loved it. Their families and guests emptied out of the church, offering hugs and congratulations all around.

After a few minutes, the photographer Jane had hired called the families back into the church for pictures. Abby smiled so big, she was sure her mouth would fall off, but it would be worth it. Once the pictures were over, the couple got into their car to head back to the Walkers' house.

Letting out a sigh, Harvey asked her, "Can you believe it?" The excitement was obvious in his voice.

Abby laughed. "I sure can! I have never been so happy in all my life." And she truly hadn't.

"Neither have I, Mrs. Nicholas."

She let a little squeal out and squeezed her eyes shut at hearing herself called by her new married name. It made her pulse quicken. "I love it, Mr. Nicholas, and I love you!"

Abby couldn't believe her dreams had come true. She had finally married the man of her dreams after two long years.

Back at the Walkers' home, a grand party was starting. The sun was bright overhead, and guests were milling around outside. Several of Harvey's family members from Charleston and Columbia were present, as well as friends from Clemson College who were stateside or not in the war. Abby's family was also present, including a few friends from school.

Set upon a table draped with a yellow tablecloth was the wedding cake Abby had made herself. Three tiers of real cake with eggs, sugar, and butter—no K rations for that cake—were surrounded with dozens of tiny little daisies. Each tier was a scrumptious yellow butter cake, topped with pure white icing. And at the base of each tier were real daisies, white with bright yellow centers. It was a magnificent cake, if Abby did think so herself.

There were tables and chairs set up around the yard for the nearly sixty people in attendance. Across the picnic table were mounds of freshly made food. Carved roast chicken piped hot in the center of the table, while steamed vegetables and fresh baked breads were spread across the table and piled high. Raspberries, apricots, and blueberries were nestled together in a colorful fruit salad. Pitchers of water and iced tea perspired in the sunlight. The aromas of abundant food wafted through the spring breeze and made everyone's stomach growl as they waited for the bride and groom to join them.

Harvey pulled the car up to the house, and the crowd gathered around to greet the newlyweds. Abby smiled through the window, and Harvey came around the car to open her door. As she stepped out and stood, Harvey took her arm. He went without his cane, as they had planned, and leaned slightly on Abby. With continued therapy, he was doing better and better on his feet. The crowd applauded as they walked up the driveway toward the festivities.

Everybody in attendance was in high spirits. Food was passed around with stories of the newlyweds as children. The cake was cut into during peals of laughter brought on by the youngest attendees. Abby and Harvey were never more than a few steps from each other all afternoon and frequently stopped what they were doing for a quick kiss or stolen glance.

Before the group broke for the evening, their fathers gave their toasts, starting with David Nicholas. He rapped a spoon on his glass to get everybody's attention.

"Everybody, please raise a glass. We may not have champagne, but our spirits are high nonetheless," he began. "Today, my only son got married to a beautiful girl. Not only is Abigail a beautiful girl, but she's smart and witty. Abby also knows to go after what she wants, don't you, Abby?" The crowd laughed, everybody knowing about Abby's life-altering decision to go to Charleston to seek Harvey out. "And that's exactly what Harvey needs. A woman—a wife—who will help him achieve all his goals and hers. These two compliment each other in a way I've never seen. The minute Harvey told us about this enchanting girl, I knew he was head over heels in love with her. And it seems the feeling was mutual. The war has brought great sadness over everybody here, but these two have defied the odds and found their way together again. Let no one but God ever come between you again. Look to Him first, and you two can survive anything. Cheers!"

Everybody raised their tea or water glass and clinked with a person near them before taking a sip. Abby and Harvey touched their glasses together and smiled.

Nathan followed with his speech. "When this young man first came into town, I knew my daughter had taken an immediate liking to him." Abby blushed when she realized her father had known. "Don't think we didn't know, Abby, when you snuck out of the house on your birthday that year. In fact, this young man is so respectable, he asked us first if he could see you that night. And that told me a lot about Harvey's character. What other young man would do that? Be so reputable and polite as to ask if you were allowed to sneak off? You can thank your momma for allowing you to go off, too, Abby. But these two do have something special—something you just don't see in young people today—a commitment to the Lord first and to each other second. May you always know your priorities and keep them straight."

Abby laughed and looked at Harvey. She hadn't known after all this time that he had arranged with her parents to let her sneak out of the house that night. And she had been so careful not to get caught either!

As the swarm of people dissipated, the two families were left, thrown together for the first time. They remained outside to talk and get to know one another, while they nibbled on leftover food. They had eaten so much for lunch, they weren't really hungry for another meal, but a few bites here and there seemed to do the trick. David and Nathan were engrossed in talking about cars, and Susan's husband, James, joined them. Abby was thankful they weren't talking about the war. She had heard enough of it for a lifetime. Abby's younger siblings and Harvey's niece and nephew ran around the house, playing tag as if they were the best of friends.

The ladies were slowly gathering up plates and taking them inside, stealing a piece of fruit here or a chunk of bread there. They were all cheerful as they talked and worked. Abby was impressed that even Harvey's mother and sister were pitching in. When everything was tidy, the women sat in the living room and fanned themselves. The summer air had a breeze, but they had gotten warm with all the hustle and bustle. When Abby went into the living room, she looked for Emmeline but did not see her.

"Momma, where's Emme?" She had wanted to give Emmeline a small gift of perfume. She had gotten one for Emmeline and one for her sister. Reba had loved hers, but Emmeline was nowhere to be found.

As Grace bounced P.J. on her knee, she looked around. "I'm not sure, dear. I thought she had come in with us. Maybe she's in the washroom?"

Abby went down the hall and knocked on the bathroom door. "Emme? Are you in there?" Abby heard coughing and the sound of stifled tears.

"Just a minute; I'm sorry."

Concern for her sister-in-law filled Abby's heart. She knew today would be hard on Emmeline. She should have spent more time with her. *Selfish me,* she thought. *Poor Emme is suffering still. Lord, give her strength!*

"Are you alright, Emme?"

The door was tossed open, and Emmeline nearly stumbled out. Her eyes were puffy and red, her face as pale as a sheet.

"Oh, Emme! I'm so sorry! Are you okay? Come lie down!" She pulled Emmeline into her old bedroom and laid her on Reba's bed. "Let me go get Momma."

As she turned, Emmeline caught her hand. "No, Abby. Stay here a minute." Abby stopped and knelt down next to her. "I'm sorry. I'm just not myself these days." When Abby started to speak, she shushed her. "Listen, I have to tell you. I did go to the doctor like you and Reba asked me to. But Abby, it's not good news." A tear slipped off her eyelash and onto the pillow below her.

"What do you mean, Emme?" Abby felt tears well in her eyes. *Not good news? What could she mean? Is she sick? Oh, Lord, please don't let her be sick.*

"The doctors say I have cancer, Abby." Her voice was barely a whisper as the words tumbled out of her mouth.

Tears immediately slipped down Abby's face and stained her wedding dress. A lump rose in her throat. She could not lose Emmeline, too. P.J. couldn't lose her.

"No, Emme. No, you're okay. We know you're still grieving for Peter. We know that. But you'll come through it. You'll be okay." She gripped Emmeline's hands in hers and kissed them tenderly.

Emmeline tried to smile. "I'm sorry, Abby. But I am sick. The doctors are going to give me some treatments, okay? So don't worry. I can't

. . . I won't leave P.J. I'm just so tired. But I'll get stronger with these treatments they'll give me; don't worry." To prove herself, she sat up in the bed and smoothed her hair. "See? I'll be okay. But promise me one thing, Abby."

Abby brushed tears off her cheeks and leaned closer to Emmeline. "Anything you want."

"If something happens to me, I want you and Harvey to take care of P.J. for me. Peter would want it that way." She spoke quietly and solemnly and didn't meet Abby's fear-struck expression.

"Don't talk like that, Emmeline. You'll be fine. I'm sure the doctors and these treatments will help you."

"I just don't know, Abby. I've known about the cancer for weeks now. It seems I've had it for a long time. The cancer is quite advanced, and they said that having P.J. probably made it even stronger. It's a miracle I had him at all. Peter's and my miracle. So if anything happens, you take him. It's just in case, okay? Promise?"

She looked up into Abby's eyes, and Abby could see the pain that resided in Emmeline's face. For the past few weeks, she thought it was pain over losing Peter when, in reality, it was pain over P.J. losing both his parents before he would ever remember them.

"I promise," Abby swore, her voice no more than an whisper. But inside, her entire body was panicking loudly. How could she care for P.J. if anything happened to Emmeline? How could she replace that child's parents? *Lord, please. Let her get stronger. Let this promise never come to fruition.*

"Thank you, Abby. Thank you so much. This means the world to me and to Peter. Now, you have a honeymoon to go on."

Emmeline rose and smiled, even though it was an unsteady smile. She took Abby's hand to lead her out of the house to her groom. "Emmeline, we can wait. We'll stay here with you. I promised Peter I would take care of you." Abby didn't want to leave her. Harvey would understand; they could honeymoon later.

But Emmeline shook her head and insisted, "No, you go now. I'm not going anywhere. I just had to get that off my chest is all. I feel so much better just having told you. It feels like a big weight has been lifted. Don't let it ruin your wedding day. Please, go. Find Harvey and enjoy your honeymoon!" She smiled meagerly and added, "Enjoy the life Peter and I never got a chance at. Please."

"Okay, Emme, if that's what you want. But you call me the second you need me." Emmeline may have had a weight lifted, but it descended onto Abby's shoulders, and she wasn't sure she could bear the heft quietly.

"I will."

Once the ladies were back outside, they realized everybody was waiting for them. It was time for Abby and Harvey to leave. Abby turned toward Emmeline and searched her eyes. Would she be okay while they were gone? Abby sighed; Emmeline was insistent that she go. Surely, she would be okay. Their family had endured enough, had they not? Emmeline hugged her tight, and Abby clung to her sister-in-law, tears swimming in her eyes. Everyone else thought it was because Abby was sensitive to Emmeline's loss; nobody else knew of her illness.

When they parted, Reba took Abby by the shoulders and led her away. Abby kept her eyes on Emmeline for a second and nodded to her. Then she turned to her sister and smiled. "I guess it's time to go!"

"Oh, Abby, you'll have so much fun! Call me when you realize where you're going!" Then Reba thought a moment. "On the other hand . . . I'll just talk to you when you get home. Have fun!"

The sisters hugged, and Abby was then given a round of hugs and kisses from her other siblings. Even Gabriel bounded over to her for a slobbery kiss.

Her father put his arm around her next and looked at Harvey, telling them both, "Be careful on the road. We'll see you soon, okay?"

"Yes, sir." Harvey said with a relaxed smile.

Nathan kissed Abby on the forehead. "I love you, Abigail. Harvey really lucked out." Abby smiled at her father and kissed his cheek.

Harvey's parents gave her hugs next, wishing them well and urging them to be safe on the highways. They then turned to their son and bid him farewell. Jane cried over her son, making Grace start as well. As she turned to hug Abby, she was weeping openly.

"Oh, Momma," Abby chided. "I love you."

"My first baby girl. My Abigail," was all she could say. She clutched her daughter tightly. When she let go, she smiled, her tear-stained cheeks looking like shiny apples.

Harvey took Abby's hand from her mother and led her to the car. "We'll call when we get there, so you know we're okay," he reassured her as he kissed Grace on the cheek. Then he looked at his bride, and she peered up at him with adoration in her eyes. "Ready, angel?"

Abby smiled, trying to push Emmeline's disturbing news from her mind. "I'm ready."

She would wait to tell Harvey; this was not the time or place. After all, Emmeline said she was fine and would beat the cancer. She had to. He opened the car door for her, and she slid into the seat. Harvey went to the driver's side and got in himself.

As the car started and moved forward, they waved to their families. When they were out of sight, Abby turned to Harvey with a grin across her face. "So, will you tell me where we're going now?"

Harvey chuckled at her. "I can't tell you that; it would ruin the surprise."

Abby laughed. She wanted to know where they were going, but she was thrilled that Harvey wanted to surprise her yet again. It was so exciting, to know he had planned it just for her. During the car ride, they told each other about how they felt during the day. How Abby felt like she was going to explode like a burst of fireworks when she made her way down the aisle. How Harvey had wanted to lift her into his arms and whisk her off to the honeymoon without stopping back at their reception. They laughed as they recalled Jake's shining moment and lamented over missing Peter. Abby avoided giving away the news of Emmeline's infirmity, reasoning that it was best to wait until they returned home. After all, Emmeline had said she would be okay and would recover soon. Maybe nobody else ever need know she had been sick.

Harvey drove north over mountains and a few rivers. Abby loved seeing all the nature around her. Leaves and flowers were blooming on all the trees, crisp green shoots exploded all around. Small bursts of pink and purple dotted the roadside as wildflowers flourished after a dormant winter. They turned off the highway and entered a small mountain village, and within a few minutes, the biggest building Abby had ever seen came into view.

"Look how big that is, Harvey! It looks like a castle!" Abby exclaimed.

He smiled, loving to see her excitement. "That's called Biltmore House. Have you never heard of it?"

"No, never. Should I have?"

"It's a pretty famous house, but that doesn't mean you should have heard of it," he replied.

Abby craned her neck out the window to look to the top spires of the house. "I didn't know they had castles here. I thought they were only in England."

"It is the biggest house in the United States," Harvey told her.

Abby nodded her head. "Where are we, anyway?" She looked to her new husband for an answer.

Harvey pulled into a long driveway, directing them opposite the castle. "Asheville, North Carolina. My parents have a little cabin up here, and I thought we would enjoy the cool air and blooming flowers for our honeymoon."

Abby took a deep breath, feeling the cool air rush into her lungs. "I love it. And we're in North Carolina? I've never even been outside South Carolina before. This wasn't too far away, though."

"No, just a few hours," said Harvey as he maneuvered the winding drive. "Here we are. The Nicholas cabin." He put the car into park and spread his arms out for Abby to see their final destination.

"Oh, Harvey, it's lovely."

The cabin was a spacious log home with a giant gray stone fireplace jutting out from the side of the house. A deep front porch with turn-of-the-century rocking chairs greeted them. Abby saw that a small path led to the front door and then off the side of the porch away from the house. It was lined with pink and blue azaleas that seemed to have waited just for her to bloom. Dogwood trees decorated the front lawn, while larger pines became thick behind the house.

While she took the sight in from the car, Harvey had maneuvered around and opened her door for her. Abby swung her legs around and stood. A flash of cool air washed over her as a breeze whipped through the trees. She smiled at Harvey—giddy, nervous. Abby thought he looked just as nervous as she.

"Let's go in!" Harvey said emphatically. Abby smiled and took his hand and followed him down the path to the porch.

The inside of the house looked as though it had been prepared just for them—and it had. The living room, dining room, and kitchen were all connected as one large room. Against one wall, the stone fireplace was full of wood and more sat to the side, a box of matches perched on the top. Before the fireplace was a large, deep couch, perfect for curling up with a loved one. A radio sat to one side of the couch, a full bookshelf to the other. In the middle of the room was a large dining table with enough room for Abby's entire family. But only two places were set on the corner closest to the fireplace, and Abby could see fine china and glasses waiting for this very night to be put to use. Opposite the fireplace was the kitchen. Fresh fruit lay in a basket on the counter for the couple to feast on. A carefully selected bottle of champagne was settled into an ice bucket with two fluted glasses resting in front of it.

Abby took it all in, one facet at a time. Every last detail was beautifully and painstakingly considered. She looked to her groom, who awaited her response. Not knowing what to say, Abby put her hand to Harvey's cheek and stroked it. She moved close to him and put her mouth to his, kissing him deeply. His arms wrapped around her as he responded.

Pulling away, his whispered, "This isn't all, Mrs. Nicholas." The words gave Abby goosebumps all down her arms, and a chill ran down her back, but her stomach grew warm. Harvey took her hand and led her down a small hall to a bedroom that was also waiting for their arrival.

Abby saw rose petals scattered all over the room from the bed to the window sills. The room was scented with the perfume from the pink and yellow petals, and it made the heat in Abby's stomach grow and spread. Two fluffy white robes hung on hooks to her right next to the bathroom, each with their own pair of slippers underneath. A smooth, red satin blanket lay over the top of the bed with matching red satin pillows at the head. A small russet-colored couch sat opposite the bed. The golden curtains were open, showcasing a breathtaking view of the mountains beyond the cabin.

Abby could barely whisper, but she had to speak. "Harvey, this is gorgeous. This is all for us?"

"All for you, my bride," he murmured in her ear as he caressed her hair.

Abby's cheeks grew crimson, and she smiled. She suddenly remembered the special nightgown tucked away in her suitcase and knew she should have it ready. She turned to Harvey and giggled. "I need to, um, freshen up."

Harvey smiled. "I'll get the bags from the car. Why don't you see what's in the kitchen? I made sure there was plenty of food stocked up for us. And there's a bottle of champagne waiting as well."

Abby had a feeling that Harvey had a plan as well, so she obliged. She went to the kitchen while Harvey went back out to the car. She opened the refrigerator and found a platter of chocolate-covered strawberries waiting for her. Alongside those were figs and other fruits covered with spices and honey. She pulled the platters out and set them onto the counter. She quickly reached into a cabinet for a plate and selected the plumpest fruits to serve to her groom. She then returned the platters to the refrigerator, just as Harvey came in with the suitcases.

"That looks wonderful; what have you got?" he asked.

"Just some fruit," she called over her shoulder as she arranged the plate to look as appealing as possible.

"Let me set these in our room, and I'll open the champagne." He disappeared for a moment and then returned to the kitchen area. "I thought I smelled honey and chocolate," he said as he came up behind Abby and wrapped his arms around her waist. "And you," he added, breathing her in.

Holding her breath, Abby wanted to both jump into his arms and run away at the same time. She was excited, yet also terrified, of their time to come.

Sensing her nerves, Harvey ran his hands through her hair. "Take a deep breath, Abby. We're in no rush. Let's eat a little something; I know I'm hungry." She smiled, thankful for a groom who understood her apprehension. "Didn't you say you wanted to freshen up?"

"I will after we eat," she said as she picked up the plate of fruit. "Shall we dine at the table?"

"How about I get a fire started instead?" Harvey suggested. "It's still quite cool up here at night." He took the champagne and glasses and walked to the couch, setting them on the table in front of it. He knelt down before the fireplace with a little effort and began to work on building a fire.

Abby carried the tray of food over to the table as well and watched Harvey. He really was improving physically. She was so proud of him. She wasn't sure if he had noticed that getting down to the floor had been so much easier now than it was just a few weeks ago. The therapy she was helping him with was working wonders. While he still relied on his cane for most walking, he could get through a house or other short distances without it now. She didn't care if he needed the cane forever, as long as he was happy and healthy otherwise, and he certainly was now.

As a small fire grew to life, Harvey turned and patted the thick carpet next to him for Abby to sit down. She blissfully joined him on the floor and handed him the bottle of champagne, while she took a glass in each hand. She did her best to look demure and appealing, unsure if she was succeeding, but Harvey didn't seem to care. He barely took his eyes off her, regardless of what she did.

"Ready?" he asked her as he prepared to pop the cork.

"Yes," she said. Her response was for both the champagne and the evening to come. Harvey pulled the cork with a great pop, and she held out a glass for him to fill and then offered the other one.

When Harvey put the bottle down, they clinked their glasses in a wordless toast to each other. Abby, wanting to be a proper, dutiful wife, picked up the plate and chose the largest chocolate-covered strawberry. She held it out, her fingers clutching the green leaves, and offered it to her husband. Harvey leaned in close and closed his eyes as he bit into the fruit. He kissed Abby's hand and then took the top from her and discarded it. He returned the favor by choosing a fig for her to taste. Abby closed her eyes and opened her mouth. She closed it over the fig and felt Harvey's fingers at her lips. She swallowed and kissed his hand as he had done hers.

Oh, Lord, she prayed silently. *Lord, thank You. Please let me be the wife Harvey deserves. I can't believe this moment is here. I've waited for it,*

anticipated it, feared it, since the moment I met him. And now, I wait with
bated breath for him, and I couldn't be happier.

They ate in silence—feeding each other and sipping their champagne. The drink was sweet and accentuated the fruit perfectly. Abby looked into Harvey's eyes and noticed just how green they were, a lighter green than she had ever noticed before. His hair brushed his forehead just the way she loved for it to do. He wore a grin that lasted the entire meal, pleasurable and relaxed.

When they finished, Abby knew what would come next. She wished she were more graceful and longed for a way to get to her suitcase without looking silly. Luckily, Harvey seemed just as nervous as she. He rose to his feet with a little wobble, then steadied himself. Saying he needed to keep the bottle on ice, he walked to the kitchen area, giving Abby a chance to escape.

"I'll be right back," she said as she dashed into the bedroom. She pushed her hair from her face and opened the suitcase. She found the tissue paper and carefully unfolded the edges, revealing the white satin nightgown her aunt had bestowed upon her. She went into the bathroom and closed the door behind her.

She stopped as the door closed. She wasn't sure how to present herself once she had the lingerie on. *Do I go back out into the living room? Were the curtains open for the world to see in? Maybe I should wait in here for Harvey to find me. Do I call for him to come back here? Oh, I should have asked someone what to do at this point! Drat! Oh well, here goes nothing!*

Abby slipped the satin fabric on over her body. The cool material gave her goosebumps, and the marabou feathers tickled her skin. She looked in the rustic mirror hanging on the wall. She looked wonderful; she had to admit. With her feet bare, the gown touched the floor.

She ran her fingers through her hair and repositioned the combs so her hair was up off her neck with a few select tendrils hanging down over her shoulders. She looked at herself and had thought to pinch her cheeks to make them rosy, but they were rosy enough. She opened the tube of lipstick she had grabbed and applied the red tint to her mouth. She pressed her lips together and swallowed hard.

Okay, Abby, you can do this, she told herself. *I've been waiting so long for this night to arrive, and now that it's here, I don't know what to do. I'm going to just open the door and find Harvey. It's that easy. I'll find him, kiss him and . . . and . . .* Abby thought maybe it would be best to do this one step at a time and not worry about the next step.

She smoothed the nightgown over her hips and smiled. Abby put her hand on the doorknob and took a deep breath, wishing her pulse would slow a little. She opened the door and stepped back into the bedroom.

All around her was a soft glow. Candles sitting on the dresser and nightstands were lit, bathing the room with flickering light. Abby smiled as she saw Harvey on the small couch, waiting for her, champagne flutes in hand. She closed the door behind her and grappled with feeling both shy and brazen at the same time.

Crossing the room toward her groom, Abby's smile grew wider. He stood to meet her and offered her one of the glasses of champagne. She shook her head to decline, the glass she had before was enough. He set the glasses down on the table beside him and led Abby to the bed. Nerves filled her head and stomach, but she ignored them, opting instead to focus on the beauty of the moment. Abby could feel herself turn red and grow warm, a mix of emotions tumbling through her mind and body.

"Oh, Abigail, my bride, I adore you," Harvey whispered in her ear as he pulled her close.

They spent the better part of a week savoring each moment as it came. Abby marveled at how much more she grew to love her groom with each passing day. When they weren't at the cabin, they shopped in the city, sipped on wine, and laughed as much as possible. Abby thought that week had to be the best on record and never wanted it to end.

CHAPTER 17

BUT THE HONEYMOON HAD TO end, and the newlyweds came home to find that Emmeline's illness had caught up with her in that short week. It progressed rapidly, and she could hide it no longer. The funeral was two months later, on a breezy day in August, right after Abby's nineteenth birthday. Emmeline did not beat the cancer as she had vowed. Not for her lack of trying—the entire family witnessed her fight to break free from the illness that made her weak, sick, and pale. But even though Emmeline won a few battles, the cancer won the war.

Abby never told anybody that she knew about the cancer before the rest of them. She had spent Emmeline's remaining time on earth caring for her sister-in-law and P.J. Emmeline didn't want P.J. to see her so weak, even though he was not yet a year old, so Abby could only bring him to his mother when she was feeling well and sitting up in bed. He would sit with her and look at books or play with toys until Emmeline tired and asked to rest.

She had made it clear that Abby and Harvey were to take P.J. and care for him until he was grown; she even put it in her will. Mr. and Mrs. Madison were not thrilled with the idea, but at Emmeline's insistence, they relented.

When Emmeline died, Abby was with her, just the two of them. Emmeline had lain in her childhood bed at her parent's house. Everybody else was gone, tending to other things. Harvey had understood that Abby wanted to spend as much time with Emmeline as possible. She sat with her sister-in-law and wiped her brow when she needed it. She covered her when she was cold and turned down the blankets when she was hot.

Holding Emmeline's hand, Abby reminisced about the past. She told Emmeline fanciful stories about the future, about how P.J. would grow up and how Peter would be so proud of his son. Abby regaled her with accounts of Heaven and parables of the Bible, assuring Emmeline that she would live forever in Christ. And in the end, she promised Emmeline that Peter would be waiting for her, his hand outstretched for her to take.

"I see him, Abby," Emmeline had muttered as Abby wiped sweat from her brow.

"Who?" Abby wasn't sure what Emmeline was talking about. She had been rambling, preferring to talk endlessly than to sit in silence.

She smiled. "Peter. I see him. He's wearing his uniform, and he's waiting for me."

Brushing a tear from her cheek, Abby realized just what Emmeline was saying. She shook her head, not wanting to believe it. "Are you sure, Emme?" She squeezed her sister-in-law's hand tight.

"Oh, Abby, he's so handsome. And he said it's time to be with him like we should have been." Emmeline unconsciously smoothed out the light blue house dress she wore, making sure she looked her best. "You'll watch P.J. for me, won't you, Abby?" She made it sound like she was going for a night on the town, not an eternity in Heaven.

Emmeline finally looked over to Abby for an answer. Choked up, Abby responded, "Of course, Emme. P.J. will be just fine. Tell Peter we love him."

Emmeline's gaze went beyond Abby, and she said, "He knows. He loves you, too. And I love you, Abby. You've been my very best friend. Thank you. It's time now."

Abby could no longer hold back the sobs, and she let them run free. "Goodbye, Emmeline. We love you. Goodbye."

Fading quickly, Emmeline echoed quietly, "Goodbye." A wide smile broke across her face, and she looked happier than she had been since the war started. Her face froze in that smile, and her head slumped to the side; her hand went limp. She was gone.

Abby had wailed loudly at that point, having never witnessed death firsthand before. How could she be gone? Emmeline had a son to care for. How could Abby overtake such an important job? She had lain across Emmeline's body until Mrs. Madison had returned; then the two of them had wept bitterly together.

Abby sought God as she remembered the scene from a few days before. *Why God? Why her? Why now? What does this accomplish? First, You take Peter, and now Emmeline. You've left P.J. without parents. And now You're entrusting him to us, Lord? Harvey and I just got married; we don't know how to care for a baby! This is unfair on so many levels; don't You know that? Of course, You do. How can I praise You in all this? I love her like a true sister. Her body is still here, but her soul is with You. Take care of her, Lord. I'll make a deal with You—You take care of Peter and Emme, and I'll take care of P.J. Oh, God, just help us all.*

Abby walked out of the church after the funeral with Harvey holding her up. They had already set up the nursery in their new house for P.J. and had moved his things in the day before. Tonight, they would take him home to become a part of their family. They would become an instant family of three. Abby, Harvey, and P.J.

CHAPTER 18

P.J. TORE THROUGH THE HOUSE after school in the spring of 1949. He was an active first grader, and Abby had a hard time keeping up with him—especially now that she was pregnant.

She rubbed her stomach, certain she could feel it expanding under her hand. Abby was worn and weary, but so thrilled and thankful to be in the condition in the first place. After more than five years of marriage, five years of praying, and five years of heartache, she was finally expecting a child. By the time fall came, Abby would be a mother.

"I can't believe I have only a few months to go!" She exclaimed to P.J., who could not have cared less. He just wanted a snack. She went to the fridge and retrieved a bunch of grapes and a glass of milk for her nephew.

"Aww, Aunt Abby," P.J. moaned, "I want cookies."

She smiled; the child had a voracious appetite for sweets, just like his father. "I know you do, P.J., but you're getting grapes. They're sweet enough." P.J. scrunched up his face and popped a grape in his mouth anyway. "Besides, your Uncle Harvey will be home soon, and dinner will be on the table."

"What are we having?"

Abby had been working on her cooking skills and had become quite accomplished. After Harvey began pastoring at Zion Grace Baptist Church and P.J. had started school, she had sat idly after her household chores were done. Harvey suggested that she enroll in a cooking class at a local school, and she had marched out the very next day and signed up. Since then, she had flourished as a cook and longed to go further. It was at that time, she had found out she was pregnant after so many years of longing.

She sniffed the air and inhaled the scent of pot roast simmering, along with carrots, onion, and potatoes, while freshly baked bread cooled on a rack next to the sink. She thought it smelled heavenly but knew that such aromas were above the palate of a six-year-old little boy.

"What do you smell, Petey?" She loved using her mom's pet name for her brother on him.

"I don't know," P.J. sighed. "Chicken?" His sandy blond hair curled closely to his head but bobbed anyway as he moved. He hated his curls and picked at them when he was bored, as he was now. His dark brown eyes rolled at his aunt as she asked him yet again to guess what she was cooking.

Knowing she should chide her nephew for rolling his eyes, Abby only smiled and laughed. "Pot roast, sweetheart. When your uncle gets home, we'll eat." She tousled his hair as she stole a grape from him.

How could I ever love a child as much as I love P.J.? I am so excited to be a mother, but I guess I've been one for nearly six years now. Almost six years since Emmeline left us. It's so hard to believe. But I've loved P.J. as if he were my own from the day he was born. Being a mom may not be new to me, but this part is. Being with child, anticipating childbirth, that's all new. And I do wonder if I could love this little baby as much as I love P.J. I sure hope God makes more room in my heart.

After dinner was eaten, P.J. was tucked into bed. Abby and Harvey stood at his door and watched him sleep for a moment before retreating to the living room. Harvey sat down with a book, and Abby picked up some yarn and knitting needles and began working on the soft yellow material. She had plans to make booties and a sweater for the new arrival.

As she worked, Harvey watched her, his book resting in his lap. Harvey had begun watching her from the moment they were married, and Abby was used to it now. In that first year of marriage, it made her shy to have him watch her, but now she enjoyed his attention—especially as her waistline expanded.

"Remember our first Christmas when you gave me the mittens and scarf?"

Abby smiled. "I sure do. I was such a novice back then. Whatever happened to them?"

Harvey got off the couch with ease and walked to her, sitting close enough that their arms touched. "I still have them. They're packed away."

Looking at her husband, Abby thought of how he had overcome his handicaps in the past several years. For those who knew him, he still walked with a slight shuffle, but if someone didn't know, they wouldn't have seen it. He hardly used his cane anymore, but kept it handy just in case. He couldn't run or jump, but he was all right with that. He could keep up with P.J. and move with little difficulty, and that was what mattered.

"I can't believe you still have them," Abby commented as she set to work. Secretly, she was thrilled he had kept them. They had even gone to war with him.

"Of course I do. They were your first gift to me." Harvey leaned in and kissed her neck. Even after several years, she still felt a chill run down her spine when Harvey did that. "What are you making?"

Abby looked sheepishly at her husband. "Baby booties. I couldn't help myself."

"I figured you would start on something like that sooner or later. We've waited long enough for this little one. I'm surprised you didn't start the minute you figured out you were expecting."

Harvey cautiously laid his hand on her stomach, his hand splayed out around the small mound that protruded from Abby's abdomen. Abby thought back to when Emmeline was pregnant with P.J. and recalled her being much smaller at this same point. But her mother had told her each person was different, and each pregnancy was different, and not to compare them.

Suddenly, Abby felt a burst of movement from her stomach. "Harvey! Did you feel that?"

"I did! Was that the baby?" Harvey put both hands on Abby's stomach and brought his face closer.

"I think so. Wow, that's amazing. I've never felt it move like that before." She radiated joy at that moment and had never been more excited.

Then her stomach rolled, and both Harvey's hands were kicked off. They looked at each other and laughed with amazement. Abby lifted her shirt and exposed her belly; the cool air gave her goosebumps, but she didn't mind. She and Harvey were astounded to watch the pitch and roll of her middle. Abby was certainly tickled to feel it on the inside and see it on the outside.

"That's one active kid," Harvey marveled. He snuggled in even closer to Abby and her expanding waistline. Abby breathed him in, still as intoxicated by his scent than ever.

"I'm glad I have a doctor appointment tomorrow. Maybe he can tell me more about the movements."

They watched their child perform acrobatics inside its mother's womb for a few more minutes, and then they retired to bed. Abby was having a hard time fitting in her nightgowns anymore. The loose, empire-waisted gowns were pulling taut across her stomach already, and she was only halfway through her pregnancy. Abby fell asleep with Harvey's hand firmly pressed to her belly and the baby settling in for a good night's rest.

The next day, Abby got P.J. off to school, and she was going to head to her doctor's appointment for a check-up. Harvey had surprised her by taking the morning off and going with her. He wanted to hear the baby's heartbeat after watching her stomach the night before.

Doctor John Thomas was a wonderful doctor and answered the first-time parents' pressing questions. Abby wanted to know about managing house and baby. Harvey, ever the typical dad, asked about the sleeping habits of newborns. Abby self-consciously asked about feeding the baby properly, and the doctor assured her that a nurse could help her when the time came.

When the questions ran out, the doctor said he would listen to the baby's heartbeat next. Abby and Harvey were excited and nervous at the same time. He brought in a machine with a stethoscope-like end, placing it on Abby's belly.

Thump-thump, thump-thump, thump-thump. The sound filled the air. Abby looked at Harvey and smiled, a tear springing to her eye. He kissed her on the forehead and held his wife's hand tight. As Doctor Thomas moved the machine around, a different rhythmic sound was heard. *Thump-thump, wump, thump-thump, wump.* The doctor furrowed his brow and began moving around quietly.

Abby's joy turned to concern as the doctor grew quiet and started to move around hurriedly. Doctor Thomas left the room for a moment and came back in with a nurse and more equipment. Abby's voice was lost as fear mounted.

What's wrong with my baby? What's going on? What happened? Why isn't the doctor speaking? Didn't the heartbeat sound okay? Oh, Lord, please let my baby be okay. I've spent five years praying and crying and waiting for this baby. Please don't take him from me. Haven't I lost enough already?

While Abby couldn't speak, Harvey found his voice. "Doctor Thomas? What's going on?"

After a harrowing few seconds, the doctor turned to face the couple with a smile. "Mr. and Mrs. Nicholas, I have a surprise for you. That excessive movement you said you felt yesterday? I suspect you have a set of twins in there. Congratulations!"

Abby let out a sigh of relief, mixed with a nervous giggle. Twins? After all this time of her womb being closed, she now carried twins? God truly was good and amazing. Tears slipped down her cheek, both from excitement and nerves. She hugged Harvey tight, and he kissed her.

She had never been so happy in all her life.

Over the next several weeks, Abby began searching for things in pairs. Two stuffed teddy bears, two cribs, two rattles—and it overjoyed her. Harvey's study was converted into a double nursery. The walls were painted a cheery yellow called "Canary," and matching cribs sat side-by-side along the back wall. A wooden rocking chair passed the time before it soothed a crying baby in the corner. A tall white dresser stood opposite the window, waiting to be filled with tiny clothes. Rattles, stuffed animals, and other toys sat in pairs atop the dresser for the children to play with once they were old enough.

Abby longed to know if her children were boys or girls. She didn't care either way, but wished she could color-code things for them. And what if she were carrying a boy and a girl? Then she would need some things pink and some things blue. She would often lay her hands on either side of her stomach and ask who were the children growing inside of her. The time before she would find out was quickly passing.

One evening, a few weeks before she was due to give birth, Harvey surprised her by asking what she wanted to name the babies. "Haven't you thought about it?" he asked.

"Of course I have. I've been talking to Momma about family names we can use, but nothing seems to fit right." Abby bit her lip as she watched Harvey mentally go through his own family tree. "Naturally, if we have boys, one will be David Harvey, the Third, right?"

Harvey pondered the idea for a moment. "I don't know. I like my name, but being a junior comes with its own set of hassles. I kind of like the name Julian."

"Julian," Abby repeated. "Hmm."

"Well, what do you like?" Harvey asked as he picked up Abby's hand and kissed her fingers. A warmth filled Abby as her husband performed such a familiar task.

"For a boy? I would like to use the middle name Michael, after my brother. And I do like Louise for a girl, since that was Emmeline's middle name."

"I like Louise," Harvey nodded. "I really like the name Eve."

Abby let the name roll off her tongue. "Eve. I like that." She rubbed her stomach, certain she could not swell any larger than she already was. These children were sure to come out huge. "Julian and Eve? Maybe it's a boy and a girl."

As if to protest, one of the babies began kicking inside its dark world. "I don't think that one agrees," Harvey laughed as he put a hand on Abby's stomach to feel the movement. He never tired of feeling his children wiggle and kick inside the protection of their mother's womb.

"Maybe it's two boys," Abby offered. More protesting. "Then again, maybe we have two girls." As suddenly as it had begun, the kicking stopped. Abby and Harvey looked at each other with marvel and laughed until they cried tears of delight.

EPILOGUE

"EVE WAS BORN FIRST WITH fiery red hair, but a calm demeanor. Juliette came five minutes later with a head of curly black hair and screaming all the way. We always said God mixed their hair colors up and that Juliette should have gotten the fiery hair. But God doesn't make mistakes."

Abby sat in a rocking chair surrounded by her grandchildren, all ten of them. Her granddaughters had asked her how she met and fell in love with their grandfather. Abby loved the story and retold it with a twinkle in her eye.

How she missed Harvey. Had it really been five years since he had gone home to be with the Lord? She had a hard time remembering things that happened recently. But ask her about the past—about how Harvey Nicholas had come into her life—and she lit up.

The grandchildren hadn't been all too interested in the entire story up until this point, but with her eldest granddaughter preparing for her own wedding, romance was on everybody's mind. The girls sighed with each kiss; the boys pumped their fists with talk of the war.

"Grandma, I had no idea you were married so long before having Mom and Aunt Jules," her eldest granddaughter, Willow, commented.

Abby's face fell. "Yes, it was a long time. We wanted a baby from the minute we got married. But just like Sarah and Hannah in the Bible, God closed my womb for a time. And when His time was right, He opened it. Almost three years later, Joseph was born, and then came our baby, Alisa. And of course, Petey was always with us. He may not have been my first baby, but he taught me everything about parenting." She glanced up at P.J.—who preferred Pete now—and smiled. "Your daddy would be so proud of you. And your momma, too."

Pete just nodded and smiled. She had been telling him that since he could remember. He may have never met his father or remembered his mother, but his aunt and uncle always made sure he was loved and knew everything he wanted to know about his parents.

"It all sounds so exciting and quick when I tell it, but I promise you, those two years before I married your grandpa stretched out an eternity. Especially that year when he was overseas. I never thought 1942 would end. And there was so much heartache and loss in those years. Losing Peter and Emmeline, almost losing your grandfather . . . to both the war and to Clarice Renard. But we overcame it all," Abby said quietly with a tear in her eye.

She sighed and continued, "And then having to wait month after month to become pregnant. Each month was full of disappointment and tears. There was a real stigma attached to not having children. We had begun to wonder if we had done something wrong that God was preventing us from having children. But later on, I realized that God made us wait so that we could focus on giving Petey our attention, and he needed it as a young boy.

"But being married to Harvey and raising the children was the best time of my life. Five beautiful children I raised to love the Lord. And now, ten gorgeous grandchildren and more on the way." She stopped and looked to her youngest daughter, Alisa, now expecting her second child. Alisa rubbed her stomach in response. "I have had such a blessed life because of you all. Harvey and I made it through everything together by leaning on God and each other."

Thoughts turned to her late-husband. Harvey had had a sudden heart attack five years before and never recovered. After a week in the hospital, he slipped away from her. Abby had never felt so lost before; she had been by Harvey's side for the forty years before his death. But her children had rallied around her, comforting her and keeping her busy. Now, they were her lifeline as Abby approached her sixty-fourth birthday.

"Now, Willow," Abby continued, turning toward her eldest granddaughter, "I know you think you and Daniel make a terrific love story. But if you want to hear a real romance story, let me tell you about your mother, Eve, and your Aunt Juliette . . . "

For more information about
Allison Wells
&
War-Torn Heart
please visit:

www.allisonwellswrites.com
www.facebook.com/allisonwellswrites
@OrangeAlli
AllisonWellsWrites@gmail.com

For more information about
AMBASSADOR INTERNATIONAL
please visit:

www.ambassador-international.com
@AmbassadorIntl
www.facebook.com/AmbassadorIntl

If you enjoyed this book, please consider leaving us a review on
Amazon, Goodreads, or our website.

CPSIA information can be obtained
at www.ICGtesting.com
Printed in the USA
LVHW080952200319
611255LV00016B/81/P